STILL US

LINDSAY DETWILER

HOT TREE PUBLISHING

MORE FROM LINDSAY

HOT TREE
PUBLISHING

Still Us © 2018 by Lindsay Detwiler

For information, contact the publisher, Hot Tree Publishing.

WWW.HOTTREEPUBLISHING.COM
EDITING & FORMATTING: HOT TREE EDITING
COVER DESIGNER: SOXSATIONAL COVER ART
FORMATTING: RMGRAPHX

ISBN-13: 978-1-925655-65-0

10 9 8 7 6 5 4 3 2 1

To anyone who has ever loved and lost
And to my husband, the love I never want to lose

CHAPTER ONE

LILA

As I stand in the barren kitchen, the dusty room screams at me of broken dreams, shattered promises, and final goodbyes. I let my fingers dance over the faux marble countertop one last time, thinking back to the first time I'd envisioned our lives melding together in this room.

On that day—a summer day, sun shining as if promising a fresh, new life—I'd ambled in on his arm, picturing all the Italian feasts, candlelit dinners, and takeout food we'd share in here. I'd touched the smooth countertop with my perfectly polished fingernails and felt the warmth we'd experience here, together.

We've had our dinners. We've made our memories and experienced the warmth. But now, this room has been sucked clean, a chilling quality left behind reminiscent of a mausoleum. Now, there's nothing left but the lemon scent from our scouring efforts and the frosty feel of knowing it's over. I'm not leaning on anyone's arm. I'm standing here alone, biting at my chipped black nail polish. I wonder what the earlier version of me would have said if she could've seen this train wreck coming. I wonder if she'd have still smiled, still wrapped her arms around him, still whispered sweet nothings in his ear as he leaned her against their new faux marble countertop, as they prepared to move in and start a new life.

It doesn't matter now. That girl, that couple, is long gone.

The wooden floor creaks under my feet as I make my way to the living room. My footsteps echo in a way that sounds unnatural, the emptiness of the rooms foreign to my ears. Glancing around, the bright rectangles on the faded walls remind me of where our memories used to hang. Now those photographs have been sealed away in boxes we'll both remember but try so hard to forget.

What happened to us?

I traipse by the furrows in the carpet left from the plaid sofa I inherited in college. I pause, seeing him in the corner, still fiddling with the final box as if the layout of tools within their cardboard home is actually important.

As he silently repacks the box over and over, I can't help but wonder if he's stalling, like the sealing of the final box is a permanent admission we're through.

But putting off the last box won't put off the final parting. We've said our goodbyes over and over again. From the first box I loaded in the U-Haul to the dance over what mugs were whose, we've maneuvered the painful division performance. Piece by piece, we've unglued our papier-mâché lives back into a cryptic, individualized version of us.

We've reclaimed our furniture and rearranged our lives. There's one final walkthrough with the landlord, a final division of our security deposit, and we'll be loosed from one another for good.

Luke finally resigns from his task, pulling out the roll of tape.

"Shit," he exclaims as he's wrapped up by the cheap, sticky tape.

Instinctively, I cross the room to help him like I have so many times.

I hate the tension between us as I grab the roll, use my nail to pry the last end loose, and slap on the final nail in the proverbial coffin of our relationship.

Three years and fourteen days started unraveling six months ago, but the slapping on of the tape on the last box makes me mourn.

"So this is the last of it," he says, hoisting the box from the floor, eyeing me with the dark eyes that used to wordlessly speak to me.

They're the eyes that used to say forever.

Now, those eyes look at me and silently, irrevocably close that door.

"I'll call you when Landlord Joe schedules the final walkthrough," I say matter-of-factly, as if I'm talking to my dentist or the man at the post office, not the man I've built a life with and torn down around us.

"Okay. You know my number."

This is perhaps the hardest of all, hearing the seriousness in his words. Three years, fourteen days, a life together, has boiled down to a barren apartment, a separation of coffee mugs, thirty-one packed boxes, two moving vans, and a "You know my number."

There's a moment of hesitation, as if we're both unsure of the true reality of this. There's a moment when I think, like so many other times, Luke's charisma and charm will set this right.

But this is, I suppose, no match for even Luke. So, in an anticlimactic yet earth-shattering move, he turns and heads for the door.

He doesn't look back.

Instead, after three years and fourteen days, I'm left in a cold, dusty shell of the life and love we once had. Wiping away a rogue tear, I'm left with the realization I have no clue what the hell I'm supposed to do now.

CHAPTER TWO

LILA

"Lila, are you sure there aren't bricks in these?" Maren asks as she hands Will the last of my boxes from the U-Haul.

"Where's this one going? Your room *and* the spare room are full," Will says, sweat beading on his forehead. The poor guy is earning his place in the family already, and he hasn't even said his "I dos."

I sigh, swiping a piece of hair out of my face, wanting to crumple to the pavement. I didn't consider that all the stuff I acquired over the past few years was quite a bit more than what I had when I moved out of my parents' house all those years ago.

Moving back in with your parents at twenty-nine is bad enough without having to solve dilemmas like where your extra boxes should go.

"Just put them in the shed," my dad says, coming up behind me and putting a hand on my shoulder. He squeezes it, and I put a hand on his. "It'll be okay, Lila Lou. We'll figure this all out."

I shake my head at his childhood nickname for me as I motion for Will to go ahead to the shed.

"Okay, are we finally done now? I'm exhausted," Maren announces, wiping her hands as if she's gotten dirty. She hobbles toward the house, yanking on my hand. "Let's get inside. Mom said dinner's almost ready. She made your favorite."

"I'm not hungry."

Maren eyes me. "Oh no you don't. You're not going into this whole emo, no-eating depression. I won't have it. Now listen. I know this is a little shitty right now, moving back home—no offense, Dad—but it's going to be fine. You made the right decision. It's going to take some time to get back on your feet, but it's all good. So come eat some damn food, drink some wine, and settle in."

I grin. Only Maren can get away with telling it like it is and not offending anyone. She hobbles toward the front door, her red stilettos not exactly the best moving shoes. But that's Maren for you—she could be dying of pneumonia and she'd be worried about what her hair looked like and asking for her six-inch heels.

Will emerges from behind the house, still sweating, the June sun pounding down on us.

"Thanks, Will. I owe you."

"It's not a problem. Seriously. Happy to help." I smile at Maren's fiancé as he readjusts his glasses, sweat now pouring from his forehead. The guy's a desk job kind of guy, not a moving day kind of guy. Still, he was here bright and early, ready to haul away my life and put it back to the place where I started.

I'm glad my sister got a good one, a truly good one.

I follow Will into the house, his designer jeans and button-up looking a little crumpled from all the exertion.

But who am I to judge? My whole life is a bit crumpled right now. Moving back home at this stage of my life wasn't exactly what I had in mind. Neither was breaking up with the guy I thought was the love of my life.

He might still be. Because right now, this sure doesn't feel like the right thing or the better thing or even the thing I want. It sucks, even if I put moving back into my childhood room aside.

But this is reality. We're over, and I'm no longer the semi-independent grown-up I've been trying to be for years. I'm now the "I live at home" woman who will be staring at the bright turquoise walls of my childhood, Justin Timberlake posters still adorning every inch. I'd like to say I'm going to tear them down immediately—but the man is pretty hot, and right now, a hot man to keep me company in the coldness of my empty bed might not be a bad thing. Plus, this is temporary, I remind myself. It's just a stopping point in this new, exciting journey.

I blow a strand of hair out of my eyes. The way things are looking, this is a stopping point only on the way to lonely old age. With my student loans needing to be paid off, going out on my own doesn't even seem to be anywhere on the horizon.

Maren offered to let me move in with her and Will, but I didn't really want to cramp her style. Living with soon-to-be newlyweds just seemed a little creepy. There's also the problem that her apartment doesn't allow dogs, and I'm not leaving the only true, loyal man in my life behind.

"Hey, big guy," Will says as Henry rushes down my parents' stairs to greet him for the tenth time today. He doesn't care that Will's been in and out of the house already. He still gets as excited as if he's someone new.

I try to get a hold of Henry's collar so he doesn't knock everyone down, but it's no use. The two-hundred-pound dog plows through, almost knocking me to the ground when he bumps against my knees. Just what I need—a broken leg on top of it.

One look at that droopy face and happy, wagging butt reminds me why I chose my childhood room and Mom's overbearing tendencies versus a life without Henry.

Although Maren promptly told me I better get on finding a sugar daddy—and soon—because she firmly believes Mom is going to drive me mad.

It's certainly possible.

Right now, though, I'm too tired to consider all the ridiculous antics my mother is sure to pull. I follow my family upstairs to the kitchen where Mom and Grandma are already setting up for dinner.

Despite my fears and the embarrassment, I sigh, telling myself it's all good. This was the right choice. It's going to be fine.

Now I just have to hope my faux positivity speaks to the

universe and all that trippy stuff. We'll see.

"There you are, honey. How's it going? Can I get you anything? Need any help organizing?" Mom asks, rushing at me and talking a mile a minute.

"Mom, give the girl room to breathe. She's going through a breakup, not paralysis. She can manage," Maren says, and Mom rolls her eyes at her.

"I'm just worried about her. She's not getting any younger, you know," Mom notes, clutching at her chest for dramatic effect. The woman should have been an actress on daytime soap operas instead of a secretary. She's got a flair for the dramatic.

"I don't think that's helping things, Lucy," my dad warns, giving her a look.

Grandma is parked at the kitchen table, her Pomeranian on her lap although Mom constantly tells her dogs do not belong at the table.

But Grandma doesn't listen to sensibilities like these, and she certainly doesn't listen to my mother. Which absolutely drives my mother mad.

Henry approaches Grandma and Cookie, who emits a vicious growl, and Henry erupts in a barking fit. Grandma chuckles as Cookie snaps at Henry's nose, and Henry darts around the table, hiding in fear for his life despite the obvious size difference. Mom and Dad argue in the corner of the kitchen about whether Luke should be mentioned, the volume rising to a level above the barking of the dogs.

Maren and Will are making out in the corner like he's just come back from war, and I quickly avert my eyes so I don't see something I won't be able to unsee. Maren's bold, but I didn't think an accountant would be so shameless at a family gathering. I guess Maren really does bring out a different side of him, as he claimed during their crazy romantic proposal last December.

My head swirls as I try to figure what to take in and what to block out. It's like I'm lost in the kitchen, my family going right along without me. I've been left behind, the Lila without Luke not worth noticing.

I guess that's okay because right now, I'm not 100 percent sure who the Lila without Luke even is. It's crazy how a few years together and suddenly I'm no longer just one person anymore. My identity melts into his and when I try to separate them, there's residual effects of him marked in me and on me. I'm not quite who I was before.

I shake my head, reminding myself I'm lucky. I'm going to get through this. I can do this.

Looking around at my crazy family, I realize I *am* lucky and I do love them.

But I don't know how anyone could survive them.

And then it happens. During the chaos, the smoke detector goes off, and everyone looks to my parents.

"Oh shit," Mom exclaims, rushing to the stove where the lasagna was cooking. Grabbing potholders, she whips open the oven to pull out dinner.

Black smoke billows through the kitchen.

Grandma screams, "Fire! Fire! Fire!"

Mom swears. Dad rushes to open windows, and Henry starts dry-heaving while Cookie barks loudly.

Yep. Things are going just swell.

How long until I can move back out?

* * *

"Oh, Harvey, you know I like to get a look at the delivery boy. How am I going to rate him on my scale when you didn't let me answer the door?" Grandma whines. "I even put on my red lips, my good Avon lipstick, because I knew he would be coming. What a waste."

"Mom, they have to keep sending a new pizza delivery boy here because of the inappropriate comments you keep making. No more answering the door. You know the rules," Dad replies, shaking his head at Grandma, who is leaning against the counter now, pouting.

Grandma winks at me. "There are quite a few nice-looking ones at that Phil's Pizza. Next time we order, make sure you get a look. Who knows, maybe you'll find a new man."

I shake my head, but can't help but grin. Grandma Claire is one of the bright spots of moving back home. I'll get to spend more time with her, and she's definitely a firecracker for her age.

Maren, Will, Mom, Grandma, and I gather around the table as Dad dishes out paper plates.

"Sorry I ruined your welcome home dinner, Lila. I wanted things to be perfect," Mom admits, looking truly disheartened.

"It's fine, Mom. Pizza is great," I reply as she leans in to put an arm around me. The lasagna, black as coal and still smelling pretty nasty, simmers on the top of the stove, Henry stupidly eyeing it with drool flying out of his mouth. That thing is so burnt, I think it's going to be lava-hot for at least a week. And that pan is definitely garbage.

In truth, we were all expecting pizza for dinner, even if our naivety let us believe we were eating home-cooked lasagna. Mom's never been a great cook, although she certainly tries. We just aren't brave enough to bring it up. We always let pizza be the backup and pretend like we're so shocked when the delivery man comes. Let's put it this way, though—Grandma Claire's rated a lot of pizza delivery boys over the past few years since she moved in with Mom and Dad. A lot.

We gather around, exhausted from a day of moving and lugging heavy boxes. I'm exhausted emotionally as well.

I nibble on a slice of cheese pizza, trying to remind myself this is good. Sitting around the table with family is great. I have a perfectly fine life without him.

"How many more days until the wedding, Maren?" Grandma asks after taking a bite of pizza. Maren pours us all a glass of wine, and Grandma motions for her to keep pouring. Mom shakes her head. Grandma's not really supposed to drink with her heart medicine, but that's never slowed her down. Italian to the core, she loves herself a good wine with dinner—every night. I think Mom's just resigned herself to this and given up.

"One hundred thirty-one," she says, a huge grin lighting up her face as she scrunches her nose at Will.

They're so in love it should make me sick. It doesn't

though. I'm happy for my wild-child sister. To be honest, I never thought she'd settle down. More than that, I never thought she'd settle down with an accountant who loves reading and Sudoku. Still, the two of them together balance each other out. When they look at each other, happiness seems to pour out of them in a sickening concoction of sweet and passionate.

I look up from my plate to realize everyone is silently gauging me, to see if I'm going to get upset.

This just frustrates me. "Okay, guys, I'm going to be fine. You don't have to tiptoe around me. I love you all for looking out for me, but I'm fine. Seriously."

"Yeah, she's fine," Grandma says, feeding Cookie a piece of pepperoni. "She's still got time to find a new one so she has a date for the wedding."

"Grandma, that's not helping," Maren says. "Although, I do know this great guy…."

"Okay. We're done here. No one is setting me up. I'm fine, really. There's nothing wrong with being single until I can figure things out." I reach for my napkin to wipe some pizza grease from my face, hoping to hell this conversation is shutting down.

"Amen," Dad says.

"Truth. Men are overrated. Although after so long without sex, it does get a little lonely," Grandma chimes in, and everyone simultaneously groans as the word "sex" comes out of our grandma's mouth.

She just chuckles and shrugs.

"Just make sure you don't end up a spinster, okay?"

Grandma adds, and I grimace.

"Oh stop. She won't be a spinster. Before you know it, she'll be engaged to a hot hunk who deserves her. This is just a rough patch," Mom says.

At this, it is my turn to groan. An edge infiltrates my voice as I respond, "Mom, please just stop."

"I know, honey. But you two were so... different. I think this is going to be such a good thing. You're going to find someone who can actually fit you. A good doctor or lawyer or something." She's making the serious face at me, a mixture between the duck face and the Mom glare.

"You know, different isn't a bad thing. And really, Mom? Doctors or lawyers? Are we doing arranged marriages now?" I ask, still feeling the need to defend Luke and me like I have so many times.

"You're going to need something different after about two weeks of this. Hell, you might even beg for an arranged marriage if it gets you out of here," Maren whispers to me, gesturing her wine glass toward Mom.

"I heard that," Mom says.

"I know," Maren says.

"Ladies," Dad says.

And so the bickering, arguing family is back, shoving pizza in their mouths, being way too loud, drinking too much wine, and yelling at Grandma for more inappropriate comments.

"Are you sure you know what you're getting yourself into?" I ask Will when my family is engaged in a battle about whether cousin Wilma should, in fact, be invited to the wedding despite the refrigerator fight from two years ago.

"I'm beginning to wonder," he whispers, smiling. "But listen, if you ever need a break, we have an open guest room. I'm sure we could sneak Henry in for a day or so."

"Thanks," I say, meaning it.

"Oh, and Lila?"

"Yeah, Will?"

"It is going to be okay, you know. You'll see. You're a strong woman, just like your sister, even if you don't think so."

I smile, thankful there's at least one sane person going to be in our family. Or at least sane until the family gets their hooks into him.

But thinking about his words, I'm not so sure he's right. Because no matter how much I tell myself I'm going to be happy or that this is the right thing to do, as I crawl over the pathway of boxes in my childhood bedroom and stare at the bright walls and Justin Timberlake later that night, I wonder how many more days I can manage this new life. I wonder what Luke's doing.

Most of all, I hear the word "spinster" circulating in my head, and I wonder if this whole breakup was even worth it at all.

CHAPTER THREE

LUKE

"Dude, I'm all for having a good time and living it up, but maybe you should slow down? You have to go to work tomorrow. You can't call off again."

Evan reaches across the sofa to snag the bottle of beer from my hand. I don't budge, aimlessly staring at the football game on television, the faded plaid couch an extension of my body at this point. I'm wearing the same jeans and T-shirt I wore yesterday, my black beanie keeping my semigreasy curls tucked away. Floyd is curled up on his back on my lap, giving me more motivation to not move an inch.

Evan goes to put the beer on the coffee table, but apparently changes his mind and starts swigging it.

I don't care. I don't care about anything.

"Did you hear me? Look, I love that you're here and I think it's awesome you're having a good time and all. But I have rent to pay, you know?"

I turn to eye Evan, who is, in typical Evan fashion, talking way too much with his hands.

"Yeah, I know. I'm going to work tomorrow. I can't stand sitting here another day anyway."

"That's the spirit. Look, I know this sucks right now, but give it a few weeks and you'll be asking 'Lila who?' You're not tied down anymore. You can have all the girls you want, and man, do I have some to show to you."

He pats me on the back now, or more like slaps me, apparently in a gesture of male bonding.

It just pisses me off. We might have been best friends in high school, but we're on completely different levels now. Evan, the eternal bachelor, is all about getting all the girls he wants. That's just not me, not anymore.

You could find me fifty supermodels right now and tell me they're mine for the taking, and it wouldn't stir anything.

Because the fifty of them... they wouldn't be her, not even close.

Evan jaunts off to the kitchen, probably to dig out some Fritos or something. I just stare, the murmur of the game blending into the background. I don't see anything that's happening. I barely hear Evan rambling on about tomorrow and bills and some bet he made with Steve.

I just keep playing the memories over and over, thinking about how I ended up here, and wondering how I'm ever going to move on from this.

Most of all, I sit and think about what a fool I've been and how I should've never let it come to this. My cell phone catches my eye on the coffee table.

It's not too late. It's only been a few days. Maybe it's not too late.

But then I think about those final words I said, and the ultimate nail in the coffin. I think about that look in her eyes when I took that last box out of the apartment. It was a teary look and a pleading look. Still, somewhere in there, I saw something else.

A look of hope.

Maybe this is what Lila needed all along. Maybe I was an idiot for thinking I could be good enough for her, could be what she needed. I'm too far gone for that, too far lost to be the man Lila Morrow deserves. It's about time I figured that out.

But it doesn't make this shitty feeling in my chest any more bearable. It doesn't make me want to stop drinking beer after beer, to go out there and live life.

The thought that Lila is no longer mine makes me want to do exactly what I've done for the two days since moving into Evan's bachelor pad—sit, stare, and fade into nothingness.

No matter what Evan says, I'm not going to just forget about Lila. I'm not going to merge into the bachelor life seamlessly.

I'm not going to stop missing her and wondering how I could've stopped this train wreck from imploding.

I'm not going to stop wishing I could get her back but remembering that she's better off without me.

So I stare at the television until I nod off, the morning alarm rousting me and Floyd from the plaid couch for the first time in half a day. I drag myself to the shower and finally rinse off the residue from the breakup days ago. I wash away the Luke I was with Lila and try to start fresh.

But the new start I thought we'd both get doesn't feel too great, I realize, as I trudge out the door to work.

* * *

"There he is. The free man," Dean bellows as I get out of my pickup truck, parked outside our latest job. It's a gray day, drizzle mercifully bringing the temperature down. I could use a relatively easy day.

Dean's already setting up at the tiny ranch house we're working on today. He's got the ladder out and is chipperly jaunting from his truck to the house, setting up tools, whistling annoyingly.

I'd be ready to choke him if it weren't Dean. That's just how the guy is. Eternally in a good mood. He readjusts his sunglasses, eyeing me as I pull out my thermos for some coffee. I know I look just as rough as I feel.

"You doing okay, buddy?" he asks, slapping my back. "You finish getting everything moved in? Sorry I couldn't help you. Cassie's parents were in for the weekend, and I had to do my time."

"It's okay. Yeah, we got everything in."

"You really doing okay? You look like shit, if I'm being honest."

I sigh. "I know. Just… it's been rough."

"I know. But listen, let's just put in a hard day's work, not talk about you-know-who, and maybe it'll help. Things will be all right. Give it some time."

"That's what everyone keeps telling me. But I don't know. I don't know if I did the right thing," I confess. Dean's been a close friend, and he's an honest friend. I know he won't sugarcoat anything. Plus, unlike Evan, he's out of the single-is-better phase.

Dean shrugs. "Just don't think about it too much. It sucks, I know. You and Lila had a good thing going, and I liked her. I really liked her. It's hard. But if it wasn't meant to be, if it couldn't work out, well, then you owe it to each other to try to move on and be happy. And, not to sound all sappy and shit, but if you're meant to find your way back to each other, you will. In the meantime, enjoy the bachelor life. Drink some extra beers. Because someday, when you get married, you'll be the one spending weekends with over-the-top in-laws eating Thai food and answering eight million questions about home repairs. Trust me," he says, rolling his eyes.

I grin. "That bad?"

"Worse. I had a full two-hour conversation with her mother about the best types of blinds for the house. Seriously. The woman can't give us an inch of space."

I smile, letting Dean ramble on about his in-law problems, happy to drown myself in someone's else's world, even if just for our shift. Dean and I spend the day ripping up the old roof, the drizzle and cool temperatures making the work easier than normal. Once we're done, we clean up, set things up for tomorrow's task, and head to our vehicles.

"You want to go out or something?" I ask, thinking

maybe everyone's right. Maybe I just need to give this whole moving on thing a try, or at least the forgetting part.

"Can't. We're going blind shopping," Dean says, grinning.

"Oh, man. They got to her then?"

"Uh-huh. Why didn't anyone tell me on my wedding day that in four years, I'd be spending my Monday night blind shopping after a hellish weekend with in-laws?"

"You love her," I say, grinning.

"Of course I do. But Jesus, sometimes, a guy needs to cling to his masculinity a little, you know? Not feel so tied down."

I nod, saying goodbye to Dean as I jump in my truck, knowing all too well what he's talking about. I head back to Evan's, which still doesn't feel like home or like mine. I head there, regardless, to think about things too complicated and exhausting for a Monday night. Mostly I think about how much freedom I have now—and how little I actually appreciate it.

Breaking up fucking sucks.

CHAPTER FOUR

LUKE

"Hey, fella, how are you? Good to see you again," Charley proclaims from behind the grill, his beer belly almost touching the grates. I wonder if his belly hair, which is visible below what is practically a crop top, is scorched onto the burgers. I try to shove aside the thought.

Charley lets out a wheezing cough, perhaps the abundance of cigarettes getting to him. His scraggly white beard is a little longer than the last time I saw him. He's only got about six months to grow it out for his gig.

"I'm okay," I say. "Need any help?"

"Nah, this is my prime territory. King of the grill, and all that. Maybe your mother needs help though, getting the potato salad and stuff ready."

I nod, relieved I don't have to make awkward small talk with Mom's boyfriend of the month, who happens to be the Santa Claus at our local mall in the winter and a sculptor the rest of the year. They met at one of his art shows a few months ago, Charley's nude sculptures capturing Mom's eye.

And the rest was history... or at least history for this month.

I wander inside the familiar ranch, eyeing the peeling yellow paint on the outside. I really should make it over to help Mom fix the place up. Of course, she'd probably just read me a riot act about how women don't need men to save them and all that.

I open the creaky screen door and amble inside, Bowser nipping at my heels. He is one piece of Charley's baggage—a five-pound Chihuahua that hates everyone and has an overactive bladder. I look down in time to move my foot from the spray of piss coming my way.

Great. Just what I need.

"Luke, there you are!" Mom exclaims, dashing from the kitchen to greet me. She leans in for a huge hug and squeezes me a long time. "It's been forever," she says.

Really, it's only been about three weeks. Mom and Charley were away on a Caribbean cruise for a while. Thankfully, Scarlet got stuck with the joy of watching Bowser.

Mom readjusts her tube top—when she gets a new boyfriend, she breaks out the faded turquoise square of fabric, feeling more confident, I suppose. Scarlet and I always give each other a knowing look when we see it reappear, knowing there's a new man in the picture.

"Dinner's almost ready. I'm so glad you could make it, especially with everything going on. This is the time you need to be surrounded by family," she says, leading me to the kitchen. Scarlet and her husband John are chopping onions and helping ice the cake Mom made. Scarlet turns to eye me.

"Mom, Jesus, it's not like she died. They broke up," Scarlet says, shaking her head and giving Mom the Scarlet eye roll. She looks me up and down for a second before continuing. "Although, he does look awful. Are you eating and sleeping? You look like hell, Luke. Really."

"Yep, family. Just what I need right now," I say, shaking my head as I run a hand through my curls. I know Scarlet's right, and I know she's not one to hide the truth.

John approaches, slapping me on the back. "You look fine, Luke. Don't listen to them. How's the single life treating you?"

I shrug noncommittally. It's crazy how my breakup seems to be the talk on everyone's lips. How is a guy supposed to move on and let it go when no one will let me?

"Will everyone stop talking about it? Give him some room to breathe," Scarlet says now. "Jesus, where is the tact in this family?"

I raise an eyebrow at Scarlet, the infernal hypocrite.

"Well, we're just worried about him is all. I know how much Lila meant. And don't get me wrong, she was a great girl. But she wasn't for you. So serious all the time. Always so… judgy, you know? Like the time she refused to eat my brownies and stuff."

"Mom, you put pot in them. Honestly, what did you expect?" I ask, squeezing the bridge of my nose between my thumb and forefinger. This family is a headache. I'm surprised Lila didn't go running sooner than she did.

"The girl needed to loosen up. We all do. But anyway, you're better off. Play the field. Live it up, Luke. You're still so young." Mom is carrying potato salad out the screen door to the picnic table, John following with the onions and condiments.

"Not that young," Scarlet says, nudging me, and I smirk.

"Hey, you're not going to be in your twenties forever," I retort, leaning on the counter to look out the kitchen window. Charley's taking the burgers off the grill, but he stops to lean in and give Mom a kiss. Their kissing turns a little heated, and John looks hellishly uncomfortable, trying to distract himself with setting the table. Scarlet peers out the window beside me, laughing at her husband's clear discomfort.

"How did you keep him around? How did he not go running?" I ask, smirking.

Scarlet shrugged. "Guess he figured I was worth dealing with Mom's bizarre ways."

"Remind me to have another chat with that guy," I tease.

Scarlet and I have always had an easy relationship despite our typical sibling rivalry. We're close enough to be honest with each other.

"Look, I know why you did what you did, and I know maybe it was the right thing to do. But Lila was so good for you. You were good together. Are you sure you made the right decision?"

Out of everyone, Scarlet would be the one to bring up this topic, to question me, to not just tell me things are going to be fine.

I shrug. "Honestly? I don't know. These past few days, I've started to wonder."

Scarlet sighs. "Things are different for you when it comes to love. You were older than me, and you were more affected by the shit with Mom and Dad. I get that. But Luke, don't let what Dad did screw up everything for you. And don't forget that you're worth it, too. Whether it's Lila or not, you deserve someone willing to look past all of this"— she motions toward the house, referring to the general dysfunction that is Mom—"to be with you. You're a good guy. Really."

"Thanks, Scarlet. So sentimental today. Are you pregnant or something?" I tease, nudging her.

"Hell, no. We're not ready for that yet. And hey, are you saying I look chubby?"

"Never."

"Did you say pregnant?" Mom says, wandering back through the screen door. That woman is flighty as hell, but she has sonic hearing, I swear.

"No, Mom. No babies," Scarlet says.

"Thank God. I'm not ready to hear the word Grandma. I'm too young."

Scarlet and I look at each other, wide-eyed.

"If you say so," Scarlet mumbles as I head to the fridge to get some drinks. Bowser dashes back toward me, nipping at my feet.

"Dammit, Mom. Will you get this dog? Did Charley really have to move this thing in, too?"

"Oh, Bowser's not so bad. He's Charley's favorite. Here, buddy," Mom says, stooping down to pick up the snarling dog as she baby talks to it. But Bowser isn't having it. Instead, the dog latches onto Mom's hand, sinking its tiny, razor-sharp teeth into the fleshy part of her thumb.

"Dammit!" she screams, flinging the dog across the kitchen. Blood spurts everywhere, a fountain of red, as I abandon the drinks to rush to Mom's help. Scarlet yells for John, who dashes inside.

"Here, let me go get my first aid kit," he announces, running to get his kit.

"Good thing I married a nurse. God knows we need medical help in this family," Scarlet says, calming now as I hold pressure on Mom's hand.

Charley's also in the house now, taking over my position. "I'm so sorry, sweetie. I don't know what got into him."

"It's okay, it's okay. I'm fine. A Band-Aid and I'll be good as new."

"You didn't make any of those brownies, did you, Mom?" Scarlet asks. "I could use a few dozen."

Mom shakes her head, laughing, as John comes in, taking over and bandaging Mom's hand. Bowser's resigned himself to the living room, perched on the couch like a king.

When all is calm again and we head outside to eat, the food is mostly cold and bugs are landing on every inch of it.

"So much for a peaceful dinner," Mom says as we all sit down. Everyone digs in—we are not a grace-saying kind of family.

"Any new art shows coming up?" I ask Charley, trying

to make friendly conversation.

"Not until September. It's in Georgia," Charley says. "I've got quite a few pieces ready to go." At this, my mom lets out a little giggle and Charley gives a creepy wink.

Oh Jesus. I was afraid of this.

"Yeah, I have quite the muse. The work is in the shed if you guys want to see it after dinner," Charley offers.

"No way," John, Scarlet, and I shout simultaneously.

I think about burning my own eyes out at the mere thought of my mom being Charley's new muse.

"You guys need to loosen up. Relax. It's all good. Charley added some leaves into the sculpture so it's appropriate."

I shake my head, and Scarlet gives another of her eye rolls.

"How the hell did we survive this family?" Scarlet asks me, and John stifles a laugh.

And the thing is, I honestly have no idea. I have no idea how the hell I turned out even seminormal or how I thought for a second I deserved someone like Lila Morrow after growing up in this loving but batshit-crazy family.

* * *

Getting back to the apartment is a relief. I promise Mom to stop by and shut down her offer to set me up on some dates. Back in my room in the bachelor pad, I inhale, taking two aspirin before lying back on my bed. My family always gives me a headache.

Don't get me wrong. Mom's a good woman—nude sculptures, questionable dates, and pot brownies aside.

She's only recently become more hippie-like, trying to get the most out of life and feel younger than her fifty-eight years. To an outsider, I'm sure she looks like an absolutely insane woman. She is not your typical church on Sunday, epitome of ladylike kind of mom. She's gritty and raw. But she's my mom, and if anyone has the right to be a little rough around the edges, it's that woman. She's had a tough go at it, and she did her best to raise Scarlet and me so we didn't know we were different. We never had a lot, her waitressing money not going very far, but we survived. We turned out semi-okay.

Mom's love life has also not been traditional. She's had more boyfriends over the years than I can count. Her relationships are unstable, and she changes men as regularly as some people change the oil in their cars—sometimes more frequently. Still, I can't fault her for that either. Dad did a number on her. I think dating gives her power. I think she wants to believe in love, craves it even, but can't let herself be committed. To Mom, I think a long, committed relationship makes her feel vulnerable.

For now, though, Charley is making her happy, and I'll take it. It's good to see her happy.

I turn over in bed, glancing at the clock.

It's Wednesday night. At this time, Lila would be getting her shower before we cuddled up to watch our favorite show. She'd use that shampoo I loved so much before brushing out her long blonde locks. On the couch, her wet hair would dampen my shirt, but I never cared. Holding her, relaxing into her in the evenings was our tradition. It's what grounded me, what made me feel ready to tackle another day of work.

Now, I lie here staring at the clock, not feeling like doing much of anything.

I don't feel angry tonight or hurt. I just feel—silence. Bone-chilling silence permeates me. I feel empty.

I wonder if it'll ever feel like home here, if I'll ever find my own routine. Because right now it doesn't feel like it.

I don't get up and put on the show we used to watch together, and I don't even move. Instead, I lie in my bed, staring at the clock, as my mind drifts back to a different time.

A time when she was mine.

* * *

Sweltering. That was the only word that came to mind as my brain fizzled, drained from the exhaustion of going up and down those damn stairs at least thirty times. The pounding July sun on my back didn't help matters—nor did the fact our new apartment had no air-conditioning to speak of. And there was no breeze, not even a single puff of air.

"Are you sure you need all these… shoes?" I asked, staring at the neatly placed label on the box in my arms.

"Are you kidding? Those aren't even half of them," she replied, smiling as she tightened her ponytail, turning from the back of the U-Haul as she grabbed another box.

"You do know this is only a one-bedroom, right? And we only have one closet?" I joked, mentally preparing myself to climb those stairs again, my calves screaming at the thought.

Just five more trips, *I thought.* Five more trips and we'd be officially moved in, officially a couple who lived together.

The thought was enough to drive me up those stairs.

"Correction," Lila said as I huffed my way up the steps, her right behind me. "I have one closet. You have a dresser."

I shook my head. "I don't even think having one entire closet to yourself is going to help. How many shoes does a girl need?" I trekked back to the bedroom, dropping the box to the floor.

"Careful, those are my babies," she said. I turned to eye her with a raised eyebrow.

"What?" she asked, putting her box down. "Don't judge. You knew I was a shoe addict when you asked me to live with you. You can't back out now."

Wiping sweat from my forehead, I walked toward her, grabbed her hands and entwined our fingers. "I'm not backing out. No way."

She smiled at me, leaning in for a kiss. Despite our dripping sweat and tired muscles, the kiss eased my exhaustion. It energized me and made me realize it was all worth it.

She pulled back. "Come on, mister. No breaks for you. We have about ten more boxes and then we're done."

"Yeah, and then we just have to organize."

"But it's exciting, isn't it?" she asked, not moving from the room.

"It is. I can't believe it's happening."

Lila lit up, that smile I'd come to love already plastered on her face. That smile I'd come to need in my life. I glanced around the tiny room, peeling yellow paint and old, decrepit windows taking away from the atmosphere of our first bedroom together but not enough to make me even blink. The thought that I, Luke Bowman, got to share a bedroom with this sexy, shoe-addicted woman was more than I could've ever dreamed of. I'd dance down the hallway and skip around the block—if I could feel my legs.

"I'm so happy we get to start our life together here. It's perfect," she said, leaning in for another kiss. I wrapped her in my arms, despite our sweatiness. Neither of us cared. We were home. That was all that mattered.

"I love you," I said, staring deep in her eyes.

"I love you, too," she replied. "But we need to finish carrying boxes. We've got more shoes to carry in."

I grinned, shaking my head. "Can't we just donate a box or two to Goodwill?"

"Luke Bowman, bite your tongue, or this happy little arrangement is going to be over before it even starts."

"Not a chance," I said as I followed her down the stairs.

"Because you love me too much?" she asked, winking over her shoulder.

"That. But also because there is no way in hell I'm moving all this shit out of here again. My legs feel like Jell-O and I'm starving."

Lila laughed. "Same. If we break up, let's just draw a line down the center of each room, deal?"

"Deal," I agreed as we paraded toward the U-Haul, smiling at the thought of it. It was a ludicrous idea, us breaking up. I was crazy about the girl who stole my heart

over a dying cat. I knew from that first moment Lila was destined to be mine. These past eight months had only strengthened the need for her, the want for her. They'd only strengthened the fact life without Lila wasn't life at all.

"After we finish these boxes, I think we should get pizza," Lila said. *"I'm starving."*

"Extra cheese and ham? Oh, and those amazing lava cakes they have," I said.

She pauses, perhaps just to put off going up the steps. "I was thinking the exact same thing. You read my mind."

"We're made for each other," I announced, propping the box on my hip to free up a hand. I offered her a fist bump.

She scrunched her nose in that adorable way that made me smile. "We're made for each other because we want the same pizza toppings?"

"Hey, it's in the details. We're made for each other," I responded, still offering her my fist.

She sighed, but obliged, bumping fists before agreeing, "If you say so."

We finished unloading our boxes, dead on our feet, and polished off an entire pizza and four lava cakes.

That night there was no hot sex or crazy celebrations. Our first night together involved falling asleep as soon as our heads hit the pillow, but we were okay with that.

Our lives were just beginning. We had so much time together, so many memories to make. There would be so many chances to make memories, we knew, as we drifted off in each other's arms, right where we believed we were supposed to be.

***

The comforter I lie on is the comforter we shared on that first night. I think about that day, the sheer exuberance of moving in, of having found the one to share my life with. I think about her bouncy ponytail and how that woman could make seventy-nine pairs of shoes sound not so bad. I thought about how I didn't care what color dish towels she insisted we needed or how she organized the living room. That day, all I cared about was the fact I was fusing my life with Lila's, and we were facing the future together.

Now, here I am, alone, the comforter that once cocooned us an empty reminder of everything good that's gone.

Those boxes didn't have a one-way ticket into that apartment, and there would be no line drawn to divide the place. There would just be some hurtful words, some drifting, and a dissolution of the love we'd packed into that apartment.

The one-bedroom wouldn't be big enough to hold our pride, our fears, and our feelings that we were outgrowing each other. That one-bedroom wasn't big enough to hold my regrets and the what-ifs.

Now, though, I'm realizing that even if I leave that place of memories behind, they won't go away. Lila won't go away.

Soul mates are built in the details, and those details follow you no matter where you go.

"Hey, man, you want some pizza?" Evan shouts from the other room.

And just like that, life goes on, the moving day memories relics from a past that no longer seems to be mine.

CHAPTER FIVE

LILA

My phone sitting on the piles of magazines by my nightstand and Henry snoring on the side of the bed where Luke should be sleeping, I battle with the unending question.

Should I call him?

It's been two weeks since we said our final goodbyes, two weeks since that last box was packed. And more than anything, I didn't expect how strange it would be to not talk to him, to not hear from him.

For three years, he was my best friend. For three years, every day started with him and ended with him. He was there when I was picking out my outfit in the morning and he was there to hear my chaotic stories from work. He was there for our pizza grilled cheese sandwiches every Wednesday and to help me come up with gym excuses every Thursday.

He was there. And now he's not.

It's like he's become a ghost in my life, vanishing into thin air with a painful goodbye.

I miss him. I want to hear his voice, long to hear what's going on. I long for the days that used to be, the easy conversations, even when things weren't perfect.

I guess that's the thing about breakups, though. They make everything seem rosier than it was. I don't sit here and long for the screaming fights or all the building tension. I don't think about the times I spent crying in the bathtub because he hadn't noticed me or the times I looked in the mirror and fretted over another fine line on my face because I was getting older and not getting any closer to my goals.

I rub my thumb over the phone screen, knowing I can't. I can't call him because to hear his voice will be my undoing. It will be too risky. I will fall for his voice that radiates through my veins. I will let go of my goals and dreams and settle. I will settle for a life that can't make either of us happy because it will be a life of sacrifice on both ends. We're different people who made a relationship work for a while but couldn't make it work forever. It's best to accept it.

Getting out of bed, stretching languidly, I peek out the window into the sunshine. It's a beautiful day, and I mercifully have the day off work. It's just me and Henry.

And Grandma and Cookie. I almost forgot that the quiet solitude of my apartment is a thing of the past as well.

I wander out to the kitchen, Henry still snoring in my bed.

"Morning, dear. Here's your coffee," Grandma Claire says, Cookie on her lap at the table. She slides a cup to me. She's already dressed, her red pantsuit screaming at me from across the table. A green hat perches on top of her perfectly permed hair. She looks like a Christmas ornament at our table. I smile.

"Thanks," I say, grabbing the cup of coffee that is lukewarm at best and has the consistency of tar. I take the tiniest sip possible and try not to gag.

"You better get that coffee down. We need to get going."

"Going? Where are we going?" I ask, confused. Mom didn't say anything about Grandma Claire going anywhere.

"To the casino, silly girl. It's Thursday. It's senior day. And since you're home, I figured I didn't need to ride up with my friends. I thought you'd take me."

I raise an eyebrow. I didn't realize Grandma had a standing casino date every Thursday. Then again, most Thursdays I'm off work, I either get a pedicure or spend the day watching Netflix.

"Um, okay. Does Mom know?"

"Of course your mother doesn't know. I'm old but I'm not stupid. It's none of that old bat's business where I go or what I spend my money on."

I smirk at Grandma's sass. It's probably a terrible idea. But for some reason, Grandma Claire's taking ownership of her life and silently pulling one over on Mom is appealing. I set my coffee cup down and say, "I'll just go get changed."

"Put something nice on. There might be some hot casino workers. And make sure you have on good underwear."

"Grandma," I say, feeling my cheeks warm.

"Just saying. I've got my Victoria's Secret on. And they're lacy."

"Oh my God," I exclaim, rushing toward my room and shutting the door. I'd forgotten how over-the-top that woman is. I think she gets worse as she ages, her censor deadening.

I shake my head, thinking this is a terrible idea. Mom would be pissed if she knew I was taking Grandma Claire out to the casino, what Mom calls the devil's arena.

This thought alone makes me rush toward my closet and shove some clothes on. If Mom disapproves, it can't be that bad of an idea, can it? Besides, it'll do me good to get out and frivolously toss some money away, although this is exactly the thing I never do. In fact, it's the kind of thing a month ago, I'd have yelled at Luke for.

No time like the present to loosen up the morals, though, and explore a little. Maybe Grandma Claire can show me a thing or two about living a little.

And who knows, maybe she's right about the casino workers. It's time I stop sulking and stop looking to the past. If I don't feel optimistic about my choice and about the future, well, I'll just have to fake it until I make it, good underwear and all.

***

"That Lou wasn't too bad," Grandma Claire exclaims as we get to *her* machine.

"Grandma, don't distract me from the problem at hand. I can't believe you brought Trixie," I whisper in a hushed voice, leading her past security and trying not to look suspicious.

Grandma just clutches tightly to her huge Michael Kors bag—which is currently housing her twenty-two-year-old cat, Trixie. I'm failing already at the whole escorting Grandma to the casino and keeping her out of trouble thing.

"First, acknowledge that Lou wasn't too bad."

Lou is the security guard at the front door. Lou is also about thirty years my elder.

"If you say so, Grandma. But we've got more pressing issues. We need to get home. We *cannot* have a cat in here."

"Oh, hush. I couldn't leave Trixie at home. She's old. What if she died? I'd never forgive myself."

"Well, shoving her in a bag probably isn't helping things. She can't even move in there. How did you even bring her along? I didn't even hear her."

"Trixie doesn't meow much anymore. And don't worry. I put some food in there, and we'll get her some water from the drink fountain. I do this all the time. Trixie's a pro. She's my good luck charm."

I cringe, shaking my head as Grandma plops down at the *Charlie and the Chocolate Factory* machine. This can't be happening.

But Grandma just sits and unzips her purse a little, the old, wheezy cat sticking her head out the hole. There's so much wrong with this scene, especially since I'm a vet.

Nonetheless, looking at the cat as Grandma scratches her chin, she does look comfortable and used to it all. Of course, she's also half-deaf and so old, she probably doesn't even know where she is. I succumb to the madness, plopping down in a seat beside her.

"Come on, Lila, loosen up. It's all good. Have fun. Spend money. May the fates be with you."

Deciding it's no use arguing, I grab a twenty from my purse and decide to go all in, my crazy Grandma and Trixie by my side.

When the minigame on my machine is triggered, Grandma Claire almost leaps out of her seat, and Trixie lets out a meow. A worker nearby eyes us suspiciously, but I cough to cover the noise. He keeps on walking.

"You got a minigame! You did it! Now we just have to hope for the golden ticket and you'll be a winner."

My excitement is short-lived. The golden ticket.

That's what I jokingly used to call Luke. Dammit, does everything have to remind me of him?

I bite my lip, trying to repress the memory of him dancing with me in the kitchen, singing the golden-ticket song from *Charlie and the Chocolate Factory*.

I shake my head, trying to get rid of the image. When the minigame is done with all its embarrassingly loud hoopla, I frown.

I've won fifty cents after all of that. I just don't think the fates are on my side, or maybe Trixie isn't as much good luck as Grandma thinks.

"Rats, Trixie. No luck here. Let's go get you a drink and then we'll head to the *Alice in Wonderland* machine."

I watch Grandma totter over to the self-serve fountain and pour Trixie a cup of water. The cat, as if trained, stretches its neck out to lap up its water. A few elderly women eye the scene but don't say a word, Grandma's glare challenging them.

I smile at how crazy my life is now, because if I don't smile, I just might cry.

* * *

It's back to reality the next day and back to the office—not that this is a bad thing after my trip to the casino and all its excitement. Grandma was thrilled because she managed to win fifty bucks.

No use explaining to her that she spent one hundred. What's funnier, she actually pointed to the gamblers anonymous hotline and made a joke of it. I didn't explain to her that she was a few more Thursdays away from needing it.

Leaving the house at the crack of dawn before even Mom and Dad were up, I patted Henry on the head, kissing him goodbye. He'd be alone with Grandma Claire today after Mom and Dad headed to their respective offices.

Oh, the horror. Hopefully he was just in for a day of game shows and soap operas, but with Grandma Claire, who knew. He could be on a plane to Vegas for the afternoon.

When I get to the office, Zoey's already organizing files. "Hey, you. How was your day off yesterday?"

"You have no idea," I say, leaning on the perfectly clean counter, enjoying the calm before the storm once office hours officially begin.

"I can only imagine. Moving back home and all. Must be scary."

This would seem rude coming from a coworker, but

Zoey isn't your average coworker. We've been best friends since junior high. She paid for my lunch on the first day of seventh grade when I'd forgotten my lunch money. The friendship blossomed over the years into sleepovers, cover stories for our high school sneak outs, and wholesome, honest truths.

"Yeah, it is. You know how good old Lucy Morrow is."

"Demanding? Condescending? Manipulative?" Zoey asks. She's been privy to the inner truth of the horror that is my mother.

"You've got it. Although, mercifully, she doesn't have any vacation days left, so she's been working a lot. Yesterday was just me and Grandma Claire."

"Oh, no. Did you two get into trouble?"

"If by trouble you mean Grandma Claire made me drive her to the casino behind my parents' backs and snuck Trixie in her purse, then yeah. But officially, we didn't get caught, so I guess that's a good sign."

Zoey hands me my cup of coffee, going above and beyond her vet tech duties. She knows I'm not a morning person. "Sounds like a blast. I'll drive Grandma Claire any day she wants."

"Please don't encourage her. Who is on the lineup today?"

"Um, let's see. You've got Carl the beagle and Julia the parakeet. Both in for checkups."

I shake my head. Julia the parakeet, owned by Mrs. Saten—yes, pronounced exactly as you're thinking and perhaps a bit accurate of a description—is in at least once a month for a checkup. The damn bird bites me every time, and every time Mrs. Saten insists I taunted it, am a horrible vet, and will be getting a terrible Yelp review for it.

"Oh, God. Anyone else?" I ask, hoping the day doesn't get much worse.

"A few new patients, a sick elkhound, and a hamster in for a checkup. Nothing extraordinary."

"Good. I could use some regular days."

"Besides Lucy Morrow, how are you doing? Really." Zoey leans on the counter near me now as I gulp my coffee.

I shrug. "Okay."

"Don't lie to me, Lila. I've known you since the time butterfly clips and choker tattoo necklaces were cool. I know when you're lying."

"All right. It sucks. I just, I hate doubting myself. I thought breaking up with Luke was going to be the best thing for me, that it was going to get my life on track and get me headed in the direction I wanted. But it just actually feels like everything is falling apart."

Zoey nudges me. "Hey, chin up. Of course it's going to feel that way. It hasn't been that long—what, like a couple weeks? Give it time. You need to regroup. You had forever planned with him, or at least the start of it. You can pack the boxes and move out, but you can't separate two lives that quickly. It's going to take time. And then, once you get over the initial shock of it all, you'll find your way. Right now, you're just thinking about all the good things. But don't forget about the things that made you call it quits. You can't settle in love, Lila. You know that."

I give her a weak grin, leaning on her shoulder. "When did you get so smart?"

"When you were busy studying to be a vet and I realized being a vet tech was easier, less stress, and more fun."

"You've got me there. Trade me?"

"Ha," she says, "you wish. There aren't enough dollar signs in the world to make me take on that damn parakeet today. No way. You can keep your bigger checks and that white coat."

I smile, thankful that even if my grandma is sneaking cats into casinos and my mom is probably going to be intolerable to live with, I do have the greatest friend a girl could ask for.

CHAPTER SIX

LILA

One word is all it takes to rock my resolve even more than it already has been. One word makes me swirl in a sea of memories, makes me dance with him in my mind. One word on my phone late at night makes me realize the empty spot beside me in the bed is where he used to be, where he perhaps could still be.

One word makes me question it all.

That word?

Hey.

A simple "hey" texted from that familiar number, my favorite picture of him lighting up my screen.

This single word texted makes me realize two things:

1.   He's thinking about me.

2.   I'm not 100 percent sure I'm ready to let go.

Because when I see that text, I think about calling him. I think about how easy it would be to let his deep, rugged voice caress me back into the familiarity of us. I think about how I could stop missing him, stop fighting this fight, whatever it is, and just give in.

The minutes tick by, too many minutes. I stare at his face, at the single word, and wonder how it got here. I wonder how the Luke and Lila who used to ride the same roller coaster ten times so we could get ten different snapshots at the photo booth got here. I wonder how the Luke and Lila whose first dance was in a rainstorm with gusting winds got here. I wonder how the Luke and Lila who had mapped out their side of the couch and their side of the bed and their side of the bathroom sink suddenly were the only side to all these things.

My fingers almost give in, my heart weak.

But then my head jolts me back to reality, like it needs to. I know I can't succumb to him, or things will never change. If I go back now, I'll be stuck in that limbo forever, stuck swirling in the world that wasn't quite enough. I'll be stuck always mourning what could've been if he'd been different or if I'd been strong enough to seek something more for life.

As much as I love that man who swept me off my feet, I also know what got me here. Zoey's right. I need to remember that everything wasn't rosy. Everything wasn't perfect and, as I've told myself since I said yes to Brian in tenth grade for the dance when I really wanted to go with Zander, I won't settle. I haven't settled in my life for anything. I can't settle on this.

So, I turn the phone over, my heart ripping silently at the thought of him waiting for a text that won't come. I know he's not guiltless, though. He made his mistakes along the way, and he has to know why I'm not texting back.

Resting my head back on the pillow, I try to soothe myself with thoughts of the future, with thoughts of how many things are going right in my life, and with thoughts that eventually, this will certainly be the best, wisest choice.

* * *

I sit at the corner table, the one completely opposite what used to be our corner.

"Where's your partner in crime?" Dot asks, hobbling over to my table now that the crowd has dulled down. I put down my peanut-butter doughnut, looking up at her. Her red lips match her permed red hair, as they always do, and she's wearing her Dot's Doughnuts shirt.

I sigh, hating to break the news to her. I gesture for her to have a seat, and she obliges.

"We broke up," I say, and Dot automatically makes a face like I've just strangled a kitten in front of her.

"I was worried about that. I haven't seen you two in weeks. I knew it couldn't be good news."

So Luke hadn't been in to see Dot either. Apparently he was putting it off just as I was. Interesting.

"I'm sorry. It's just... well, you know what this place means to us."

"And you know what you two mean to me. I was getting worried. When neither of you called in for your weekly deliveries or popped in to say hello, I was starting to panic. I miss you, both of you."

She reaches across the table to pat my hand, and the

guilt does really creep in. Dorothy—known as Dot by her customers and her family—has been a great friend to both of us, practically a grandmother. How could I blow her off?

Dot's Doughnuts opened about four years ago, the brainchild of Dot herself. She always loved baking, especially doughnuts, and she just thought our town could use a shop. Competing with the chain doughnut shops, she even added a delivery feature to her restaurant, hiring her own grandsons to do the driving. Luke and I have been known to eat our share of doughnuts from here, popping by at least once a week together and even ordering delivery throughout the week. We're hooked.

It's not just about doughnuts, though. It's about Dot. She's been there from the start of us, and she's been more like family. We get her gifts on the holidays, and we always keep her updated on our lives.

Just not this, apparently.

"I'm sorry. I feel awful." And it's true, I do. It's just another way this whole thing with Luke is throwing everything off.

"Honey, don't feel awful about not telling me. I understand. This place has so much meaning for the two of you. But don't you think the fact you can't bring yourselves to come in says enough?"

"What do you mean?"

She smiles the mysterious smile, raises an eyebrow, and stands. "You know exactly what I mean. You two are beautiful together. I knew that from the first day you crazy kids wandered in here right before closing time. Do you think I would've worked overtime for any old couple? No way. I knew you two were special. I was excited to be able to witness the magic from the beginning. Honey, let me tell you, that kind of magic doesn't just come along any old day. Trust me."

She leans in to kiss my cheek before sauntering back to her position at the counter to wait on a group of teenagers. I find myself misty-eyed.

Looking over at the wall, I see the wedding picture of Dot and Louie, her late husband. I think about all the wonderful stories she's told Luke and me over the years, all the times she smiled and talked about how lucky she was.

If anyone would know love, Dot would. She had sixty-two beautiful years of it. She made me want to believe in love, in marriage, in the whole lot.

But now, even Dot can't make me see clearly. Even Dot can't make me believe it's all going to be magically okay.

I finish my doughnut and stroll out after saying goodbye, the sun angering me with its incessant brightness.

Dot's words roll over and over in my mind, but I try to silence them.

I can't look back. Not everything can be solved with a doughnut or with misty-eyed magic.

This is real life, and sometimes in real life, a girl's just got to know when it's time for a change.

* * *

"I want a major change," I say, exuding confidence I don't really have. I take a breath, parading into the hair salon like

I actually am ready to let go of the long blonde locks I've been growing since high school.

But, as Maren and my grandma always say, a woman who cuts her hair is making a change. Perhaps the reason I'm not ready for change is because I haven't cut my hair. At least that's what I'm telling myself.

I set myself in Jacque's chair at J's Jazzy Cuts, our local top salon. Jacque just gives me a nod, scrunches his nose in appraisal of my ends, and spins me around.

And for the next three hours, he yanks on my hair, trims it, colors it, fluffs it, and styles it.

In complete silence.

If you think having a chatty hairdresser who just asks you all kinds of questions for hours is tiresome, you should sit in the silent chair of Jacque. For part of the time, I wonder if I should spark conversation, but his scrunched face tells me he's deep in concentration, and I don't want to interrupt the *artiste*. For another large chunk of time, I try to cough to cover my growling stomach, since Jacque—the only stylist in the place—does not believe in playing music. I feel more like I'm in my high school library than a salon. Not quite a day of pampering.

The rest of the three hours are spent with me in silent terror, my armpits a little sweaty at the thought he's cutting way more than I wanted. I start picturing myself with a supershort pixie cut and wonder how that will work with my forehead. I also start picturing myself with a Bieber-like haircut, which also would not be flattering on the forehead. I shudder at the thought and start saying a few Hail Marys that Jacque is as worthy of Maren's stellar review as I hope he is.

When the blow dryer is placed on the counter and Jacque silently spins me around, I take a breath and stare in the mirror.

My hand automatically moves to touch my hair but Jacque, who towers over me, slaps my hand away.

"Touching equals frizz. Don't."

His voice is deep and smooth, actually sending a shudder through me, despite the fact he's basically threatening me. I slowly force my hand to retreat and return my gaze to the mirror.

It's actually good. Like *really* good. Maren was right.

He's given me an inverted lob, but the side bangs totally make it look chic and not fifth-graderish. He's added in some dark caramel lowlights that makes the blonde pop and somehow makes my pasty white skin not look so drab.

I find myself smiling at Jacque. Jacque does not smile back.

"I love it. Thank you," I say as he shoos me out of the chair. I jump up and down a little bit, thrilled as I do a little flick of my hair. Jacque glares.

He leads me to the counter and I hand over my card for an exorbitant amount, which really should be going to my move-the-hell-out-of-Mom's-house fund. Still, a girl's got to prioritize sometimes, and this was clearly needed. I feel like a new woman already.

Jacque, not really one for customer service or niceties, simply snatches my card, processes the payment, and heads to the area to clean up. He's not exactly a five-star for friendliness, but his talent clearly makes it worth it. Next time, I'll just bring headphones, although I'm pretty sure Jacque wouldn't be okay with that.

I find myself strutting out of the shop onto the sidewalk, hoping there are crowds to see my new hair.

There is, of course, no one, and I simply retreat home, feeling like a new woman but not having anyone to show that fact off to. Nonetheless, I think the haircut is just what I needed to feel like I'm starting a new life.

Judging by the new hair, maybe it won't be such a bad start after all.

* * *

By dinnertime, I realize the error in my ways and the miscalculation. It wasn't a new haircut I needed—it was either a new living arrangement or a new mother to make me feel okay about the future.

"Oh my God, what in the hell did you do to your hair? You were so pretty and now you look like a Backstreet Boy or something," Mom proclaims when she comes home from work and finds Grandma and me watching *Jane the Virgin*. Grandma already has the hots for Michael and Rafael, and it's only episode three.

"Wow, thanks Mom," I say, shaking my head.

"Oh, Lucy, stop badgering the girl. It looks good. I mean, they say long hair is good to grab, but I think short hair just says powerful. Men like powerful in the bedroom. This will up her chances of—"

"Oh my God, Grandma, please stop," I shout, pausing *Jane* on a very unflattering facial expression and covering my ears with my hands. It's too late to protect myself, though, from Grandma's horrific observations.

"Well, I think it's not the best. Did you go to that creepy place Maren swears by? You should've known better, Lila. I mean, your sister had purple hair last summer. *Purple.* What's gotten into you two?"

"For starters, Mother, we grew up. And now we make decisions about our hair. We think outside the box. We mix it up. Not all of us have had the same hairstyle for eighteen years," I utter without thinking.

Even Grandma Claire knows I've gone too far and groans.

Mom gives me her "game on" look. "I'll let that slide," she says, "because I know right now your life's a disaster. But don't take it out on me."

"My life's not a disaster," I retort, although the words don't really have confidence behind them.

"Well, that haircut is saying you're a disaster. It's just not flattering is all I'm saying. It looks like a boy or something."

"First," I say pointedly, actually getting up from my seat, "that's kind of the point. I'm trying something new. I'm free to explore who I want to be. And second, I don't think some lowlights and a few inches off is crazy or boyish."

Feeling like a teenager, I stomp back to my room and shut the door. Sitting on the edge of my bed, I bury my head in my hands. How the hell is this happening? How am I back here under the gripping clutches of my crazy, helicopter mother?

Most of all, I wonder how the hell I can make enough money to get out of here as soon as possible. Either I need to pick up some more hours, or perhaps I need to get myself a good-luck-charm cat and join Grandma on Thursdays more often.

I try to take a calming breath and remind myself I knew what moving back in would be like. I knew it wouldn't be easy. I chose this. I thought this would be best.

Listening to Mom and Grandma argue over how to unfreeze the television for five minutes, ultimately resulting in a swearing match—Grandma being the one to let the first vulgarities fly—I again ask myself what the hell I was thinking.

Was it worth it? Was letting my stubbornness and my plans and my need for signs get in the way of us worth it? And most of all, were we really that far gone, that far apart that I couldn't have worked a little harder to make it work?

Was giving up on Luke really what I needed?

I lean back on my bed, staring at the same ceiling I stared at all through high school as I wondered when life was going to get good and when I was going to be happy.

Lying here now as an adult with my life falling apart, I start to question whether the problem isn't life. Maybe it's me. Maybe I just can't hold on to happiness when I find it, or maybe I set the bar too high.

Or, maybe, just maybe, my mother is right—not that I'd ever admit it.

Maybe this is just grief talking, and maybe it's going to

take more than a haircut and a hilarious show to make me feel ready to face the unknown future.

Maybe it'll just take time.

***

"No pity coming from me. I told you moving home was a horrific idea. I think you'd have been better to live in a tent by the river," Maren says the next morning as we sip coffee. I've got an evening shift, so I agreed to go dress shopping with her this morning. Maren, like with all things, has decided to wait until way too close to the wedding to go dress shopping. I think she did it just because Mom has been on her case. That's Maren, though—a go-with-the-flow girl. I swear she could be happy picking out her dress the morning of the wedding.

Our dress shopping venture is a secret because Maren wants a chance to browse dresses before Mom gets involved. We'll go a second time when Maren's basically settled on a choice so Mom doesn't make her crazy.

It seems like we're harsh on Mom, and maybe we are. I know, deep down, her intentions are the best. But she's just always been one of those over-the-top moms. Seeing Maren kiss a boy in eighth grade led to a way too detailed talk about babies and pregnancies and single motherhood and, in Mom's views, the destruction of dreams. We were always warned about ill intentions of others, the dangers of drugs, and the necessity to avoid kidnapping. Mom, the ultimate worrier, has her reasons. She lost her own sister, Julia, when Julia was only fifteen. She died of a drug overdose. I guess

Mom has always carried that with her.

Still, it's made her compulsively paranoid and compulsively controlling. This frustrated *me* as a teenager, and did not fare well at all with Maren. The two have had only about three civil conversations in their lifetime. I usually end up as the mediator. Such is the case with the wedding.

"She's trying to help, in her own way," I defend, looking around the tiny café as we sip our lattes.

"You tell yourself that. I mean, the woman needs to get a grip. We're grown up. We're going to be okay."

"Well, you're okay in her eyes. I'm a complete screwup right now," I say, rolling my eyes.

Maren laughs. "It's kind of funny because for all those years, she thought I was going to be the screwup."

"Thanks a lot."

"I'm just kidding, sis. You know that. Don't let Mom make you feel bad."

"Or like a spinster? An old maid? Because these are the words that have been not-so-smoothly slipped into conversations lately. It's like we're in the 1800s. Since I'm the oldest, I clearly have to be married first or face a lifetime of singleness. She's been going on and on about Cousin Martha all of a sudden. Like this is making things so much easier for me. Like I don't know I'm getting older."

Maren groans.

Cousin Martha is our thirty-eight-year-old cousin who hasn't married yet. In Lucy Morrow's world, this is a grave disaster. Being single is a swear word in her language.

Of course, in reality, I guess I can't judge her too harshly. But things are different for me. It's not that I don't feel like I'm not a successful woman without a man. It's not like I feel like I have to be married by a certain age.

I just…. I do want that commitment eventually. I want a family, I do.

But I don't think Mom calling me a spinster is helping things, at all.

"I honestly thought she'd be happy I broke up with Luke. He's nothing like the guys she would pick for me, and it's not like she ever really liked him," I say, shaking my head.

Maren shrugs. "Maybe Mom hoped Luke's singing would take off and you'd be a wealthy, famous wife of a celebrity. Then she could get her moment in the spotlight. Now you've dashed her dreams."

"Who knows. But anyway, it's just driving me crazy."

"Speaking of Luke, have you heard from him?" Maren asks.

"A text. I ignored it." I bite my lip.

"Lila, did you really?" she asks, as if she doesn't trust me.

"Yes. But I thought about answering it."

Maren shakes her head. "Lila, when you decided it was done, you were so sure. You have to trust your gut, you know? You broke up for a reason."

"But what if I was being an idiot? What if I was being unreasonable? What if Mom's craziness growing up just tainted my view of love?" I ask, confessing my fears for the first time.

"Love is never reasonable. Get that straight right now. And so what if you were, Lila? Look. Contrary to Mom's beliefs, you're not ancient. You're young. You deserve to explore a little, which you didn't really do. If you weren't sure about everything, you did the right thing. Go out there and scope out the field. Have some fun. See who you could be as just Lila for a while. There's nothing wrong with that."

"What if I made a mistake? I still love him, Maren."

"Of course you do. You don't just shut off love like a switch. But love isn't the only piece of the equation. Seriously. And you know what, Lila? If you did screw up, if you do realize someday that you were an idiot, there's nothing saying you can't fix things. Love is crazy and winding and, quite frankly, fucked-up. Call me a romantic or whatever, but since Will, I've learned that you don't figure out love, and you don't plan it. It comes for you when it's ready, and when it does, you know it's the real deal. You know when it's right."

I chuckle, shaking my head.

"What?" she asks. "I give you this beautiful advice, and you laugh? Screw you, jerk."

"No. It's just that only you could use fucked-up and romantic in the same monologue and make it work."

"Well, it's true. Listen, I get to sound wise about love, since I'm not the spinster of the family. Just trying to help you out."

I kick her under the table, and a kicking fight ensues. We laugh loudly, and a few other customers stare at us. "Are you ready to go find your dress?" I ask.

"Are you sure you're okay with it? I know the timing isn't exactly great."

"I know. You bitch, how dare you get married when I decide to break up with my boyfriend. You should at least call off the wedding for a year or two for my period of grief, as Mom calls it."

"Well, Mom would have me call off the wedding for a year, but only so your hair can grow."

"You're right. She scowled at it this morning. You'd think I got some pornographic picture shaved into my scalp or something."

"Good old Lucy's not a fan of the lob, apparently. I love it."

"You only love it because Mom doesn't."

"Yeah, sort of. On second thought, this whole shopping for my wedding dress without Mom first might not work. I don't think I'll be able to pick one without knowing which one she hates the most, you know? What if I pick one she actually ends up liking? That would be devastating."

"You are such a jerk. She's your mother."

"She's *your* mother. I don't claim her," Maren says, and I smile.

Maren and Mom have had their moments, it's true. I know, though, behind the surface-level anger is love.

Maren's right. Love isn't always this clear-cut, movie-like emotion. It's freaking complicated and messy.

It's just that we have to decide, I guess, whether or not it's worth the mess.

CHAPTER SEVEN

LUKE

It seemed like a good idea at that time, a text to see what she was up to. In reality, I was just missing her and under the influence of Evan's insistence that Jack Daniel's would make me forget her.

Days later, though, that unanswered text on my phone stings worse than the final goodbye. She's really done. Those years together weren't the building of forever.

I suppose that's really my fault, though, because I wasn't living like I was playing for forever. I messed it up, and it's no one's fault but my own.

They say heartbreak makes for good songs, but standing at the corner of Montgomery and Fifth Avenue, I don't really feel like the songs are great tonight. My guitar case is open as I stand in front of Dot's Doughnuts. Usually, after a night of playing to the sparse crowds, Lila standing nearby watching with a smile, we'd go inside, order our favorites, and chat up Dot.

Not tonight, though. Things are different now. Here I stand, just a singing wannabe, strumming on my guitar, playing a sad song that even I can tell isn't quite right. A few stragglers take pity and toss a buck into the guitar case. This doesn't make me happy, though. This was never about money. It was about being heard. It was about my passion for it.

Lila was the one who inspired me to keep singing. Her smile at my song, the look in her eyes as I played her favorite, that was what I did it for.

Now, standing here, just a lonely guy with an unanswered text on his phone, I don't feel like there's even a point. I pack up early and hurriedly wave to Dot without going in. I can't face the prospect of a table for one tonight. I can't sit there with my three peanut-butter glazed doughnuts alone, remembering how we'd always share the third one, breaking it exactly down the middle but still fighting over the best half. I can't stand the thought that life without her is empty and pointless.

I can't stand the fact I did this to us.

More than that, I can't stand the fact that my damn pride or my messed-up family or whatever else a psychologist would say is standing in my way won't let me back down. Because as much as I miss her, I can't find it in me to give in and admit I was wrong. I can't find it in me to want to change things, to be the Luke she deserves and to map out the path to a future she needs.

"Screw it all," I say as I put my hood up and lug my guitar case back to Evan's, not home but home for now.

***

"What the hell is that, Luke? Are you serious?" Evan exclaims the next morning when I call him out to the front of the apartment building to check out my new ride.

I've traded in the ancient Ford for a bit of an upgrade—a Dodge Charger.

"How the hell are you affording it? I mean, you've been working on some roofing jobs, but Jesus, if it's that profitable, maybe I should come work with you," Evan says, staring at the glossy paint and shaking his head.

I shrug. "I took out a loan."

"Can you make the payments?"

I smile from the driver seat. "Settle down. I can still make rent, if that's what you're worried about."

"So is this your plan? Buy a babe-magnet car?"

"No. My plan is that I always wanted one, and Lila said it was too expensive."

"So it's a 'fuck you, Lila.' I see," Evan says, hopping in the passenger seat to check out the interior.

"No. It's not like that."

"I think it's sort of like that."

I shake my head as Evan turns up the radio and demands I take him for a ride so we can see what the top speed is.

I drive through town and find the highway exit, slamming my foot on the gas pedal and driving like a bat out of hell, Evan cheering me on.

As we fly by the other cars and the scenery becomes a blur, I think about how good it feels to let go. The payments are ludicrous and it wasn't wise, but wise was never my thing.

That was hers. She was the one who helped me budget and helped us save for the future.

But the future's screwed now, so I might as well have a little fun, right?

"Let's go out tonight," I say, and Evan looks like he's seen a ghost.

"Are you serious?"

"I'm serious. Luke Bowman isn't done just yet. You're right. We're young. Let's get out there."

Evan lets out what can only be classified as a rebel yell, and I run a hand through my hair as I slow down to a normal, civilian-like pace.

Evan talks a mile a minute about hot places, good times, and sexy women, but I don't hear him.

That's sort of the point, though. I don't want to hear anything, feel anything. I want to just be, to just breathe, and to maybe just have some fun away.

The Luke I was with Lila is gone. I'm back to the old Luke, the I-don't-give-a-shit Luke. I'm back to the guy I was before her, just with a little less belief in love and a little more heartbreak. I'm the badass who was one choice away from making a huge mistake. I'm the rebel without a cause who was one bill away from financial ruin.

I know I should care. I've turned it all around these past few years with her.

But we all know how that turned out. So screw it.

I stomp on the accelerator again and fly down the road, not looking back.

CHAPTER EIGHT

LUKE

Before Lila, this was my routine. Work throughout the week, sing a little on weekends, and get shitfaced on weeknights with Evan, hoping to get some action. In short, I was a wreck of a man. I was an asshole in many ways. I didn't know what it meant to actually feel something, to look ahead.

I could blame it on daddy issues. I could blame it on Mom being too busy to keep an eye on me. In truth, though, I think I was born to just be a little free-spirited and a lot anti-authority. In school, I was the kid racking up the detentions and skipping class when I got a clear break to the door. I was the kid who was never going to college—even if I had the grades, we didn't have the money. The only thing that made me slow down even a little was music. Put that guitar in my self-taught hands, and I was different. I was calmer and more focused. I was a person with feelings instead of just a smoking, curly-haired bastard.

After high school, the roofing job helped give me a

steady income. I didn't use it to get myself on track or to plan ahead. I used it to party a little more, to have a lot more fun. Looking back, I was just meandering through life.

And then she came along. Within a few weeks, I realized life wasn't about drinking and smoking and just existing.

Life was about her. It was all about her.

Everything changed. I know that sounds cheesy and overdramatic, but it isn't. Lila helped me become the man I couldn't. She saw something in me I didn't even see in myself.

But now she's gone, and here I am in old habits. Sitting on the edge of my bed, a hangover from hell, I realize I'm getting too old for this shit. I'm not as young as I'd like to think. I'm not as used to this as I'd like to believe. Last night was fun when it was happening, but the aftereffects aren't so much.

And once you get a glimpse of what a normal life with meaning and love can look like, I suppose the wayward straggler's life of my past isn't as attractive.

I stumble over Floyd, who lets out a shrill cry as I step on his tail. "Sorry, buddy," I mutter, cursing myself for keeping him. I should've let Lila take him. I love that cat, I do. But even he's a painful reminder now.

In the bathroom, I glance at myself in the mirror, the stubble and bloodshot eyes making me look like a disaster. I don't recognize the man in the mirror, the man who only a few years ago was me.

I grab for the Advil to dull the pain, shaking off the thoughts. I can't change things now. I've got to stop psychoanalyzing everything.

In my boxers, I trudge to the kitchen for some coffee and some food. I'm starving. I'm exhausted. I feel like shit in every way.

In the living room, I find Evan, passed out on the couch with a girl from the bar. I think her name is Sheila. I reach for a bottle of soda from the fridge and head back to my room to rustle up some clothes. This is a scene I don't want to be a part of.

I feed Floyd his gloppy cat food before heading out, needing to get some air, needing to walk this off and feel a little bit alive again.

I head for the park, my favorite place to think ever since I was a middle schooler. I walk past the tiny excuse for a lake, hands in my pockets, thinking about things way too much.

What am I doing?

It's the question that never plagued me before, but now seems to be the number-one thing on my mind.

What the hell am I doing?

Staring at the lake, a bird cawing annoyingly in the tree beside me, I realize what I need to do. I need to call the only other person in the world who always tried to warn me to get my shit together, the only person in the world who 100 percent understands. I call the woman who's been there for me even when Lila wasn't. I call the woman who knows what a fuckup I am but loves me anyway.

Standing by the lake, hungover and lost, I call her, asking her to meet me.

I know without a doubt she'll come. She always does.

* * *

"What is your sorry ass doing here?" Scarlet asks me, not pulling any punches as usual.

I turn to look at her as she meets me at the bench.

"Thanks for coming," I say.

"Well, I figured it must be bad if you were here."

She pats the bench, the one that has come to symbolize so much over the years.

"Yeah, things are messed up."

"I gather that. So what do you want me to do?" she asks, smiling. That's Scarlet for you, though. Always jumping right in.

"Tell me I'm not an absolute disaster, I guess."

"Too late for that."

"Okay, then," I say, smiling in spite of the situation.

"Luke, listen. I know you're beating yourself up over this and you're trying to psychoanalyze the shit out of it. Lila knew what she was getting into with you. And I don't always agree with your way of thinking, but I also can't judge. I wasn't hit by what Dad did like you were. I wasn't you. I didn't have the same experience. So I can't understand completely how you feel. I get it, to an extent. I understand how he left a mark on you, and I get how that carried over into your relationship with Lila. But you've got to stop trying to mold yourself into what you think you should be. You did your best with Lila, and it wasn't enough. Do I think you could've been good together? You bet. But it isn't about me or anyone else. It's about you and what you want. I know you love her. If you think that love is enough to change, then do it. If you think that maybe you aren't willing to bend on certain issues, then move on. You've got to man up, though, and own it. It's your life. You've got to start living it."

I sigh, staring at my feet kicking up the dirt. "Why do you always make so much sense?"

"Because I'm brilliant. Now come on. You owe me ice cream for dragging my ass the whole way out here."

I roll my eyes but haul myself off the bench. Scarlet puts a hand on my arm as we stroll down to the sad excuse for an ice cream cart at the edge of the park. We spend the next half hour eating huge sundaes and talking about Scarlet's work, about Mom's boyfriend, and about everything except Lila.

When Scarlet decides she needs to get going, I give her a hug. "Thanks for always being there for me," I say.

"Chin up, big brother. You've got this."

Not believing her, I give her the fake Luke smile as she walks to her car. I head back to the bench, deciding to sit for a while and think about where it all went so wrong so many years ago.

***

"He's gone. He's fucking gone," Mom shrieked as I rubbed the sleep from my eyes.

It was Thanksgiving morning, and I had expected to get my twelve-year-old body out of bed and smell Mom's turkey and stuffing in the oven. Dad would be sitting quietly in front of the television, probably nursing a beer since he was off from the factory. Scarlet and I would go and play in the crisp autumn leaves out front until Mom would make us come in for dinner. It would be a perfectly ordinary day.

But it wasn't. Because when I woke to Mom's stupefied look, I was just confused.

"Where did he go?" I asked stupidly, expecting Mom to say he went out to the grocery store or got called into work.

"Don't you understand, Luke? He's gone forever. Gone for good. We weren't enough anymore."

I stared, my prepubescent brain not quite understanding it.

Dad had certainly been a little different these past few months. He was always the silent, serious type. I couldn't remember receiving a hug or a kiss or an I love you from the man. Still, he was here. He was always here. The last few months, though, he'd been quieter than usual, more distant. He'd been working a lot of overtime lately, gone from our family dinners. My sister, only eight, didn't understand why Daddy wasn't there to say good night to her anymore.

But now he was gone? Gone where? How could he be gone? Where did he go? Why would he want to leave?

Mom sat on my bed, sobbing, as I stared, having no idea what to do.

"Maybe he'll be back," I offered weakly.

"He's not coming back, you idiot," Mom shrieked wildly. "He left a goddamn note. I knew he was running around with that slut Monica."

I squinted at Mom now. How could she talk about Monica that way? She was Mom's best friend. What the hell was happening? I was certain I was just dreaming. I actually scratched my arm, hoping to wake myself up. I didn't.

"What's wrong, Luke?" a sleepy voice asked as Scarlet wandered into my room in her pink pajamas. Staring at Mom in confusion and horror, she turned to me. "Is Mommy hurt?"

"No, she's fine. Come on. Let's go get breakfast," I said, ushering Scarlet out to the kitchen, already knowing my role as protector was necessary.

I got Scarlet some cereal, still confused.

That's when I saw it. The note, crinkled and crumpled in the corner of the counter.

Cindy,

I'm done with this shit. I can't take it anymore. I thought I could hang in there for the kids, could keep up the façade, but I can't. I love her too much. We're taking off for Florida. I'll call sometime to check on the kids.

Dan

It was like reading a note in hieroglyphics.

What the hell happened? What possibly could've made Dad do this to her?

Sure, my parents weren't like some of my friends' parents. They weren't going away for gag-worthy romantic weekends or making out on the sofa like teenagers. But they were married. They loved each other… didn't they?

But as the weeks went on, I didn't know anymore. At twelve, I realized something apparently my parents hadn't figured: love screws you over. Big-time.

* * *

Thanksgiving ruined love for me.

But a few months later, my dad ruined everything.

He'd called, told me all sorts of things about Mom, blaming her for the relationship falling apart. Then he'd asked me to move in with him in Florida.

I was twelve, I was stupid, and I was tired of feeling like the adult in the house—Mom was still going on regular crying stints.

At twelve, I wasn't thinking about the right thing to do. I was thinking I needed my dad, asshole or not. So I moved out, abandoned Mom and Scarlet, and moved in with Dad and Monica.

It would be only one month until I figured out what a joke my dad was. I would end up right here on this bench, waiting for Mom to come pick me up after the bus dropped me off. I wouldn't look back at Florida or at Dad and, when I did, it was with guilt.

I vowed a few things that day while sitting on this same bench.

One, I would never abandon Scarlet and Mom like that again. I would man up. I would be the man Dad couldn't.

Two, I would never let marriage screw me over like it did Mom. I would never be blindsided.

And three, most importantly, I would never put myself in

the position to do what Dad did. I would never vow to love someone for a lifetime only to pull the rug out from under them. Marriage, in my opinion, was a joke. It was just a tool to hurt each other. It couldn't possibly be forever.

So, sitting here, I realize that even though I miss the hell out of Lila, I can't possibly change enough to make her happy—my dad ruined any prospect of that. In truth, though, maybe my dad being an asshole did me a favor, because he taught me early on that you truly can't rely on romance, love, marriage, or anything of the sort.

Because even though he gave it all up for Monica, she would leave him a year later for a newer model... and he would die from a heart attack, alone, all alone, never even bothering to look back at the family he left behind wondering why.

CHAPTER NINE

LILA

"Lila, it's so good to see you," Pastor Rick says, putting a hand on my shoulder as I sit beside my mom and dad in the church basement, enjoying the weekly breakfast after mass.

"Great to see you too," I say, guilt rising. It's been years since I've been here. Usually Luke and I spent Sunday mornings saying *God* in a very, very different way. I try to tell myself not to blush at the thought. "It's been getting— er, I mean—I've been busy."

Having sex instead of coming to church, and lounging in pajamas drinking extra coffee.

Oh, Lord. That isn't helping the blushing scenario.

"We understand," the elderly pastor says, no judgment passing. It does make me wish I'd come here more frequently, his kind eyes reminding me why church was never a chore for me.

"Well, I hope God does," Mom chimes in, offering a

weak smile at the end so Pastor Rick thinks she's being funny. I know better.

I shove in another bite of my glazed doughnut ring, eyeing Grandma Claire. She's wearing her hot pink dress that plunges a bit too low to be tasteful for church. Who is going to question her, though, at her age?

Still, I shake my head and smile as I see her leaning in way too close to the twentysomething missionary from Colombia who is here for the month. He looks terrified, and I can't blame him. I think about saving him—and myself from my mother's comments—by walking over and distracting Grandma.

I don't get the chance.

"Oh, well look at this. Hi, Sophie. It's so good to see you. What a surprise. I know you usually go to the Saturday evening mass, but look at this. Lila, you remember Joseph, don't you?"

I look up to see Sophie and Joseph "Sniffs" Goodman standing beside me. I'm taken back, way back, to high school, when Joseph had a crush on me and announced it over the PA system at school, making me the laughingstock of the district my senior year. I try not to visibly shudder, reminding myself we're grown now. We're out of those immature high school days. I'm sure Joseph is a nice guy, and I'm sure this is just a coincidence.

But then I see the conspiratorial wink between my mother and Mrs. Goodman, and I know. I just know.

It all makes sense. Mom's extra attention to my outfit and hair this morning. Her insistence I do a better job on my makeup.

My mother is setting me up with a church boy. And not just any church boy—Joseph Sniffs.

I paint on the smile I've mastered when a veterinary customer is being an absolute pain or when I'm convincing myself that life isn't so bad.

I'm sure Joseph isn't in on this, and I'm sure he's a great guy. He looks cute in his button-up plaid shirt, pleated pants, and glasses with three-inch-thick lenses. *He's cute. Be nice. Just be nice and friendly.*

And then Joseph sniffs.

I'm not talking a tiny sniffle or a tiny breath in. I'm talking a dog hacking on grass kind of sniff, a snort-like, everyone in the room turns around, noise.

Hence Joseph "Sniffs" Goodman, the nickname mercilessly following him through high school.

You're a grown woman now, I remind myself. *Be kind.*

"Love that hair. Looks super sexy," Joseph says, winking. And I'm reminded that the sniffing habit isn't the only bad thing about Joseph.

I guess some people really don't change.

"Why thank you, Joseph. That's sweet. So what are you up to?" I ask, trying to turn the conversation anywhere from the word "sexy."

"Well, right now I'm working on a start-up in Mom's basement. You see, it's an app that is going to revolutionize internet chatrooms. I've been working tirelessly, right, Ma?"

"Yes, sweetie," Mrs. Goodman says, putting an arm around her son. "That boy just basically hibernates in the basement all day, working on his computers and things. I could only lure him out today at the promise you'd be here, Lila."

I glance over at Mom. So this *was* a conspiracy. Mom just gives a smile that seems to suggest "You can thank me later."

This can't be happening.

"Chat rooms, huh?" I ask. "Is that still a thing?"

"Obviously, Lila, or Joseph wouldn't be working on it," Mom interrupts.

I look to Dad for help. He just keeps eating his pancakes, averting his eyes from the disaster happening. I'll have to remember to thank him later. He finally catches my eye and then smirks, thinking this is hilarious. I'm sure Maren will too.

"Well, it's great to see you, Joseph. Good luck."

"Actually, I was hoping we could get a bite to eat tonight. I could tell you all about my app. I'm looking for a pretty woman to be the face of my business, and it seems like you'd be perfect."

I stare at him, blinking, reminding myself to stay calm and kind.

Calm and kind.

"Sorry, Joseph. I can't. Really busy tonight."

"No, you're not," Mom interjects.

"Yes, super busy," I respond through gritted teeth. My mind starts to race. What am I going to use as an excuse? I don't want to be rude and say, "Sorry, Joseph, your creepy startup in your mom's basement makes me want to call the police, not go on a date. Also, I can't stand your sniffles or anything about you. I'd rather stab myself in the eye than go on a date with you where you will make sexual advances."

Yeah, not exactly church-like.

Apparently, though, I'm not speaking a language my mother, Sophie, or Joseph understand.

"Would eight work?" Joseph asks, turning to my mother now like I'm some pawn.

"That would be perfect," she answers for me. Oh my God, where the hell are we? Are they bartering with me like this is an arranged marriage?

No. Just no.

I stand up. Some of the other church members look over at me. "I'm sorry, Mrs. Goodman, Joseph, but this isn't going to work. You see, I have to get my treatment for the syphilis I contracted sleeping around town. All around. And now my mother is trying to hook me up with your son to get my reputation back in line, but I can't do it. I need some time to repent for my sins before I'm worthy."

Mrs. Goodman's jaw drops, and Joseph actually jumps back like he's been bitten. My mother gasps in horror, and my dad stares at me, wide-eyed, like I've gone way too far—which I clearly have. Pastor Rick also stares and then blesses himself. Some elderly women look at me like I've just cried witch.

Oh shit. This was too far. Way too far. Syphilis? What the hell was I thinking?

I wasn't. Mom's annoying, over-the-top behavior just got to me and mouth diarrhea happened.

Unrecoverable mouth diarrhea.

The room is quiet for an awkward amount of time. I don't know what to do. I'm frozen, too afraid to move a muscle, hoping this will all just go away.

"Well, I think we are just going home now," Sophie says, leading Joseph away from me. I offer a weak smile and wave and sit down.

"Don't worry," Grandma Claire shouts from across the room, cupping her mouth with her hands to make a mock megaphone. "Lila, I've had the syph before. It's not a big deal. A few treatments, and you're good." She gives me a smile, a wink, and a thumbs-up. As if things aren't bad enough.

I try to retreat into myself, head down on the table, my hair getting stuck in a swatch of maple syrup.

"What in the hell were you thinking?" Mom shrieks. "Are you serious? We can never set foot back in this church again."

I put my head up. "Sorry, Mom, but maybe next time, you'll ask before you try to arrange a marriage for me."

"I just wanted to find you a nice boy."

"I don't need help in the dating department, thank you very much, especially if you thought Joseph Goodman was my match. What were you thinking?"

"Well, at least with him, you know he's traditional. You know you won't have to save him. You tried to save Luke from his disastrous self. Look how that turned out."

I point now. "Don't make this about Luke. This is about you and your ridiculous 1920s belief that I need to get married right now to be happy, that I need to be married at all costs."

"Well, isn't that grand coming from the girl who was obsessed with getting a ring," Mom says, tossing her napkin down as she storms out of the church. Dad finishes his pancake before rounding up Grandma Claire and following, urging me to come along.

Tears start to fall on the way to the car. Tears of embarrassment, tears over the thought of Mom thinking Joseph was the best option for me, and tears that in many ways, Mom is right about me being a hypocrite.

* * *

"Oh my God, Lila, syphilis? In a church? Are you freaking kidding me?" She is crying with laughter as we sit on the swing in the backyard later that evening. Maren's come over for our weekly Sunday dinner. Mom cooked again. So yes, we got pizza. Grandma Claire was devastated because they sent a female pizza delivery driver.

Maren and I are in our favorite spot out back, just the two of us and Henry, who is snoring on his side under my feet. Will's working tonight; some major client's books apparently are a mess and the firm is in a tizzy. It's good to have my sister to myself, the two of us on the swings Dad made us when we were little girls. The rope is dangerously thin, but we don't care. There's a peacefulness here.

"It just came out, Maren. I was desperate and angry and wanted to make sure they got the point."

"Oh, I think they did. Pretty sure Joseph won't be coming

within fifty feet of you. This is priceless. This is *so* out of character."

"I know."

"I mean, this is something Mom would expect from me, not her precious Lila."

"Thanks for reminding me. I can't show my face in town."

"Oh, stop. It's all old women at that church anyway. No one is going to think twice about it."

"Grandma Claire won't stop giving me tips about treating it."

"Ugh. Didn't need to know that," Maren says, shaking her head. "Love that woman though."

"Me too. It's been good hanging with her. It's been the bright spot of moving back home."

"So how long until you ditch this joint? Get back out on your own?" Maren asks, swinging a little higher despite the precarious state of the swing. She's never one to be afraid, though.

My feet still carefully on the ground, Henry snoring beside me, I shrug. "I don't know. I mean, I need to get in better financial shape first."

"Of course you do."

"What's that supposed to mean?" I ask, raising an eyebrow.

"It means you always have to have everything perfect. Lila, when I moved out at nineteen, I had what, like ten bucks in my pocket? Was it smart? No way. But am I okay? Yes. Sometimes you need to stop being so rational and just live, you know?"

"You sound like Luke now."

"Do I?"

"Yes. That was part of the problem," I say, looking off into the sunset, wondering if maybe everyone's right. Maybe I'm too careful. And where does that get me? With money in my bank account and an almost aneurism from dealing with my infuriating mother? A breakdown at church leading to everyone thinking I have syphilis? Not exactly my prize moment.

"Well," Maren says, swinging quite high now, "luckily, you can't break up with me. You're stuck with me forever."

"Maren, even you realize, though, that sometimes in life you need stability. You need that conventional promise and that acknowledgement that you're heading somewhere."

Maren slows down the pumping of her legs. "Listen. Yes, it's nice that Will and I are on the same page with that. But does that mean this ring on my finger is the only way I know he's it for me? No way."

"So if he hadn't wanted to get married, you'd be fine with it?" I ask.

"I don't know. But I do know this. You and I are different, and we need different things in life. If you didn't feel like you had everything you wanted, you deserved to go out and try to find it. We've been through this."

"You're right," I say, shushing the gnawing questions and fears inside. "And it wasn't just about the commitment situation."

"It was about a whole lot more. Lila, this is eating you up.

You need to let it go. Stop questioning yourself. You made your decision. Now get out there and live. And save money if you must, but make your first goal as a newly single woman getting the hell out of Mom's house. I mean, really, don't you just feel like a teenager again?"

"Yes. Dreadfully so."

"Then let's make step one on your new-Lila life checklist getting an apartment. I'll help you."

"Deal."

"And let's make step two finding you a real date, not that sniffly basement dweller," a deep voice bellows. We turn to see Dad ambling toward us, hands in his pockets. "Glad those swings are still getting their use. Mom wanted me to tear them down, said they're an eyesore. I couldn't bear it."

"Thank goodness there's a sane voice of reason in the family," Maren says, smiling.

"And it sure as heck isn't you," Dad replies to her, laughing.

Dad walks over and pats Henry on the head before taking a seat in the grass in front of us. "Listen, I need to talk to you. You remember John Mathews? Well, his son Christopher is back in town and—"

I toss my hands up. "Daddy, I love you. But stop right there. No more conspiracies to set me up. I need time to breathe."

"Listen, I understand after the debacle this morning, you're a little gun shy. Your mom, although unarguably crazy and controlling, loves you. She was trying to help. Her attempt at helping, though, was clearly a disaster.

Christopher doesn't have the sniffles and he doesn't live in his parents' basement for his work. He's an engineer and, at the risk of sounding weird, he is pretty good-looking. He's a nice guy. Trust me."

"Wait, Christopher Mathews? I went to school with him, right?" Maren asks.

"You did. But I promise he won't hold that against you, Lila," Dad says.

"He's good, Lila. Truly," Maren agrees, nodding.

I shake my head. "I don't know."

"Listen, you don't have to marry the guy, contrary to your mother's belief. I just want you to see that there's more out there for you. Luke was a good guy, and I know he ended up winning the family over, but I was never sold on him. He was so different than you, Lila. I think Christopher might be just what you need. But no pressure. Just think about it, okay?"

He pats Henry on the head again, gets up, and walks away. Before getting too far, he turns around. "Love you, girls. It's good to have you here."

I smile, thankful for a dad who is so chill and balances out my mom's crazy. But this gets me thinking.

Dad was so worried about me and Luke being so different, yet he and my mom are night and day—and they make it work.

"Daddy," I yell, and he turns around. "You and Mom are so different. Isn't that a good thing?"

Dad smiles, staring at the ground before answering. "It can work, Lila. But it takes a lot of effort. It's exhausting.

Is it worth it? Yeah. But sometimes in life it pays to go the smoother route, you know?"

I shrug, and Dad walks away.

I know he loves Mom, even in her worst, craziest moments. But maybe Dad's right. Maybe work isn't always the answer.

"That Christopher Mathews is good," Maren says when Dad walks away. "He's superhot. Dad has good taste in men."

"Well, that's a little odd."

"Hey, no odder than Joseph Sniffles. Go for it, Lila. What do you have to lose?"

I kick at a stone in the ground. "Okay. You're right. I'll do it. Just one date."

"Just one date," Maren says. "That's exactly what I said and look at me now." She flashes her huge ring and the sun glints off it, almost blinding me. "Now, more importantly, get your horse of a dog to move so we can have our jumping contest."

"Maren, this swing doesn't look safe."

"Nothing's ever safe. Now come on. Just jump."

So I do.

***

"Shit, is this dress too tight?" I ask, yanking up on the neckline, wiggling and trying to pull the fabric from my hips.

"Are you kidding? The tighter the better," Maren says the next weekend as I'm getting ready for my date. I've been nibbling on crackers like I'm pregnant—which I'm not—trying to quell the nausea in my stomach. It's been so long since I've done this first date gig, and I was never great at it anyway.

Thankfully, Maren came over to help me get ready. She also was brilliant enough to schedule a dress fitting for Mom so she'd be out of my hair.

I look at myself in the full-length mirror, my lob curled into a puffy but, according to Maren, sensuous updo. Maren's already insisted I trade my ballet flats for a pair of stilettos, which seems like an awful idea. We'll probably end up in the emergency room instead of the Italian restaurant downtown he's promised to take me to.

"Will you relax? You look hot. It's going to be fine."

"I just don't know if I'm ready for this."

Maren puts her hands on my shoulders. "No pressure. Just go and have fun. Stop trying to make everything so complicated."

"That's what I do."

"And I love you for it. But not tonight. Tonight you're Lila the carefree, the simple. You can be Lila the worrier tomorrow."

"Okay. You're right. I've got this."

As if on cue, there's a knock at the door.

"I'll get it!" Grandma Claire yells as Henry and Cookie race through the house barking.

"Oh God, no," I gasp, dashing out in my stilettos—which is more like a careful snail crawl.

She, of course, gets there before Maren and I can. I swear

that woman is an Olympic runner when men are involved, cane and all.

"Oh, my. I'll just get my purse and I'm ready, dear," Grandma Claire says, winking at Christopher.

"Grandma, this isn't your date," Maren states.

Grandma Claire turns and winks at us. "I know, silly girls. It was a joke."

Maren and I shake our heads. We know for sure it wasn't a joke. We've seen Grandma's sly tricks firsthand.

Grandma Claire turns, winks at Christopher, who is holding a lovely bouquet of yellow daisies. "These are for you, Lila." He adds my name as if he needs to clarify.

"Beautiful. I'll just take these and put them in a vase," Grandma says, grabbing them before I can hobble my way to the door.

I smile, knowing damn well those flowers will end up in Grandma's room. It's okay, though.

Right now, I'm not looking at flowers or thinking about Grandma's incessant lusting for men. I'm thinking about Christopher Mathews, all six feet of him. He's wearing tight, dark-wash jeans and a suit jacket with a button-up. He looks professional, strong, and handsome.

"Are you ready?" he asks, flashing me a smile that reveals perfectly straight, white teeth, a nice accent to his strong jawline.

Maren's right. He's superhot.

"As ever," I say, feeling the awkward schoolgirl smile and giggles coming on. I try to gracefully sashay to the door, but I'm pretty sure I look more like a trotting antelope.

I hear Maren exhale, probably wondering how I can be a woman and not walk in heels.

"I'm sorry, I just can't," I say when I get to the door and Christopher reaches for my hands.

I see his face freeze. I lean down, take off a stiletto and chuck it into the house. I plop my foot down, pull off the other, and chuck it, too, before grabbing my ballet flats from beside the door. My feet almost audibly sigh in relief as I slip them into the shoes. "Much better."

"You're impossible," Maren yells from inside as we shut the door.

"I think you're impossibly beautiful," Christopher whispers as he leads me to his Corvette.

I blush and, surprisingly, feel like tonight might just be a good night after all.

* * *

"So what made you want to be a vet?" Christopher asks as I try to gracefully eat my spaghetti and meatballs, which is basically an impossible task. Note to self: when going on a first date, don't go for spaghetti. Get ravioli or something instead.

"Well, growing up, Mom wouldn't let us have a cat. She claimed to be allergic and all that, which is clearly not true considering my grandma's cat now lives with us. I believed her though, and I desperately wanted one. I found these three stray kittens when I was seven. Mom refused to let me keep them, so I built a little treehouse for them and raised them. I should clarify. By treehouse, I basically mean a huge refrigerator box I made Maren help me carry out to the oak tree. Dad eventually found out and helped me build a much more stable kitty shelter. When the cats got older, I had Dad build me a playhouse, complete with a sofa. I raised the cats, and loved doing it. I guess it was just always in me to care for animals."

"That's sweet. Do you like it? Being a vet, I mean?"

"I love it. It's hectic and weird hours. But the feeling of helping an animal or helping someone save their beloved friend is the best. I get to work with cute pets all day. Wouldn't have it any other way."

Christopher smiles after taking a glass of wine. "I can tell. You light up when you talk about it. And when you talk about Henry, of course."

I grimace. "Sorry, I know I'm a little obsessed with him." I mentally scold myself for telling at least five Henry stories tonight and for showing Christopher an entire phone worth of pictures chronicling Henry's four years of life.

"I think it's sweet. I have a lab named Candy that I'm obsessed with."

"Maybe Henry and Candy could have a playdate."

"Not likely," Christopher says, shrugging. "Candy hates other dogs."

"Oh. Well, probably not then. Anyway, tell me about you. What's your family like?"

"Just me. No siblings. My parents are great. Mom was a librarian until she got married, and then she was a stay-at-home mom. Dad works at the electric company a town over. It was a good childhood, although a quiet one."

I smile, taking another bite of spaghetti. It's weird getting used to small talk again, having to be the model of politeness. Looking across the restaurant, I see a family arguing wildly and I almost turn to Christopher and make a joke about my family. And then I realize he wouldn't get it. He doesn't know me like that, not yet. We're not at the joking phase.

It's weird to not be in the joking phase.

The rest of the night is good. Fun. We laugh about childhood memories and share controlling mother horror stories. I'm having a good time, and realizing maybe there is potential. Christopher is mostly serious and very focused. He's kind and nice. He's very... average. Not in looks, but in personality. He seems safe.

Maybe safe is what I need.

But after dinner, Christopher asks if I want to walk with him downtown. He wants to show me this great place he absolutely loves.

We're talking and laughing, and I'm not thinking that in a million years, he'll take me where he does.

But when Dot's Doughnuts is in front of me, and we don't walk past, my heart stops.

"They have the best doughnuts. Seriously. It's worth the ridiculous calories."

My chest tightens, and I want to run away. I want to dash down the street, tell Christopher I'm sorry but this is a bad idea.

And then I see him. On the corner, *his* corner.

What used to be our corner.

There's a sad, dark tune coming from his guitar. He's wearing his beanie that strangles his curls. He's got a beard growing, and he's staring at the ground, the streetlight casting an eerie glow on him. I hear the words, I hear Christopher asking me to go in, and yet I don't.

Because staring at the man who was once mine while I'm on a date with another, I can't think straight.

I pause for a long time before agreeing to follow Christopher inside, my insides wrenching tight. As Christopher leads me to a table and asks what I want to order, I'm not present, not really.

My mind is flashing back to another first date, one quite different from this one in so many ways, the devastation of what was up ahead unknown to me.

CHAPTER TEN

LUKE

Ringing the doorbell, I inhaled deeply, trying to do some yoga-like chanting to calm my racing mind—not that I knew yoga-like chants.

What was I doing? This girl was out of my league. From that first encounter over Floyd, I was drawn to her. I knew then, though, that she wouldn't give me the time of day. Still, when I'd seen her a second time at the gym, I felt like I couldn't ignore it. The way she looked, the way she looked at me. The sheer fact that choices or circumstances or fate brought us together a second time—it seemed like it was a sign, even if I wasn't one to believe in them. It was unexpected, and I still didn't quite believe it was true. But we'd find out tonight. It was our chance.

The door opened, and I tried to orient myself. I expected to see Lila or even her dad. But as I extended the bouquet of yellow roses, I was shocked to see an elderly woman in a huge sunhat.

"Why, these are gorgeous!" she said, taking them from me. "You do know yellow roses are for friendship, though, right?"

I just stared, not sure how to respond.

"Grandma Claire, those are for me," a voice echoed from down the hallway.

"Of course, dear. I'll just put them in water." The elderly woman winked at me and hobbled off. When she did, I caught sight of her.

Lila.

She wore a stunning lilac dress, not your typical first-date red or black. I liked the softness of it. I liked the simplicity of it, like she wasn't trying too hard.

"Sorry about Grandma Claire. Ever since Grandpa died, she's a little bit man obsessed. I'm pretty sure I'll never see those flowers again, but they're beautiful. Thank you."

I smiled, feeling like the yoga chanting to calm myself down wasn't needed. I liked her sincerity. I liked how even in jeans and a Grateful Dead T-shirt, I felt just right. It felt like with this girl, there weren't any pretenses or acting.

"You ready?" she asked, and I said I was, leading the beautiful blonde to my beat-up truck, wondering if I could really pull this off.

Wondering if Luke Bowman was finally going to get the girl, a girl he clearly didn't deserve but was already mad about anyway.

"So how's Floyd?" she asked when we got in the car after I explained how to jiggle the passenger door handle just right to open it.

"He's great. A gorgeous vet fixed him right up, and he's going to be good as new now."

"Glad to hear it. He's such a nice cat."

"He is. So do you like Chinese?" I asked.

"Of course."

"Great. There's this little buffet on the outskirts of town I was thinking we could try. Nothing fancy," I admitted, wondering now if this had been a mistake. A girl like Lila probably liked fine dining.

"Fancy isn't my thing," she said, and I believed her, her blue eyes sparkling as she reached for the radio and flipped it to the country station. "Oh, and I'm really sorry, but I had to bring my pager. I'm on call tonight. Hopefully no one needs me, and Dr. Osgood is on call, too. But just in case."

I grinned, turning to her at a stop sign. "Are you sure that isn't your emergency exit plan? You know, in case you decide I'm creepy or boring?"

She shrugged. "A girl has to plan ahead for these things, right?"

"Yeah, I can't blame you. But I promise I won't bore you or be creepier than I can help."

"Sounds promising."

"I do what I can."

We pulled up to the restaurant, and Lila jumped out of the car. "I love Sesame chicken. I haven't had it forever."

"Well, date's over. I only date girls who like General Tso's. I'm particular."

"I don't think you have an emergency pager as an excuse, so looks like you can't back out," she said as I held the door *to the restaurant open for her.*

I smiled at our easy banter. That was what I'd noticed about her from our first meeting. It was easy. It was like I'd known her for years, like we'd been together forever. There were no first-date niceties or discussions about the weather. There was no pressure to talk about the family or careers or anything. It was just us, a guy and a girl, going for Chinese food and having fun doing it.

We got into the restaurant and ordered, chatting about Henry and Floyd. She showed me a few dozen pictures of her mastiff, but I didn't mind. I liked her enthusiasm. Plus, I'd always been a little obsessed with animals too... although cats were my pet of choice.

When the food came steaming hot and we were ready to dig in, a loud beeping echoed.

"Shit," she muttered. She looked down at the number and then picked up her cell phone. After a few minutes of conversation, she turned to me, looking nearly teary-eyed. "I'm so sorry."

"Oh, Jesus. I thought I was being perfectly uncreepy," I said, pretending to be exasperated. "Was it the chopsticks joke?"

"No, seriously. I feel awful. I'm having a good time. But there's an emergency on its way to the office. A car wreck apparently. I have to get back. I feel awful."

"It's fine. I get it."

"It's not fine. I wanted to eat my Sesame chicken," she said, pouting as she looked at the platter.

"Oh, so it wasn't about me?" I asked, flagging down a

waiter and asking if we could get to-go containers quickly due to an emergency.

She smiled, gathering her things as I headed to the cashier to pay the bill. "Of course not," she said. "I only saved your cat, stalked you at the gym, and flirted with you to get some free Chinese."

"Well, mission accomplished," I said, teasing as I handed over a twenty to the cashier and then grabbed the to-go containers the waiter graciously had filled for us. We hurriedly grabbed the food and dashed to my car as I floored it toward the vet office.

"I'm really sorry again," she said when we got there and she dove out of the car.

"Rain check?" I asked.

She nodded, thanking me again as she rushed into the building with her Chinese food. When the door closed, I sighed, pulling out of the vet office parking lot.

I knew the emergency was real, but a piece of me wondered if I'd see her again. Maybe she didn't think I was creepy, but I still worried I'd be filed away into the "that was sort of fun" file.

Hours later, though, as I sat watching reruns with Floyd, an empty Chinese food container on the coffee table, my phone rang.

"Hey, I'm sorry again. I just wanted to apologize for bailing."

"It's okay. Did you handle the emergency?"

"Yeah, we saved the dog. He had a few broken bones, but he's going to be fine. I'm home now, safe and sound."

I tapped out a rhythm on the couch armrest, wondering if I should be bold.

I decided to go for it. "So, since the night's still young and we're still relatively young, I was wondering if I could cash in that rain check."

"When? Now?" she asked, not sounding off-put, just surprised.

"Yeah. There's this cool place downtown that I just discovered. It's amazing."

"Luke, I'd love to, but I just had a shower and my hair is soaking wet. I'm in my pajamas and not really presentable."

"Okay, is this a beeper kind of excuse, like to avoid going out, or is this serious?"

"No, I'm serious. I'll Snapchat you if you want proof."

"I believe you. But listen, the place we're going is low-key. You can even go in your pajamas. I'll pick you up in ten."

I hung up before she could protest, feeling emboldened.

When I pulled in front of her house ten minutes later, she was waiting for me on the front porch of her house. Her hair was wet, but she was wearing jeans and a nice top.

"No pajamas?" I asked.

"I thought that might be a little too low-key. The wet hair is bad enough. I look like a drowned rat."

"You look perfect," I said, meaning it. We drove on, Lila telling me about the emergency. It was like we hadn't skipped a beat.

We pulled up to the downtown area, and I parked the car. When we hopped out, we stood in front of the lime-green *building, the light-up sign for Dot's Doughnuts blinking.*

"Doughnuts? Now?" she asked, looking suspiciously at me.

"Oh, no. Please tell me you're not one of those calorie-counting kind of girls."

"Hardly. But I've never heard of this place. Are they still open?"

I looked at the sign, then my phone. "For another twenty minutes."

"Well, then let's go. Get a move on it."

Inside, an elderly lady smiled. "Hey, I'm Dot. Are you two lovebirds here for some doughnuts? We've got all kinds of gourmet specialty flavors."

Looking like a kid in a toy store, Lila walked down the row of bakery cases, staring at the flavors, shouting out "Tutti-Frutti" and "Mocha Latte."

"These look amazing," she proclaimed. "I don't know what to get."

"Let me pick for you. Let's see if I can pick one you'd like," I said, and she smiled.

"Deal. But if I hate it, no second date," she announced, heading to claim a table in the corner. Dot smiled at me.

"You better choose wisely," Dot whispered. Her soft yellow sweatshirt read World's Best Grandma.

"Any recommendations?" I asked, feeling the pressure.

"Yes. The peanut-butter glazed have been flying off the shelves. I've got three left. Simple, understated... but amazing. Nothing fancy."

"Nothing fancy is exactly right," I said, as Dot packed

up the three peanut-butter doughnuts and I paid her.

"We'll just eat and leave," I said, but Dot waved a hand.

"You two take all the time you need. I have to clean up anyway. Take some time to win the lady over. You two are so adorable together."

I grinned and thanked her, heading back to the table.

"So, Luke Bowman, are you going to wow me enough to make me want more?" Lila raised an eyebrow at me.

I stared at her confidently. "Oh, yes. You're going to want more."

I slid the plate of doughnuts toward her.

"All three peanut butter?"

"I'm that confident you'll love it, that I bought you one, me one, and an extra."

"That's unfortunate."

"Why?" I asked.

"I'm allergic."

I paused, wondering how my luck could be so bad. Then I noticed the corners of Lila's lips forming into a smile.

"Just kidding."

"Come on, give a guy a break." I shook my head, taking in her gorgeous smile as she beamed at her ability to fool me.

Lila reached for a doughnut, still smirking.

She winked at me before carefully taking a bite. After a moment, her eyes closed, and she let out an audible groan that made me tighten a little inside.

"Delicious," she said, smiling.

We sat in the corner of Dot's that night, picking up

the conversation right where we'd left off. When we each finished our doughnut, we grabbed the third one and split it in half.

"You're going to ruin my figure," she complained as she shoveled in her half of the third doughnut.

You're going to ruin me, *I thought, staring at the blonde-haired woman who had, in the course of one night, sucked me into her world.*

Sitting across from her, I realized without a doubt this girl was different, so different, than the women I'd dated before. She was wholesome and sweet, but she had a side of sass. She wasn't the dull, sickeningly agreeable girl I always pictured a "bring home to Mom" kind of girl would be. She was a balance of serious and fun, of kind and confident.

As we walked out the door into the summer night, saying good night to Dot and promising to be back, I turned to her right there.

First date or not, I didn't want to play by the rules with her. I couldn't.

I grabbed her hand on the corner by Dot's Doughnuts, the streetlight shining down on us, and I pulled her to me, almost like a dance move. When she was close enough, I tilted my head and bent down, claiming her mouth with mine, parting her lips with my tongue until I was sure she was feeling the electricity too.

We kissed under that streetlight, the taste of peanut-butter doughnuts swirling around us, but we didn't care. It was with that kiss we knew we were both goners, our hearts no longer our own.

***

It was our first kiss and our first date, but it wouldn't be our last. We'd kiss on that street corner countless more times over the years. We'd go to Dot's once a week, sometimes with Henry in tow, to get exactly three peanut-butter glazed doughnuts. We'd, in many ways, memorialize and commemorate that first strange but strangely perfect date.

Singing my dark song under that very streetlight, watching Lila walk into our place with someone who isn't me, my heart snaps a little. Maybe a lot. I think about how I had no way of knowing that night that I wouldn't be enough, and that I might win a second date, but I wouldn't win forever.

I don't know if Lila saw me, but I don't know how she couldn't. Still, it was like I was a ghost. In many ways, I am. I'm just a haunting from her past now, the new guy leading her to the future.

Dot strolls out, a plate in hand. "Were you really going to sing that sad song out here and not stop in for a pick-me-up? I thought I was your favorite baker in town."

I smile, reaching out for the plate before leaning in for a hug. "I'm sorry, Dot. I've just been…. Well, things have been shitty."

"I know. Lila filled me in a while back. And I saw her come strolling in with some new guy. Heard you were out here and knew it couldn't be easy."

"It isn't. Thanks for the voice mail the other week, by the way. I just couldn't bring myself to talk about it."

"I understand. Sort of."

"What do you mean?" I ask, setting my guitar down so I can enjoy the doughnut.

"I don't understand what you two are doing, in truth. You're both miserable."

I shrug. "Lila can't be that miserable. She's here with someone new already."

"Oh, stop. Trust me. She's not happy."

"She looked pretty smiley to me."

"It's her fake smile," Dot says, shaking her head.

"How do you know?"

"Because she never smiled like that for you," she says, staring at me. "Never. Not even on the first date."

"Well, apparently I was her fake smile inspiration then."

"No way. What you two had was real."

"How do you know, Dot?"

"Wow, really? Saying I don't know what I'm talking about? I'll remember that the next time you call in for a delivery." Dot's hands are on her hips, and I get a vision of the formidable force she must have been in her prime. Hell, she still is a formidable force. I grin at her, and she eases up her stance.

"I'm not saying I don't trust you. I'm just saying I don't know anything anymore."

"You've got that right. Because if you did, you'd be in there fighting for that girl."

"I've tried. It's too late."

"It's never too late. You young kids think a few weeks is too late. Honey, my Louie and I were apart for two straight years when he was deployed. Thought we were done.

I'd thrown in the towel. But you know what? We weren't done. It wasn't too late. Did you know I was engaged to another man? Louie stopped the wedding, actually. Came in like a maniac and stopped the wedding minutes before I said my vows after we'd barely seen each other in years. So don't tell me it's too late because Lila has some stupid date with that guy."

I look at Dot incredulously. "Wait, so you almost didn't end up with Louie?"

"Almost doesn't matter. What matters is what actually happens. I will advise you, though, not to wait until that close to the wire. Louie took quite a few punches that day." She smiles now, chuckling at the memory.

"You never told us that story," I say, finishing the doughnut. Dot had told Lila and me so many stories about her life with Louie and their three children, but she'd never told us the wedding story.

Dot shrugs. "You didn't need to hear it until now."

I smile at the woman's wisdom. She's such a smart lady... and she makes damn good doughnuts. "Thanks, Dot. I'll keep that in mind."

"Do more than think about it," she demands, winking before heading back in.

I pack up my guitar and leave the glowing light of the streetlight where it all began and where, tonight, all hope has been snuffed out. I walk down the dark street alone, reminded of how lonely life is without her, and reminded of how much of a damn idiot I was to think I, Luke Bowman, could change enough to keep her.

* * *

"Easy, buddy. It looks like you've got an axe to grind with that tile," Dean says, taking off his sunglasses to get a better look at me as he straddles the top of the roof. I'm perched near the bottom, breaking up the hot roofing tiles like I'm going to tear down the house.

Maybe it's seeing Lila last night, maybe it's jealousy. I don't know. But I woke up this morning feeling angry.

"I want to get the job done," I mutter, not even in the mood for Dean's easy humor.

"Well, why don't you take a break. I don't need to have an injury to deal with today."

I keep chipping away, standing to get a better angle. "I'm fine."

And, as if Dean is a warlock with prophetic abilities, it is then that my boot slips, and I realize I should've taken a break.

* * *

"Well, looks like you're getting more than the ten-minute break I was offering," Dean says six hours later as I hobble out of the ER, the crutches already digging into my armpits. The anger has dissipated into sheer dejection.

So this is what rock bottom feels like.

"Yeah, just what I need. Well, looks like I'll get to play some Xbox for the next few months while I'm out." And also sulk in Evan's apartment, self-pity radiating from me already.

Dean slaps my back as we head to his truck. "Chin up.

Think of it as a restart. Look, while you're on disability, you'll get more time to work on your music, right?"

"Lot of good that'll do," I mutter, feeling exhausted.

"Hey, come on. This funk you're in isn't like you. Where's the go-get-it, humorous guy we all love?"

"Don't get all mushy and sentimental on me. I don't want a motivational speech right now," I grumble.

"Well, you're getting one. Listen, take some time. Pour that heartbreak into your songs. I know you think Lila was what set you straight, but I knew you before her. Sure, she helped you get your wild ass together. She was good for you. But even before Lila, you weren't all that bad, you know. You've always had spirit and confidence. You need to find that again. If you and Lila aren't meant to be, then pour that energy into your music and jumpstart your career. Stop feeling sorry for yourself. It's pathetic."

I exhale. "You're right. It's time for me to man up. I'm going to have to figure it out without her and without my right leg, I guess."

"You know what they say about rock bottom," Dean says as he slaps on the steering wheel to the beat of the rock and roll song blasting on the radio.

"That there's nowhere to go but up."

"No. Screw that cheesy shit. My dad always said rock bottom hurts like hell when you hit, but sometimes it knocks some sense into you. Now, I'm not an expert, but maybe that broken leg will be a good reminder for the next few months that moping about Lila isn't going to get you anywhere except on your ass. So get writing some songs, get yourself together, and we'll go out and find you some women to have a little fun with."

"Maybe," I say, looking out the window as we near Evan's—correction, my—apartment.

"Get your sorry ass out of here and go start making a plan. I'll check in on you later this week."

"Thanks, Dean. For everything."

"You're welcome. Now I need to get going. I'm sure the other guys on the crew have been screwing around all day, and we've got a roof to get done. Not all of us can leap off the roof to get out of work, you know."

I shake my head and grin before hobbling up the steps—very precariously—and heading into the apartment to sit and think.

CHAPTER ELEVEN

LUKE

"You know, if you wanted attention, you could've got a mohawk or something. No sense throwing yourself off a roof," Scarlet teases on Friday when she takes me to breakfast.

The good thing about being off work with a broken leg is I have plenty of time for socializing.

The bad thing is I can't drive, and I have to depend on my crazy sister to get me around.

We pull into the Waffle Hut, and I limp into the restaurant on my crutches, Scarlet joking about racing me and all that.

"You're not really helping things," I complain when we get inside, me completely out of breath as a kind waitress leads us to the booth closest to the door.

"Oh, and when I broke my nose in seventh grade, you were nothing but kind."

"Okay, that was different."

"Yeah. I was a poor, defenseless preteen with confidence

issues and you took advantage. You're just an idiot who fell from a roof."

"Thanks for your sympathy."

"Anytime. Now, question. When are you going to get it together, big brother? Because right now, falling from the roof seems to be the least of your problems. You're falling apart."

"Again, your kindness is overwhelming."

When the waitress comes, we both order coffees and put in orders for chocolate-chip waffles, our mutual favorite.

"Seriously, all jokes aside, I'm worried about you. You haven't been the same since... well, you know."

"I know. It sucks. I miss her. I want to man up and pretend it doesn't matter, pretend I can just go out and find someone new, but I just can't. She was everything to me."

"Can I ask you something?"

"You're going to anyway," I say, and she shrugs.

"True. Why did you let her go, then, if you love her so much?"

I shake my head, averting my eyes. "Because I knew she needed more. It was becoming clear to me that I couldn't be what she needed."

"Why not?"

I look her in the eyes, raising an eyebrow. "Are you crazy? You know why."

"No. I know what you're blaming. But really, Luke? Is that what made you walk away and be miserable? Was it worth it?"

"I don't know, Scarlet. But I knew I couldn't give her

what she needed. She made it clear she couldn't settle for less."

"But why couldn't you give it to her?"

Now, anger starts to bubble. The feelings of inadequacy fester. "You know why, Scarlet. You know I can't promise her that."

"Luke, you're not him."

"You and I both know how similar we are. The music, the hair. Hell, even Mom knew it. After he left, she could barely stand to be around me because I was so much like him."

"But Dad wasn't all bad. You're the good of him."

"We don't know that."

"You wouldn't do what he did," Scarlet says, reaching for my hand. I soften at her touch.

"We don't know that. In his position, hell, maybe I would. And I won't risk that. I won't risk doing that to Lila or to a kid. I'm not dad material, and I never will be."

"But with Lila, you could be," she says softly.

"I won't take that risk. I won't hurt a kid the way Dad hurt us, and I won't risk it with Lila."

"Did you tell her all this? Does she know why you feel the way you do?"

"She knows the story about Dad. She's smart, Scarlet."

"But sometimes in love, it's not that easy to see. Maybe she's reading your hesitancy differently."

"Well, it doesn't matter," I say as the waitress sets our coffees in front of us. Scarlet stirs in some half-and-half while I warm my hand on the mug. "It's over. I can't give

Lila what she wants, and I can't ask her to settle for less. She deserves a stable man, a family man. I don't want to risk the idea I won't be that for her. She wants stability and promises I can't give."

"Because you're scared."

"Because I'm realistic. I've seen what marriage does to people."

"But look at me. I'm happy," Scarlet observes.

"You're just a freak," I say, smiling now.

"Luke, I'm just saying that you ended such a good thing based on fears of the future. Are you happy though?"

"It's not about my happiness."

"Which is exactly my point. The fact you're willing to walk away out of fear of hurting her shows that you're not Dad. You're not him."

I sigh, watching as the waitress carries our waffles out. I want to believe Scarlet. I wanted to believe this idea when Lila and I were having those conversations that would eventually lead me to here. I wanted to believe it when we officially ended it, when we were boxing up the life we'd shared. I wanted nothing more than to give Lila exactly what she was silently asking for. I wanted to assure her and myself that forever could work, and that we could start a family together.

I wanted to give Lila the life she deserved.

But as much as I wanted to turn around and promise forever to her, I couldn't.

Because as much as I want to believe I'm not my dad, the selfless prick who up and left all those years ago, leaving a scar on my mom, my sister, and most of all, me, I can't believe it. When I look in the mirror, I see him looking back. I see the wandering musician rooted in my soul. I see the need for fame, and I see the pull of the stage. I see the man who walked away at the lure of another woman, who didn't look back to serve his selfish lusts.

I see a man who isn't the picture-perfect, stable man a woman needs, a child needs.

I see Luke Bowman, the rebellious, rambling man who settled down for a while but probably can't settle down forever.

In her eyes, I saw forever... but in the mirror, I see a man who couldn't possibly get it right. I see a man too afraid to mess up because he knew what that felt like.

Now, looking into my coffee cup before I drown out the musings, I see Luke Bowman, the man who walked away from the love of his life because he couldn't get the courage to promise her what she needed.

CHAPTER TWELVE

LUKE

"Sounds okay," Evan says, handing me a beer as I look up at him. I've commandeered the front stoop to the apartment building, working on my songs. Evan was working on some business on his computer and told me my sad song was depressing him, so I came out here, the sun shining in my eyes.

"Thanks, I think," I mutter, taking the beer as Evan has a seat.

"Do you write happy anymore?" he asks.

I shake my head. "Do you want to pour some more salt in the wound?"

"No. But I'd like to take you out."

"Really?" I ask, motioning toward my foot. "Pretty sure I'm not going to be rocking the club in this thing."

"First, let's be clear. I'm not sure Luke Bowman could rock the club with two able legs."

"I was a master of the club in my day."

"And those days are long gone. But it's time to reacquaint. Come on, I've got another hour of work and then let's get out of this joint. Go have some real drinks, hang out with some real people. Because as much fun as it is watching you watch reruns of *Game of Thrones*, I just can't anymore. Even Floyd is depressed watching you."

I sigh. He's right. My life's become this morose, revolving door of singing sad songs and watching television. Without even work to keep me going, it's been pretty sad.

"Okay. I'll come. But you owe me the first round. I'm unemployed, after all."

"I think you owe me the second round for having to listen to your depressing songs. Although, speaking of it, bring your guitar. It's open mic night."

"I don't know, man. I'm not in the mood."

"Seriously? You've been waiting for your big break since high school. I don't think you're going to get it on this stoop playing to stragglers walking by."

"I don't think I'm ever going to get it, let's be real."

Evan looks at me seriously. "You're good, Luke. For real."

"You kicked me out and said my song depressed you."

"Oh, it did. It's hellishly depressing. But women go crazy for that thing. So at the very least, you might not get a recording contract, but maybe you'll snag a chick out of it. Girls dig that shit."

"I'm not looking for a girl."

"Well, you should be. Maybe then you could write an upbeat song. Get your ass inside and get yourself looking presentable."

"I don't know why I agreed to move in with you," I say as I pull myself to my good foot.

"Because you were desperate. And no one else would take your sorry ass in."

"Truth."

I hobble up the stairs and get ready for a night out, not really feeling it. I guess that's life, though. Sometimes you have to put yourself out there, go outside what you want to do.

CHAPTER THIRTEEN

LILA

Queasy from all the birthday cake I ate, I wander out on the back porch with Henry to look at the stars.

Another year gone by, another sad wish on the candles at my mom's insistence. Another year of wondering when life is going to be what I thought it would.

Maren and Will have gone home, and Grandma Claire is snoring on the couch. Mom and Dad are watching *Survivor* on television now that the birthday bash is over—complete with caviar, thanks to Mom.

Here I am, alone, sitting on the porch watching the stars with just Henry to keep me company. There's no hot birthday sex happening tonight. It's just me in my frumpy sweatpants with a greasy ponytail and worries about where I'll be sitting next year at this time.

Christopher called yesterday to see if I wanted to go out today. He, of course, has no idea it's my birthday. How could he? We've only been out twice. Two dates. Two great times, one sweet kiss, and numerous calls.

It should be enough.

But inside, every time I talk to him, I know it's not. There are no butterflies. There's no spark. He's a great guy, absolutely amazing, and he's extremely good-looking. He could give me what I want—the steady life, the commitment, the houseful of kids. We'd have this magazine-worthy, snapshot life.

But there would be no butterflies. There would be no tingle when he touched my hand, no light in my eyes.

Biting my lip, I study the constellations I learned in high school, wondering if that spark's forever gone.

Staring at the sky, I think of the first time I realized the spark was real, and that the butterflies of movies weren't the thing of fantasies. I think back to the moment that ruined every other man for me, every other moment.

Nothing, nothing, could ever be as magical as that first time we met.

* * *

Standing in the hallway of Park Lane Animal Hospital with my freshly pressed white jacket, I could barely stand still. My shift didn't start for fifteen minutes, but I could hardly wait. I'd been working for this moment for eight years— eight years of nose-in-the-books work, of spending every cent toward this education. I'd earned the title, I'd walked at graduation, and I'd earned my parents' pride. I'd done it.

And now my future began.

I was a little nervous. I'd interned at Park Lane Animal

Hospital and, in truth, knew it better than I knew anything. Still, the first official day as Dr. Morrow was intimidating. I wanted to do a good job.

"Ready for the patients to roll in?" Zoey asked. We'd been friends all through high school. She'd actually helped me get the internship here, knowing the Park family so well.

"I hope so."

"I've learned you never know what's going to come through these doors," she said, smiling as she handed me a cup of coffee. "Here, you'll need this. I'd suggest one-shoting it because who knows when you'll get a chance after those doors open. Of course, you know that. Relax. It's not really your first day here."

"Well, I just hope everything goes smoothly."

And that's when it happened.

The pounding on the glass out front, the man standing in the rain, holding up a carrier and desperately yelling for help.

So much for having a few minutes until opening. My first job was happening, and it was happening now.

***

"I'd like to just keep him overnight," I said, writing down notes in the chart, finally feeling like I could breathe.

I looked across the room at the curly-haired man; Luke Bowman, the chart said. He was slouching in the chair in the office, looking visibly relieved. I knew what he was feeling. I wiped some sweat from my sticky forehead.

It'd been touch and go for a few hours. The truck that hit

Floyd had been merciless, smashing the poor cat's back leg and almost killing him. Floyd was just lucky to have gotten away enough to save his life.

"Is he going to be okay?" the man asked, his voice smooth and intriguing. It was endearing to see him so worried about Floyd. I could tell from the moment he walked in that he genuinely cared about the fluffy gray cat, and it made me smile to see a man so open about his concern for a living creature. I could tell animal lovers from a mile away, was drawn to them. Maybe it was just that. Maybe it was the curly hair. Maybe it was the voice.

Regardless, I cleared my throat, trying to clear my head and the faint feel of warmth spreading to my cheeks.

"He's going to be fine. You got him here just in time."

"Thank God. That cat is such a pain in the ass. But I'd be lying if I said I didn't love him. I'm glad he's going to be okay." He looked up at me now, and I met his eyes with mine.

The exhaustion from the surgical procedures and the stress of saving Floyd melted. "Thank you," Luke said, and I could tell he meant it.

"You're welcome. I'm glad things worked out. I'll keep a close eye on him personally."

"Are you working all night?" he asked, standing now from his chair.

"No. But I'm going to stay. I want to make sure he's okay."

"No one would expect you to do that," he said, obviously feeling bad.

"Hey, Floyd's special to me, too. He's my first official patient."

"Wait, you're just out of vet school?"

"Don't worry. I know what I'm doing."

"I know that," Luke said. "I wasn't insinuating.... It's just, you seem so knowledgeable. It seems like you've been doing this forever."

I grinned, feeling playful. "Really? Do I look that old?"

Luke grimaced, covering his eyes with his hand. "I'm sorry. No. I'm just screwing this all up. What I mean is, thank you, and I'm glad Floyd came to such an amazing vet. You're amazing, Dr. Morrow. Seriously."

And for whatever reason, I decided to step away from the professional cover of the coat and say, "Call me Lila."

"Lila. Thank you. Are you sure you're okay with staying?"

"Positive. I'll call you if there are any changes."

"Okay, then. I'll see you soon?"

"See you soon. Don't worry."

"I won't. I know Floyd's in the best hands."

He paused a moment, lingering with his hand on the doorknob. I thought he might say something else, might continue the conversation. It felt weird having this... whatever this was... under the circumstances. Still, those eyes....

"Lila! Porcupine incident in room four. We need you stat!" Zoey shouted.

I snapped back to work. "Duty calls. I'll be in touch," I shouted, rushing out of the room, glancing back at Luke

Bowman one more time before carrying on with my day.

* * *

"Lila, don't be crazy. Go home. It's been a long day." Zoey had her keys in her hand as she stood in front of me. I was perched on the sofa in the emergency holding room in the back, where Floyd was being kept. He was doing great, sleeping now after eating some food.

"I just want to make sure he's okay. He's really important to Luke."

Zoey raised an eyebrow. "First-name basis, huh? Wait, this is the sexy curly-haired guy that pounded on the door this morning, right? Hell, honey, you're right. Stay. Do anything to win that one over. He's hot."

"It's not like that. It's strictly professional."

"Uh-huh. You tell yourself that. But listen, if you need anything, Dr. Benson is on call, and I'm just down the road."

"I'll be okay."

"Okay, crazy. I'll see you Wednesday then. Enjoy your day off tomorrow. You better be gone when I get here at ten in the morning."

"I'll try. I might still be sleeping."

Zoey shook her head, mumbling something about psychosis before leaving. I cuddled under the scratchy throw someone had left after spending a night like mine, tucked in and ready to sit vigil over Floyd, thinking about the man who had rocked my first day at work.

A knocking on the front door startled me a few minutes later. Thinking Zoey had forgotten something and her key, I stretched, ambled out to the front, and paused at the sight of a familiar curly-haired man peeking in the window.

I opened the door. "Luke? What are you doing here?"

He handed me a coffee, holding one for himself. "I came to bring you coffee and to keep you company. That Floyd can be a difficult one. I thought I should come help you keep him under control."

I smiled. "He's been sleeping. He's doing great, though."

"Glad to hear it."

"Follow me, he's back here." I led Luke back down the hallway to where Floyd was, feeling a little self-conscious about my melted-off makeup and greasy hair. I aimlessly twirled my ponytail, feeling suddenly antsy.

I'm sure he just came to see Floyd, *I told myself. Deep down, though, I wondered how many other customers would do this.*

Luke visited with Floyd, the cat purring at the sight of him.

"I can tell you have a special bond," I said. "Did you have him since he was a kitten?"

Luke nodded. "Found him when I was fifteen. He was just a tiny thing, abandoned. Let's just say I sort of knew how he felt at the time. We had a bond right away. He drives me crazy sometimes, meowing all night and keeping me up, but I love the big guy. I'm so glad you saved him. Crazy Floyd got out and was wandering by the road this morning, I guess."

"Floyd, next time you want to come see me, you don't need to get hit to do it, okay, buddy? Just come for

a checkup," I said to the cat, reaching in the cage to pet him, my hand accidentally touching Luke. "Sorry," I said, yanking my hand back and heading to the couch. "Do you want me to give you some time alone?"

"No, it's okay. I don't think Floyd's too private of a cat. I'm pretty sure he's okay with you hearing our conversation." Luke grinned, and I suddenly felt like an idiot.

I sat on the couch, sipping my coffee. After a few more pets, Floyd put his head back down and Luke came to sit on the sofa beside me.

"So, are you from around here?" Luke asked.

I nodded. "We moved here my senior year from South Carolina. Dad's job relocated him. It was the worst thing ever at the time, but now I'm glad. I love it here in Oakwood. How about you?"

"Born and raised. Never left this place."

"What do you do for work?"

"Roofing. I sing on the side too."

"Oh, that's so cool," I said, truly intrigued. I always loved the artsy types.

"Any pets?" Luke asked.

"Are you kidding? Every vet has to have pets, right? Here," I said, reaching for my phone to show Luke the hundreds of pictures of Henry.

"That's one awesome dog. I'd love to meet him sometime," Luke said, and I felt my stomach flutter that familiar flutter I'd felt only once before junior year.

Junior year, though, it had ended with a tearful goodbye, a move states away, a promise to keep it going long-distance, and an eventual broken heart.

Sitting on the sofa with the curly-haired hunk who was a singer and an animal lover, I couldn't help but wonder if this might just be different and if Luke's desire to see Henry might turn into something more.

"I'd like that too."

We spent the next few hours chatting about school, childhood memories, animals, and life. For those hours, it didn't feel like Luke was some man I'd met less than twenty-four hours ago. It felt like he was someone I'd been meant to talk to my whole life, like the piece of me that was missing.

When we woke up in the morning to Floyd's cries for food, I awkwardly stumbled to my feet. I'd been leaning on Luke's shoulder, a wet spot on his shirt showing where my drooling mouth had been. I flushed with embarrassment.

"Oh my God, I'm so sorry. We must've fallen asleep. I'm so sorry," I said, cupping my mouth in embarrassment.

Luke looked at his shirt, then at me, and started laughing. "It's fine. Just a little drool, right, Doctor? Nothing you haven't dealt with before."

"I'm mortified."

He shrugged. "Could be worse."

"Not really. I just fell asleep on a patient's owner's shoulder and drooled on him. Not quite professional."

"Well, there's one solution for that."

"What's that?" *I asked, rushing to get Floyd some food from the cupboard, mostly to busy my hands.*

"Let's not make this professional. Let's make it personal. Go out with me tonight."

I froze with a can of cat food in my hand. I turned to look at Luke, trying to avoid looking at the drool spot. "I don't know. That's not very professional. I mean, what would people think?"

"People can think what they want. Who cares. Go out with me."

He took a step forward now, and I felt that familiar flutter. I wanted to say yes, to see where this feeling would take me.

But with the haze of the evening gone and the bright daylight streaming in, I realized this could lead me down another path to heartbreak. I didn't know much about Luke, but I knew he seemed too good to be true. Those eyes were inviting, but they also said trouble.

"I don't know. I'll think about it."

"That means no."

"It means I'll think about it."

"Dammit, Lila Morrow. Just go out with me."

I sighed, shaking my head. "I can't. But I think Floyd is okay to go home. Call me if anything changes."

Luke stared, those eyes piercing into me. For a moment, he hesitated, as if he was going to push me further. "Okay. But you call me if anything changes on your end, okay?"

I smiled, shaking my head. "Okay, I will."

I helped him get Floyd ready for the ride home, giving him medicines and instructions and things to watch for. As I walked him to the door and thanked him for the coffee, he turned around to me.

"Lila Morrow?"

"Yeah?"

"Just one more thing."

He leaned in and gave me a kiss on the cheek. I froze, shocked by his boldness. He pulled back so we were almost nose to nose, his eyes glinting in the sun's rays floating through the door. "I don't think this is over. I think you haven't seen the last of me. I think we could be good for each other."

I sighed again, the fluttering intense now. "Well, for starters, that was more than just one thing, FYI."

He shook his head now. "I'll see you soon, soul mate."

"Soul mate? Really? Don't you think it's a little soon?" I said, unable to stop the smile from spreading on my face.

"Nope. Not at all. Come on, Floyd. Let's get out of here before Dr. Morrow makes a move. We're not ready for marriage yet, you know."

"You're unbelievable." I was flabbergasted by his confidence, more accurately labeled as arrogance. From his smirk to the way he walked out of there, it seemed like Luke Bowman knew I would be his.

Which was both frustrating and surprisingly intriguing.

"Well, thank you," he said, whistling as he walked to his pickup truck, loaded Floyd, and drove out of the parking lot, leaving me to stand and wonder what the hell kind of trouble I'd gotten into.

***

"Maren, this is a terrible idea. I have no rhythm," I whined, yanking down my hot pink exercise top and feeling completely out of place. I had no idea why I'd let her talk

me into it.

"Come on. Zumba's great. Plus, that guy I've been telling you about works out here, so come on. Just go with it."

"Wait, that Will guy?"

"Yes, idiot. Hence the hour it took me to get ready for Zumba. Didn't you think the eye makeup was a little over the top?"

"Still do. But I don't see what your obsession has to do with me."

"Because I need a Zumba buddy. Only creepos come alone. I don't want Will thinking I'm a creepo."

"That seems like seriously flawed logic," I said.

"Okay, doctor lady. You get that white jacket and you think you know everything," Maren said, rolling her eyes but grinning.

I shoved her into the wall, and we started yelling and pinching each other like the preteens we still were when together. After we'd settled down, I turned to the right, eyeing the muscular guys on the machinery, taking a peek.

And then I froze, putting a hand on Maren's arm. "Oh, shit. Are you serious?" I asked, seeing the familiar curls.

He was in a T-shirt and shorts, but even from here, I could appreciate his amazing biceps at work. My heart started to beat faster.

"What?"

"It's him. That guy from the other day. You know, the whole Floyd thing?"

"Oh, Lila, he's gorgeous. Go get him." Maren let out what I thought was supposed to be a Latin growl, but

sounded more like a cough.

"No. I can't. He's crazy. Super bold. He's trouble."

"Trouble is what you need," she hissed. "You're so boring. He could liven you up. Now go talk to him."

"Not in this outfit."

"Absolutely in that outfit. Now go, or I will."

"I thought you were here for Will," I observed, staring at my crazy sister.

"I am. But if you let that fine man go to waste, I'll just have to move in on both."

"You're ridiculous," I said. "But fine. And besides, there's Will. Go make eyes at him," I said, rolling my eyes now. We pinched each other one more time before heading off in separate directions. So much for using the gym to get fit.

"Are you following me?" I asked, pretending to sound angry. Luke looked up, smiling instantly at the sight of me, which made me feel even more fluttery.

"Looks like you're following me. I've been going here for years. You?"

"Um, just today," I admitted, shrugging. "How's Floyd?"

"Good, thanks to a gorgeous new vet. He's all better. But he could probably use a house call just to make sure."

"I think he'll be fine, but he's welcome to stop by during office hours for a professional visit," I replied, putting emphasis on the word "professional."

Luke stepped away from the weight machine, coming closer. "Now that I think about it, Floyd actually is feeling a little sad. You see, he's super thankful you saved him, and he feels bad you didn't get a proper thank-you. He was really hoping I would take you out for a fancy dinner, just as a thanks. Professional, of course."

"Do you know how creepy you sound talking about your cat like that? People are going to worry."

"Let them worry. I only care what one person in this room thinks, and I'm looking at her."

"You don't even really know me."

"So let me." His eyes never left mine, his words piercing me. This man just strolled into my life, and now he just stood in it like he belonged there. It was unsettling. But it was also sexy.

"You're so confident."

"No, I'm just sure. Sure you and I could be good together."

"And how could you possibly know that?" I asked, raising an eyebrow, grinding the toe of one of my sneakers into the weird foamy material on the floor.

He shrugged. "Because I just met you, and I already can't stop thinking about you. Come on, just go to dinner with me. Just one dinner. If you think I'm creepy or you don't feel it too, you can bail. Floyd and I will find another vet, and you won't ever have to see me again."

I sighed. "You're impossible."

"I've been told that a time or two."

"But okay."

"Wait, okay? Like, yes?"

"Like yes. But only for Floyd." I couldn't fight the grin

forming on my face, and I couldn't stop the feeling in my veins I got when he stared at me.

"I'll take it. Okay. Here, put your number in. I'll pick you up at six tomorrow?" he asked, his grin spreading as he handed me his cell phone.

"Oh, she'll be waiting," Maren said, putting an arm around my shoulder. "She hasn't stopped talking about you since you met. Don't let her cold exterior fool you. She's crazy about you."

"Maren, shut up," I said, mortified, but Luke just smiled even wider as I handed back the phone with my number in it.

"See, I knew it. See you tomorrow," he said, going back to his weight machine like he hadn't just sealed our date and potentially our life.

"I'm going to kill you," I whispered to Maren.

"No, you won't. Because I'm going to tell this whole story so adorably at your wedding, as maid of honor of course."

"How's Will, in other news?" I asked as we headed to Zumba, the music already blaring from the group room as the warm-up started.

"Good. We're going out on Friday."

"Well, you sealed that deal quickly."

"Are you surprised? Who can resist my charm? Besides, when you know, you know."

I wished at that moment I could be more like Maren, so open to the whims of life, so willing to accept with confidence what I felt.

We strolled into Zumba class, though, trying to avoid the in-sync women who looked like they were professional dancers and getting way too many glares from them as we maneuvered through the crowd to the back.

"Class starts at five o'clock. Be on time," the little blonde instructor shouted, clearly directing her words at us.

"Sorry, we were too busy finding the loves of our lives while you bitches were line dancing," Maren shouted.

I froze, already mortified but now over the top. "Maren, you can't say that."

"I just did," she said, jumping in line, ignoring the glares as she painted on a fake cheerleader smile and started sashaying to the beat while I fumbled in the corner to try and stay in step.

"Good thing we lined up our dates because I think we might be banned from the gym after this."

"Whatever. Zumba is overrated anyway," Maren said way too loudly over the Latin beat of the music, shimmying her hips offbeat but with confidence.

"You dragged me here."

"Yeah, to get a date lined up. You didn't really think I was into exercising, did you?"

For the next hour, we giggled as we were off-step more than we were on, sweating up a storm and looking nothing like dancers as the other women in the class. By the end, I was pretty sure I'd pulled an ass muscle, and Maren had fallen to the floor, once because of an untied shoelace and once out of laughter at me.

"What a story for the wedding," I said. "You might have

to clean up your toast a little bit."

"No way. I'm including Zumba bitches, word for word, in it."

I shook my head as we giggled the whole way out of the gym, feeling giddy from the endorphins, the ridiculous jokes we made during class, and most of all, the possibility of love we both found.

* * *

Tossing my hair into a ponytail as I zoom through the door of Park Lane, I'm barely able to breathe. I have two minutes to spare until I'm officially on the clock, but patients are already lined up in the waiting room. Staying up thinking about all those memories last night was both masochistic and stupid.

I fly around the woofing dogs and cages of hamsters, birds, and Herbert the snake to get behind the counter and toward the offices.

"Here," Zoey says, practically shoving a cup of coffee into my hands.

"Thanks. Sorry I'm running so late."

"No worries. Calm down. You have a minute. Gosh, your hair is all over the place," she says, eyeing me.

I shrug. "Who cares."

"You will in a minute when you see our new intern," Zoey says, winking.

"Why?"

"Because he's freaking gorgeous with a capital *G*. Seriously. Go and fix that messy ponytail. Oh, hell, who am

I kidding. You're perfect, crazy hair or not."

"Slow down, matchmaker. We work together. It'll be strictly professional."

"Yeah, okay. See all these women in the waiting room drooling worse than their dogs? It's because he walked through a minute ago. He's amazing."

"I have to get back there."

"Uh-huh. Exactly."

I take a swig of my coffee, which is piping hot, almost choke on it, and then head down the hallway.

I walk past the room where I met Luke, brushing it off in the flurry of activity already happening. I don't have time to reminisce.

"Hey, you must be Dr. Lila Morrow?" a warm voice says. I turn around and am face-to-face with the intern.

I take a breath, trying not to exhale my nasty coffee breath into the new guy's face since we are very, very close.

My heart flutters. Dammit, Zoey wasn't kidding. I nibble on my lip so I don't risk my jaw dropping.

He is more than gorgeous with a capital *G*. He's gorgeous with a capital everything.

Dimples on the cheeks, strong body, tall, and tanned. He's got a day's worth of dark stubble, just the way I like it, and spiky hair—what Zoey and I call Edward Cullen hair. He looks much, much better, though, than a sparkly vampire ever could—and I was always team Edward, so that's saying something.

"I'm Oliver Waynesboro. First day, and man, I'd be lying if I said I wasn't nervous."

He flashes me perfect teeth. This guy might be nervous, but I bet I'm more nervous than him. He extends his hand to shake mine, and I hesitantly oblige, afraid there might be sparks when we touch.

There aren't, but his hand covers mine, and I smile. "I'm Lila Morrow."

"Yeah, I know. Zoey's been talking all about you from the second I got here. Told me you're newly single, too."

I blush and laugh way too much. It's my nervous laugh, the one I think is atrociously annoying.

"Well, patients will be rolling in. Don't want them to have to wait too long. Let me know if you need anything," I say, feeling the need to escape.

"Oh, I thought Dr. Jones told you. I'm paired with you all morning, you know, so I can learn the ropes. You're not getting rid of me anytime soon, Dr. Morrow."

"Oh, wonderful. Paired with you will be perfect," I say, and then inwardly groan. Oh my God, I'm like a smitten fourteen-year-old around this guy. I can actually feel my palms sweating. How the hell am I going to keep my cool all morning?

Before I have time to think too much, Zoey is announcing our first patient.

"Guess we better get to it, then," I say, reminding myself to be professional.

"Can't wait," he says, winking at me, practically sending me into a tailspin, and then following me into the room.

And by the room, I mean *the* room. The room that started it all with Luke. How's that for a slap in the face from the universe?

CHAPTER FOURTEEN

LILA

"You know Maren's going to kill you, right?" Zoey asks as she sets up the vegetable tray in the Oakwood Fire Hall. There are fall-colored streamers and balloons everywhere, cutesy baby pictures of Maren, and photos of Maren and Will lining the food table. Zoey and I have been working all morning doing the traditional setup—party games and cakes and guess the bride's favorite whatever stations. We've ushered in friends and family and run through the schedule.

I want this to be perfect for Maren.

Although, Zoey's right. She's still going to kill me.

"Look, just because Maren said she didn't want a wedding shower doesn't mean she actually meant it. Besides, she can't be too pissed. She's lucky I took the reins and refused to let Mom lift a finger other than to make potato salad and buy some prizes. She should be kissing my feet. If I hadn't taken over, she would've had a five-hundred-guest affair."

"I think with Maren, she meant she really didn't want a shower."

"Well, what kind of maid of honor would I be if I didn't embarrass her with a shower? She'll forgive me."

"Well, if not, I call dibs on maid of honor. It's so much easier to get laid at the wedding when you're wearing those horrid, silky dresses. Drunk men just go crazy for them. Weird fantasy or something." Zoey winks at me, and I just shake my head.

At this very moment, Will's mom is leading her mother by us. She gives Zoey a glare. Zoey mouths "sorry" and shrugs. Once they're seated at their round table out of earshot, we both giggle like teenagers.

The fire hall is pretty sparse. Maren wanted a simple wedding, only about a hundred guests. There are only about thirty women here. Still, even in the small setting, there's already one woman too many.

Great-aunt Lula.

"Oh my God, these streamers are so tacky," the eighty-five-year-old woman screams to no one in particular. I shake my head.

Maren hadn't even wanted to invite Grandma Claire's sister. The two have violently hated each other their entire lives. Still, with Mom's side of the family dwindling, she'd insisted that Great-aunt Lula be there to represent the Statelys at the wedding.

Maren had said no.

Mom had sent out an invite anyway.

I hadn't invited Great-aunt Lula to today's event.

Mom found out and invited her anyway.

Are you seeing a pattern?

"God, give me some of that alcoholic punch," I demanded, and Zoey hooked me up with a cup.

"Oh, they should be here in a minute," I state after my phone buzzes with the text from Mom. "Get everyone situated," I tell Zoey.

"Where does Maren think she's going?" Zoey asked.

"To lunch with Mom and Grandma Claire."

"And how did you get out of it?"

"Told her I had a hot date. That shut her up. Other than a million questions, of course." I take another swig of my punch, getting ready to play hostess for the next two hours.

The door flies open. "Surprise!" the crowd yells.

Mom ushers Grandma Claire, who is wearing her floppy red sunhat, in through the door. She waves excitedly. Maren, who is standing beside Mom and Grandma, smiles and covers her mouth in genuine surprise.

Once the room has quieted down, Maren heads my way.

"Fuck you," she whispers into my ear as she hugs me and the crowd "awws."

"You love me," I say, handing her my punch. "Oh, and it's alcoholic."

"I guess you can be forgiven. But so help me God, Aunt Lula better not…."

"Oh, my, jeans at your own bridal shower? Couldn't someone have had her dress properly for this? Good Lord," a shaky but loud voice bellows from the crowd. Maren closes her eyes and sighs.

"Sorry. Mom's fault. Now go sit in your special seat. It's time for party games."

Maren shakes her head, tosses back the rest of the punch, and heads to her seat as I prepare to read from my script and organize the room into a wedding shower extravaganza.

* * *

"Yes, that's correct, Maren's favorite restaurant is Olive Garden," I say animatedly as Zoey hands out another prize—probably another air freshener, judging by the wrapping paper.

I'm getting ready to read the next question, the room alight with murmurings and laughter, when the door flies open. We all turn to see three unknown women strut in, very scandalously dressed. They look like they've just come from a very, very skanky runway. I'm pretty sure their dresses, which are a satiny red, are about eight inches long total.

"Can I help you?" I ask as the room goes quiet.

"Where's the bride-to-be?" one asks, practically licking her bright red lips as she says it. She's eyeing me in a way that feels oddly sensual, her blonde hair curled perfectly and her makeup magazine-worthy. She's got huge breasts bulging out of her halter-top dress. Are these Maren's friends? Are they Will's family? What the hell?

"Um, right there," I say, deflecting them toward Maren, who looks just as confused as me.

"Perfect," the tall blonde says, heading over to Maren.

The three actually gather around her. The last one in line, a tall brunette, hits a few buttons on her phone.

Some crazy, swanky music starts playing, and the three start gyrating around Maren, who is looking at me.

Horrified, I shake my head, eyes wide, as they do a lap dance for Maren. The blonde reaches behind and starts unzipping her dress.

"Oh my God, what the hell?" Maren screams, and I rush over to stop the music, grabbing the phone from the brunette. There are gasps and questions all around. The girls look at me, also confused.

We all stand in shocked silence for a moment before Grandma Claire speaks up.

"What the hell is right! I ordered three male strippers for Maren. What are you three doing here?"

We all turn to Grandma Claire. "Grandma, are you kidding?" I ask. "You ordered strippers?"

"Well, yeah, of course I did. Girl's got to get her kicks in before she's tied down."

"Grandma, first, you order strippers at a bachelorette party, not a wedding shower, for Christ's sake," Maren says, shaking her head and staring at the ceiling as the three strippers awkwardly step to the side.

"Don't take the Lord's name in vain," Mom yells.

I turn to her, standing in her pink skirt suit. "Are you kidding?" I ask. "We've got three female strippers at the shower, and you're worried because she said Christ?"

"Lila, I mean it."

I throw my hands up. "Oh my God. Grandma, this was wildly inappropriate."

"Well, of course it is. They were supposed to be men,

137

LINDSAY DETWILER

I swear. I know Maren's not a lesbian, I wasn't suggesting she was...."

I groan audibly, wondering what I'm going to do with this one. Pretty sure no maid of honor book on the planet tells you how to deal with your grandma ordering female strippers for your sister's wedding shower.

I look over to Will's family's table. They look horrified, confused, and like they need counseling.

Join the club, I suppose.

"Well, I mean, when life hands you lemons, or in this case, lots of melons, you might as well make the best of it," Grandma Claire says.

Maren, who hasn't moved, just exhales.

"What? I mean, I paid good money with my son's credit card for this. We might as well get our money's worth, am I right?" Grandma Claire looks around the shower, hoping to strum up some support for her cause.

"No, Grandma. Just... no. Thank you, ladies. You're, um, lovely, thank you. Your services are finished," I say, placing a hand on the shoulder of the closest lady and then awkwardly pulling it back.

The three look at me, shrug, and strut out. Grandma's right, though. They've already been paid, so I'm sure they don't care. One actually has the nerve to steal a cookie off a tray on the way out. I've got bigger worries at this point.

"Mom, how did Grandma have access to Dad's credit card?" Maren asks. The rest of the women at the shower are either fiddling with their wedding favor pretending they're not hearing our family conversation, or staring at us, mouths agape, taking it all in so they can report back to their friends at work on Monday about the Stately/Morrow wedding shower debacle.

"Maren, I don't know. Your father's an idiot sometimes."

Still standing up front, I realize all the women are looking at me, including Maren, like I'm going to make this better somehow.

I do what I do best—I turn to Zoey.

She looks at me, looks at the crowd, and says, "Time for cake?"

Everyone stands at once, rushing to the dessert table, insisting it's a fabulous idea and they can't wait to try the vanilla bean cupcakes and the chocolate lava cakes we've had made.

The room erupts into nervous energy.

Finally able to get attention off me, I shake my head before laughing hysterically.

What the hell else can I do?

***

The shower is mercifully winding down.

"I told you I didn't want a shower. You should've listened."

"Okay, well, it will be quite a great story for your kids someday," I say, shoving another cupcake into my mouth, nervous eating one of my bad habits.

"I don't think I'll be telling anyone about this. I'm not a prude, but Jesus."

"Maren, watch your mouth," Mom says, sneaking up

on us. That woman has sonic hearing, I swear.

Maren rolls her eyes, and Grandma Claire stumbles up toward us. She nudges me in the ribs with her elbow. "Okay, be honest. Those three were pretty gorgeous. I mean, the men I ordered were way better, don't get me wrong, but they were knockouts. I really got my money's worth."

I pinch the bridge of my nose. "Grandma, please. Let's just not."

"I'll say. Mom is probably rolling over in her grave," a grating voice announces. It's Lula, who is now about a foot from Grandma Claire. "How could you?"

"Sorry, some of us aren't prudes. You're just jealous, you ugly cow."

"Grandma," I scold. "Stop."

Aunt Lula scowls, turning to me now and shaking her head. "Oh, it's fine. I might be an ugly cow, but at least I was married. You, on the other hand, should be mortified. Your younger sister's getting married before you? Embarrassing. In my day, we had a word for that: spinster."

Now it's my turn to be angry.

I don't have time to defend myself, though. Because before I can react, Grandma Claire is doing what she does best.

Acting crazy.

The vegetable tray is on the table beside her. With lightning speed for an eightysomething, she grabs the entire tray and flings it at Aunt Lula.

More gasps ensue as we look to see Aunt Lula covered in glopping ranch dressing after being pelted with celery, carrots, and a variety of garden vegetables. There's even a baby carrot stuck in her overly hair sprayed perm.

Grandma Claire lets out a loud cackle. Maren and I freeze, clueless yet again about what to do.

"Take that, you wench," Grandma yells as Aunt Lula, horrified, flings ranch off her hands.

At this very moment, the door opens again. At this point, it's like shell shock. I'm terrified about what else could possibly go wrong.

Will walks through the door, a huge bouquet of roses in his hands. "Am I on time?" he asks, referring to the time I told him to come.

"Oh, right on time," Maren says, rushing over to him and leaping into his arms. "Right on time to take me away."

Will, hugging Maren, looks over at us. Grandma Claire, ignoring the fact her sister is still standing coated in ranch dressing, smiles and waves.

Will eyes Aunt Lula and me. I shrug. "Can't wait for the wedding," I say as Mom rushes over with a towel to wipe off Aunt Lula.

"I think I'm eloping," Maren yells as she leads Will to a table to fill him in on the stripper escapade, the Aunt Lula drama, and the realities of life in the Stately/Morrow family.

***

"What are you going to do with five toasters?" Zoey asks as she carries a carefully stacked tower of presents into Maren and Will's apartment. She's graciously offered to help with cleanup since Mom thought it might be best to get Grandma

Claire home and settled down.

"Make a lot of toast, I guess," Will says as he holds the door open for us. I am carrying a comforter set and a tea set, hoping not to drop either.

"Thanks for everything, guys," Maren says as we stack our individual piles of presents in the living room. Figuring Will can get the last stack, the three of us plop down on the tan sofa, sweat beading on our foreheads from the trips back and forth to the loaded-down Suburban.

"Do you mean that?" I ask, smiling.

"I do. It was good to feel loved, despite Aunt Lula and everything. I appreciate it." Maren squeezes me in a side hug, and I relish the moment, happy to see my sister so happy. She deserves it. "But now, on to more important items. Who are you bringing as your date?"

I pull back from our hug. "Zoey."

"Come on. I know Zoey's coming. But who is your date?"

"I don't have one. I don't need one."

"Shut up. Of course you do. What about Christopher?"

I sigh. "He's not really my type. He's called a few more times, but I don't know. There's just something off."

"Honey, you don't have to marry the guy you bring. He's just got to be a fun date and maybe even a fun romp."

"Maren, you're starting to sound like Aunt Lula. I don't have to have a date to have fun."

"Besides," Zoey says. "She doesn't have to go with Christopher when there's a new, sexy man in her life."

I flash my glare to Zoey, who shrugs.

"What? You've been holding out on me? I need details," Maren says, squeezing my hand so hard I jump.

"I'm not holding out. There are no details. We have a new intern who Zoey thinks is hot."

Zoey laughs. "Come on? Just me? You've been ogling him all week."

"What's his name?" Maren asks, leaning forward from her seat as her interest is piqued.

"Oliver Waynesboro. And he's gorgeous and he hasn't taken his eyes off your sister," Zoey pipes in before I can get a word in.

"Perfect. And he's a vet in training? Match made in heaven. Yep, he's the date."

"Hi, hello, I'm Lila, and I'm still here. I'd appreciate being a part of the conversation about my date to the wedding."

"It's settled. You're bringing Oliver. I'm the bride. I get what I want."

"That's ridiculous. I barely know him." I flop backward, sinking deeper into the sofa and staring at the ceiling.

"So what a perfect way to get to know him. Bring him to my wedding or else."

"I'm not asking him. That's weird. Unprofessional," I argue, exasperated.

"Then I'll ask for you," Zoey says. "It's settled."

"You two are unbelievable."

"You love us," Maren says, and Zoey nods.

"What are you three girls giggling about?" Will asks, walking into the living room from the kitchen.

"Just Lila's supersexy date," Maren says.

"Not as sexy as the groom, of course," Will adds, and we all smile. Maren shrugs, and he grabs her around the waist, tickling her until she screams.

"And that's our cue to get out of here," I say to Zoey, who is already standing up from the sofa.

"What, and leave me with all this unpacking?" Maren says, batting Will's hands away.

"You two can manage," I say. "Love you, sis. Talk to you soon."

"Make sure she doesn't weasel her way out of asking Oliver," Maren shouts at Zoey as we head out the door.

"Oh, she won't," Zoey replies, nudging me.

It's bad enough when you have a plotting, stubborn sister. But when she ropes your best friend in, too? It's impossible.

CHAPTER FIFTEEN

LUKE

"Get in," Dean shouts through the open window in his pickup truck, honking the horn over and over. I'm sitting in my regular spot, working out a new song that I'm actually liking.

"For what?" I ask. It's been a few weeks since I've seen Dean in person.

"You're getting the hell out of here and going out. It's Friday."

"Have you forgotten?" I ask, pointing to my leg. "Not much hardcore partying you can do with a bum leg." In truth, the trip to the club with Evan didn't go so well last time. Open mic night got overtaken by some soulful singer with his guitar, someone I couldn't compete with. I ended up drinking way too many beers and wallowing alone at the bar while Evan flirted with about five different girls. I guess a guy in a cast isn't all that appealing.

"Are you kidding? That's the lamest-ass excuse I've

ever heard. Now throw your guitar in the back and get in. We're going out. It's karaoke night at the Renegade, so you can even try out your new song, see if it goes over well with the ladies."

I sigh. I don't feel like going out, in truth, or even singing, at least on a stage. The old Luke, the one from years ago, would've been jumping in the back of the truck in a millisecond, broken leg or not. He'd have been doing a shot on the way to do shots.

I get to my feet, though. No use sitting here all night. I am turning into a creepy recluse. Wouldn't hurt to get out.

"Thatta boy," Dean says as I hobble to his truck. He gets out to help me load the guitar. "Now let's get you back out there, see what Friday nights are really supposed to look like."

"I'm pretty rusty," I say, and it's true. It's been a while since I've really let my guard down, let loose, and got out.

"Well, it's time. No creepy cat man tonight or lonely song player. By the end of the night, you're going to be batting women off you, broken leg or not."

"We'll see about that. But damn, I could use some drinks."

"Say no more." Dean stomps on the gas, peeling out onto the road, blasting songs to get us pumped up for a night of fun.

* * *

The crowd actually cheers, and I can't stop smiling like a damn idiot.

"Thank you," I say into the mic as I hobble off the stage. I feel like I'm glowing, probably partially from the buzz I'm feeling. Dean's been pumping me full of liquor since we got here, telling me I need to loosen up.

Part of it, though, is that the crowd actually seemed to like my song. I sort of turned karaoke night into open mic night, deciding to go all in—again, probably the alcohol talking—and sing my new song. It's called "She Walked Right By."

Yeah, it's about her. Of course it is.

I hobble off the stage, Dean whooping from the back corner. I'm heading to claim my next drink, which Dean promised he'd pay for if I got on stage.

"That was beautiful," a voice says from behind me. I turn to see a woman with long black hair. She's wearing a tight red dress, halter style, her breasts bulging out. She's got the bright lip thing going on, and she, in truth, looks like she walked off the page of one of those women's magazines Lila used to leave lying around the house.

She's damn gorgeous in an overt way. I breathe out, trying to play it cool. "Thanks. It's a new song I've been working on."

"Well, it was perfect. What are you doing singing here, though? I feel like you should be playing somewhere bigger."

I shrug. "I'm not really that good. Just do it as a hobby."

"Humble, too. Wow. And gorgeous. Definitely a star. Let me buy you a drink," she says, her voice lingering.

"Isn't the guy supposed to buy the girl a drink?" I ask,

feeling flirtatious but not quite sure how to proceed. I'm off my game.

"I'm not like most girls, I think you'll find. Much less complicated. Now come on." She yanks on my arm, and I feel electricity at her touch. I smile, feeling the glowing sensation for the second time tonight.

Less complicated. Absolutely gorgeous. Sounds like just the kind of woman I could use tonight.

I'm feeling high on the rush from being on stage, on the booze, and on the fact a sexy woman is on my arm. I'm feeling good enough to forget everything, all the heartache and longings and regrets. I want to sit a little closer to the woman at the bar, to lean in and tell her all sorts of things. I'm ready to forget about the past and live in the present a little bit. I'm feeling good enough to wonder what those breasts would feel like, what she would feel like....

So when the red dress woman leans in very close, a hand on my thigh, and says, "You know, I'd be okay if you wanted to kiss me," the smell of tequila on her breath, I don't take my eyes off her.

"I don't even know your name," I whisper, staring into her hazel eyes and feeling her hand creep up. I shudder, my breath ragged.

"It's Margot. Margot Lane. Can you kiss me now?" It's more of a command than an offer, her eyes drawing me in like a siren's song.

Staring at her, I see a woman of mystery, of intrigue, and of wildness. I see a woman not afraid to take a risk and to let her heart lead. I see a woman a little more rebellious and a lot more forward than most.

I see a woman so different than Lila's polite, humble, rational character.

But maybe that's the point. Maybe my heart needs something different, something new, something less complicated. Because if I can't have Lila, what's the point of rational and concrete? What's the point of playing it safe?

So it is probably for these very reasons that I, without any thought, lean in and take Margot's lips with mine, kissing her voraciously, hungrily, like I can consume her.

Something tells me, though, sitting on the barstool and coming up for air, that it's Margot who could potentially consume me, mind, body, and spirit. This girl isn't one you rein in. This girl isn't one who will be looking for a ring on her finger or a baby stroller.

This girl has a fire I've never seen.

Pulling back, though, and seeing her smile, I realize maybe I want to be consumed by a fire burning too hot to touch. Maybe I need to be a little scorched and seared.

Margot Lane isn't what I was looking for or even what I want right now.

But maybe Margot Lane is exactly what I need.

CHAPTER SIXTEEN

LUKE

I almost say "no" when Margot asks me to take her to dinner the next night, calling me when I'm debating tossing her phone number. It's not that I'm not into her. It's just, in the clear-headed light of day, away from the booze and the plunging neckline, I wonder if I'm ready.

I'm not a saint, don't get me wrong. I, like many men, can appreciate a good body when I see it. I'm human. The thought of washing away the memories of Lila with a drunken night of wild sex and fun times is tempting. But I'm not that Luke anymore. I've got this crazy thing now called guilt I'm susceptible to.

So, even though Dean and Evan think I'm crazy, I swear the next day I'm not calling Margot, that the kiss we shared was just a one-time thing.

A damn nice one-time thing, but nothing more. Margot Lane wasn't the type you called back, I convinced myself.

I guess I was right because the next day, she called me.

And, to my surprise, I found myself agreeing to let her pick me up at six.

I greet her at the door with roses, jeans, and a T-shirt. She told me to dress comfortably. She's taken the lead on the date, which feels odd.

She's wearing micro-short shorts that show off a lot of thigh, and a plunging neckline again. I clear my throat, handing her the roses.

"Why roses? So expensive. Next time pick wildflowers," she says, and I'm momentarily stunned. She takes them from me, and I follow her out the door. "Thank you. It was sweet. But come on, we're going to miss all the good stuff."

"Where are we going?" I ask, wondering if I'm dressed right.

"The fair in Colverstown."

"Oh. Never been."

"Are you kidding? It's only the best fair in the entire state."

I smile, watching her talk animatedly as we head to her truck. "Best lemonade and funnel cakes ever. Plus, I'm a sucker for carnival games. Are you going to win me an awesome prize?"

"You know they're rigged, right?"

"You know that's only what men say who aren't man enough to win them, right?"

She grins at me as I climb into the truck. She tosses the roses on the dash as I situate myself. Her hair is long and straight again, and I can't stop thinking about what it would feel like to run my hands through it, to yank her mouth close to mine, to kiss her again.

I stop myself. I try to tell myself I'm getting ahead of things. I don't know her. Who knows what she's like.

Then again, I let my mind keep going. Maybe it doesn't have to be this deep love connection. Been there, done that. Maybe fun and sexy and passionate is what I need.

We start driving the half-hour trip, and Margot is alight with conversation. She talks about her childhood and asks about mine. She talks about her cat named Lola and shows me pictures on her phone at a red light. She talks and talks like she's got nothing to hide, like she has no censor.

I can barely get a word in, but when I can, I ask, "So what made you settle down here in Oakwood?"

She shrugs. "My roommate at the time, her name was Candy, decided to come here from Florida. She met some guy online who was living here, so I decided to come on a whim."

"So you just picked up and moved across the country?"

"Why not? I was young, and it sounded like an adventure."

I shake my head. "You know most people wouldn't do that, right?"

"I'm not most people. I told you I'm different."

"I'm beginning to think I like different," I say, looking over to appraise her. She smiles back.

"Good. I was hoping you would."

We finish the drive, Margot singing loudly to a Pink Floyd song that comes on the radio and making a list of things we just have to do at the fair.

***

My second kiss with Margot Lane happens at the top of the Ferris wheel, a picture-perfect moment after we've eaten a ton of funnel cake and lemonade. The September night air has a bite to it, a chill suggesting we're easing into autumn, the clear sky giving us a gorgeous view of the constellations. There's a giant stuffed cow between us—I proved my masculinity on the ring toss. The kiss is slow and sensuous this time, Margot's hand planted on my jaw, keeping me close. Not like I'd be going anywhere anyway. When she pulls back, her eyes are warm and hungry. I feel all sorts of things I haven't felt since....

"I think I'm falling for you," Margot says. I'm shocked. It's so soon for an admission like this. Most girls are more guarded with their hearts.

"You barely know me," I respond, not wanting to shoot her down but wanting to know where she's coming from.

"I know enough. I knew it when I first saw you on that stage. We could be good together, Luke Bowman."

I sigh, looking out at the skyline for a second, taking it all in. I think about the depth of the words she doesn't even realize. I think about how not so long ago, it was my mouth uttering similar words to a woman who is now in my past, or at least should be.

"Margot, I— You should know I just ended a relationship I'd been in for a while. It was pretty serious. I still—I'm not—"

"Shhh...," she whispers, putting a smooth hand over my lips. I look into her eyes, still seeing the lust there. "It's okay. We've all got a past, Luke. We've all got someone we're not quite over. But maybe I could help with that. Maybe together, we could find a new version of serious. No pressure, just the present. Just you and me and whatever we're feeling. I know your heart's not 100 percent mine yet, but I'm okay with that. Explore with me. Live a little. Be adventurous. Because otherwise, what's the point of all this, you know?"

It's a rambling monologue coming from a flighty girl with an obvious tendency to wear her heart on her sleeve. It's from a girl I barely know anything about, who might not be completely sincere in her words and actions. Somehow, though, sitting at the top of the Ferris wheel rocking gently in the warm breeze, it makes sense. It all clicks.

Maybe I'm just afraid of serious after what happened. Maybe I just need a break, or maybe I just need someone who in no way, shape, or form reminds me of her.

So when Margot leans again to kiss me and the Ferris Wheel starts up again, I keep kissing her this time, knowing with each second our lips are together, I'm more and more hers.

I'm more and more glued to this wily girl who isn't going to be easy to keep a hold of... but somehow, that's comforting to me.

* * *

A few weeks of late night walks and coffee dates, and I'm sold on Margot. A couple of karaoke dance nights and trips to the club and dancing in the fountain at the park, and I'm also sold on the fact she might be the death of me. She is everything Lila isn't. She's the wild to Lila's rational. She's the carefree to Lila's plotting. She's the crazy and sometimes obnoxiously chatty but super sexual woman I'm getting more and more attached to.

As the weeks go on, I'm convinced she's not Lila and never will be. But right now, it feels good.

So in the first weekend of October when I reclaim my annual gig at the Oakwood Fall Fest, Margot squeals with delight at getting a front row seat. Things are different this year. I'm different this year, and my relationship is definitely different. But I'm excited to look out and see the vivacious, sing-out-loud Margot in the seat.

My music's shifted this month too. I call Margot my muse, but she thinks the word sounds too stuffy. Whatever she is, she's livened up my music. There's a new edgy vibe to it, a new life. Even Evan thinks the songs sound pretty good and "less depressing." I think he also just thinks Margot is hot as hell—but who wouldn't?

"You ready?" the lady in charge of the festival asks as I stand off to the side of the stage, waiting for Banjo Bill to wrap up.

"You bet," I say, pumped up to play, even though the crowd is thin in front of the stage. Families and Oakwood residents mill about from stand to stand, buying cotton candy and lemonade. It's a small venue, but it's one of my favorites. It's nice to play to a crowd where you know the faces.

I step out to the microphone, ready to start the first song. I see Margot animatedly waving from the seat up front reserved for her. I smile as I start the first song, singing right to her. Looking up for a second, though, someone else catches my eye.

Actually, three someones.

I keep singing, but I barely hear the words. My eyes are glued on the sight in front of me, beyond the reaches of the tiny crowd gathered.

It's her.

Lila.

She's standing in the middle of the street fair in an orange sundress, leaning on his arm.

A tall, skinny man I've never seen before says something to her, and she throws her head back and laughs. He's holding Henry's leash, and the three look like the picture-perfect family out for a September stroll. Standing on the stage singing my song, I feel my chest tighten. Suddenly, it's not Margot I'm staring at, thinking about.

It's her. It's them.

When I finish my song, I take a second to soak in the applause. I think about what song I'd planned on singing, the one I wrote about Margot. I turn to see her clapping animatedly. I smile. Inside, though, I know no matter what she says, this isn't okay. It isn't okay that I should be thinking about Margot but I can't stop staring at my ex.

But I can't stop wanting Lila to notice me. I can't stop wondering why she isn't even looking, why it's like I don't exist. She's so drowned in the world of Mr. Tall and Handsome, she doesn't even see me up here. How many Oakwood Festivals did she sit right here, front row, and listen to me sing? How can she not notice?

On a whim, I change it up. I pull out an old song.

I play the song she always loved, the one I wrote about her.

I play "Under the Streetlight."

It works. She freezes, presumably midsentence. Her hand falls to her side, and she turns to face the street. I stare at her, and she stares back, two hearts that have lost each other seeing each other for the first time in a while. I sing the song right to her, forgetting about Margot and the crowd. For a moment, everything fades and it's just Lila and me again, two souls in the middle of a crowded street. I wonder if the song is taking her back to the first kiss, to the first time, to everything else. I wonder if this song is enough to remind her that we were, at one time, good together. I wonder if it makes her miss me like I've missed her.

I wonder, above all, why I have this need for her to remember.

There's a silence for a while, a frozen moment. She doesn't seem to move, to breathe.

When I sing that final note and the crowd claps, she doesn't. She stares for a long moment, still frozen. Then she snaps out of it, pulls on the guy's arm, and leads him away, Henry in tow. She walks away, down the street, as I stand on stage staring at the empty space that once held her.

I don't know why, but this time, seeing her leave, it hurts even more than the first time.

I realize now, no matter what, I don't think I can get Lila to remember who we were together. I don't think we can ever be us again.

No matter how much I tell myself I'm moving on or how sexy and perfect and wonderful Margot is, I don't know if I'll ever stop looking at the empty space in the crowd wondering why Lila can't be there. I don't know if I'll ever stop looking for her.

I don't know if I'll ever let go of "Under the Streetlight" or the feeling of knowing she was once mine and isn't anymore.

CHAPTER SEVENTEEN

LILA

"So, I finally did it," he said, shoving a strand of hair out of his eyes as we sat on the tailgate of his truck, staring down at the lights in Oakwood.

"Did what?" I asked, kicking my sandaled feet back and forth, looking up at the moon and the stars. It was beautiful out here in the park atop the town, not a soul in sight. It was our own private piece of land. It felt good to be alone with him.

"Wrote you that song you'd been asking for. I mean, I don't think it's that good, you know, but if you want to hear it...," he said sheepishly.

I nudged him with my shoulder, the feel of his T-shirt scratchy on my bare shoulders and arms. "Of course I want to hear it! Oh my God, no one has ever written me a song."

"Well, I'm glad I get to be the first."

He flashed me that smile that could melt me no matter what was happening. I stared at him, the bite of the night air *chilling me, but once his warm voice started singing in its gritty, raw style, I forgot about the chills and the mosquito biting my ankle. I forgot about work the next day and all the complexities of life. I forgot about everything except for Luke Bowman, the man who had swept me off my feet four months ago and had never let my feet touch the ground.*

His lyrics echoed through the desolate park, and I hung on to every word about the streetlight and the first kiss. I blushed when he talked about the sexy blonde who'd saved his cat and helped him be a better man.

It was our story, and to others the song probably sounded odd. To me, though, it was a beautiful reminder of the surprises life and love sometimes brought you. I never in a million years thought I'd fall in love with that guy who brought in a dying cat that morning. Most of all, I never expected that four months later, I'd be sitting under the stars listening to him sing a song he'd written about our love story. I never thought I'd be so crazy about him so fast.

When he finished singing, the words came out before my rational self could step in. "I love you, soul mate."

Once the last word was out, I froze, biting my lip. It was too much, too soon. It was cheesy. Soul mate? The word had just jumped off my tongue before I could stop it. This was it. I'd scared him.

Instead, though, he put down his guitar in the bed of the truck and leaned closer. He took my face in his hands. "I love you, too. Soul mate."

And with that reflection of my words, I eased into myself, into the kiss he planted on me. There was a mutual understanding between us that our worlds had shifted and that our hearts were stuck to each other now. In four months, I'd gone from questioning if love was even real to believing this man was my soul mate.

But he believed it, too.

The kiss intensified. Before I knew it, Luke was stretching out a blanket in the bed of the truck, and I was climbing backward, kissing him hungrily, pulling him on top of me. It was hardly the lovemaking atmosphere of the movies. Sure, the starry night was gorgeous and the solitude of the wilderness provided an intimate backdrop. But the bed of the truck was hard on my back, and the blanket barely served as a buffer. The truck was dirty and worn from Luke hauling all sorts of things for work. There'd probably be a roofer's nail in my backside before it was all done, I'd thought.

Still, I couldn't bring myself to care or to move. I couldn't stop for a second; the need to have Luke was so strong. We kissed voraciously, our hands exploring each other in a way encouraged by our revelation that this was serious, real. Luke pulled down the straps on my sundress, and I shuddered as his lips found the skin at the top of my collarbone.

"Make love to me," I whispered, pulling on his hair.

Luke leaned up just enough for me to see the hungry lust in his eyes. "Are you sure?"

"I'm positive," I said, needing him so badly I could barely breathe.

My lips felt swollen from kissing, but when he dove back in to claim them again, electricity jolted through every inch of my body. We clawed at each other's clothes like we were starving. In many ways, I guess we were. We were starving for that first passionate promise of forever, that first feel of skin on skin, of being connected in every physical way.

When he pulled back gently after plenty of foreplay to reach for a condom, I glanced up at the sky, the stars shining and dazzling against the deep blackness of the night sky.

"I love you, Lila Morrow," he whispered as he positioned himself, and I smiled up at him.

"I love you, too," I said before succumbing to him in every possible way, the feel of him inside me helping me know, without a doubt, that this was all I ever wanted.

***

Turning over in bed, the sun streaming through the blind and Henry snoring loudly, I lazily come to.

It was just a dream. A very real dream, a memory, but still not real.

Dammit, Luke. Why did you have to play that song last night? Why did you have to look at me across the crowd while your lips sang the words they'd sung that night under the stars?

I exhale loudly, feeling the sexual tension and longing in me dissipate as I groggily snap out of dream world. Things are different now. That song is just a memory, and that night under the stars, although perfect, is long gone. Things changed. People changed. We aren't the soul mates Luke and Lila anymore. We'd been wrong.

I stretch, sleepily heading to the bathroom to get ready

for work. I pull out the ponytail from my hair, undress, and jump into the shower. I think a cold shower is exactly what I need this morning.

My head aches, and I feel like I'm hungover. I guess lying awake until two in the morning analyzing everything about Luke on stage wasn't the wisest idea.

I'd tried to shrug it off last night. Oliver, Henry, and I had scurried off to the funnel cake stand. We'd had a great time, and I feel Oliver worming his way into my thoughts more and more.

But seeing Luke last night threw it all off.

Which then makes me feel guilty. What am I doing? How am I ever going to move on? As soon as I find a guy I like, who has potential, I sabotage myself by clinging to memories that aren't reality anymore.

I soak my hair, wondering if I'm ever going to stop thinking about what could've been or what was. I wonder if there will ever be a time when I can look at Luke and not feel a pang of missing him. I wonder if I can ever give my heart to someone else.

Maren keeps telling me it's normal, that when you build a life with someone as intricately as I did with Luke, there are bound to be doubts about leaving. Still, it's been months and I feel like I haven't made any progress. Worse, I feel like I'm being such a jerk going out with Oliver, talking about dates and flirting when my heart isn't free yet.

I finish getting ready and head to Park Lane, smiling as I glance at my phone before getting in the car.

Oliver: Got your coffee waiting for you. Starbucks.

Hope Zoey doesn't think I'm trying to replace her.

He's amazing. He is. And I feel myself wanting to let go of the past for him. It's a good sign.

Maybe it'll just take time, but maybe, if I let myself, I'll build new memories. I'll build new moments, new soul mate revelations.

Things change. People change. Our hearts change.

We just have to be ready to accept that.

***

"Maren, breathe. It's all good."

"Lila, you don't understand. The cake decorator backed out. Claimed bankruptcy or something. We don't have a cake, and my friend Casey said the deejay we picked is a disaster and...."

I hold the phone about five inches from my ear, but Maren's voice is still blasting. Zoey gives me a sympathetic look, and even Oliver turns to mouth "yikes." We're on lunch break at the office.

Maren's wedding is next Saturday, and needless to say the once calm and mellow bride has morphed into the traditional bridezilla. To be honest, I didn't expect this from go-with-the-flow Maren. I guess pre-wedding jitters can create an emotional wreck out of anyone.

Add to that Mom's constant interference and meddling, and I guess you have the recipe for a Maren explosion.

"Listen," I say, taking a deep breath for her. "It's going to be all good. Seriously. What matters most is you are marrying the man of your dreams. It's going to be perfect no matter what."

"Not according to Mom. She's calling this the wedding from hell." I can tell from Maren's voice that tears are flowing. This is a disaster.

"Mom would call Kate Middleton's wedding the wedding from hell. You know her standards are impossible. Forget what she says like you always do. Focus on you. Focus on Will. As for the cake, no worries. Zoey and I will come up with a backup plan. I'm sure the deejay is great. Even if he isn't, you've got an open bar. One hour in and everyone's going to be so drunk, they won't care if he plays polkas all night."

I hear Maren take a few breaths on the other line. I think I've talked her off the ledge.

"Okay. You're right. I don't know why I let Mom get me so stressed. I think I just lost my shit."

"I'll say. Now listen. Leave the cake to me. Relax, and I'll see you at five."

"Five? Tonight? For what?"

"I'm taking you to the spa for a massage and then out for a drink afterward. My treat."

"Lila, I don't have time for that."

"Of course you do. Give me your to-do list and I'll give something to Mom to keep her busy and out of your hair. Relax. This is your time. Enjoy it."

"Okay. You're right."

"Aren't I always?"

"And you did ask Oliver to be your date, right?"

"No. But Zoey took over like she promised. He will be

accompanying me."

Oliver looks up at me and gives me a smile. Zoey had not so casually broached the subject a few weeks ago, tossing out the idea as we sat at lunch. Oliver had been happy to oblige, and I was actually happy Zoey forced my hand.

Over the past few weeks, Oliver and I have been on a few low-key adventures—I guess we could call them dates. From the fall festival to coffee to a few lunches, we've been taking it slow and getting to know each other.

And despite the vivid sex-dream memory, I've found something surprising; he's been taking my mind off the whole Luke situation. I'm finding myself open to exploring whatever this is with Oliver, which is a big step for me.

I hang up the phone and literally wipe my brow. "Oh my God, my family is losing it."

"Weddings do that to people. I'm surprised Maren's getting caught up in it all."

"I think Mom's getting caught up and it's stressing Maren out," I say. "Who knows. I guess there's a little bridezilla lurking in all of us."

"Not me," Oliver says, shrugging.

"Smartass," I retort, and he laughs.

"Whoa, easy now. Is that how professionals speak to each other?" he asks.

I raise an eyebrow. "No, but I also don't think professionals go on dates and all that either."

"Oh, Lord. If you two are going to spend the rest of lunch with these sad little excuses for flirting like you did all last week, I'm getting out of here. Honestly. Just kiss each other already. Hell, have sex with each other, I don't care. But get it out of your system so I can go back to my non-gag-worthy lunches, okay?"

"Oh my God, Zoey," I proclaim, burying my face in my hands.

"Come on. Like you two haven't been thinking about it? Please." With that, she exits the breakroom to go who knows where, leaving us alone.

"That was awkward," I say, not really sure what else to say.

"A little. But I mean, I can't argue with her," Oliver says before he, too, leaves the room as he eats the last piece of his sandwich.

Suddenly, I'm alone staring at photographs of cats and dogs with a few bites of salad left, stressing over where the hell I'm going to find a wedding cake in less than a week, and curious about whether or not sex with Oliver is actually a possibility at this point.

* * *

The next day, both Oliver and I are off work, so he asks if he can pick me up for lunch. In order to avoid the craziness that is my family—which is extra crazy this week with the wedding and all—I ask if I can just meet him.

Maren is definitely feeling better after our spa visit last night, and I managed to find a cake baker who wasn't booked for next weekend. Who knows what the cake will look like, but again, I'm counting on a lot of drunkenness to cover for the possibility of a lackluster cake.

All in all, though, everything is going smoothly, I think, as I drive myself to Los Hombres, our local version of Mexican cuisine—which in reality is a restaurant serving fancy, overpriced tacos with a few old guys who know nothing about true Mexican food. Still, it's one of Oliver's favorites apparently, and although I'm not a fan, I figured it would be tacky to argue.

I pull into the parking lot, sporting some simple jeans and a T-shirt, not feeling like going over-the-top on my day off. Grandma Claire insisted I slather on some red lipstick, though. I hadn't told her I was meeting Oliver, but I swear that woman has a sixth sense when it comes to dating.

Not that we're dating, dating. Sure, it's clearly a lunch date. But it's just a one-time thing. Or five-time thing, if you count the festival and the coffee and the other random lunches. But this is a one-time official date, not a relationship. Which is why I didn't put a lot of effort in. I didn't want to look like I was trying too hard.

Because I'm not even sure if I want to try too hard.

Then again, he is my date to the wedding, so I better get used to that word.

Oh dear. This is just a hot mess.

I don't have time to think about it, though, because as soon as I park, he's pulling in beside me, his red Mustang revving as he slides into the parking spot.

When he gets out, I notice he's dressed much nicer—much more datelike—for the occasion. He's got on a button-up and some tan pants. I feel like crap now, embarrassed to get out of the car. It's too late to peel out, though, because he waves animatedly.

"Hey," he says. "So good to see you outside work."

I notice he eyes my outfit, but he doesn't say anything.

I can tell, though, he's wondering if I just rolled out of bed.

I try to brush the insecurities aside as he hands me some roses. "These are for you," he says.

"Oh, that's sweet," I say, not sure what to do with them, not used to the whole dating awkwardness, to be honest. After a moment of running through the options in my head, I open my car door and toss them gently on the passenger seat, giving a little giggle as I do to soften the weirdness.

"Shall we?" he asks, offering me his arm like we're going to prom.

I shrug, taking his arm and marching into Los Hombres, feeling all sorts of tension about being on Oliver's arm. Still, he looks gorgeous—and he smells even better, a rich cologne dancing around us. I need to just breathe. I know Oliver. We've been working together closely. But knowing someone in the office is very different than being on a date. Very different.

We stroll into the restaurant, which is pretty empty since it's Tuesday. We're led to a back booth, mariachi music blasting through the restaurant so loudly, it's hard to even think.

"Nice place, huh?" Oliver shouts once we've ordered our drinks—he's taken the liberty of ordering us both margaritas, although I'm not a lime person. I shrug it off.

"It's very—nice, yes," I agree, smiling.

In truth, I've only ever been to Los Hombres once. With Luke.

And we ended up just ordering a water and a serving of nachos, deeming the prices of the place outrageous and the atmosphere mediocre. We'd laughed about how if this was fine, authentic Mexican cuisine, we were clearly royalty.

But Oliver is smiling and chomping away at the expensive appetizer tray he ordered—the service is fast since the place is empty. He's going on and on about how he found this place during undergrad and is crazy about it. He talks about how he actually had his first date here, which was also in undergrad, and proceeds to tell me all about Melissa.

I just smile and nod, the music providing a weird soundtrack to the encounter. I feel tense. In fairness, it's not Oliver's fault. He's still got the warm smile and the inviting eyes, and he's talking away animatedly.

It's just, like I said, it's been so long since I've done this. It feels so weird to be somewhere with Oliver, a man I barely know, in a booth sharing nachos and talking about the past. It feels weird to be with anyone but *him*.

Still, as Oliver opens up about his family life and his siblings, I smile, sensing the joy in his spirit and the excitement for life. He talks about how he wants to open up his own practice someday and how he hopes to have a big family. He talks about his plans for the future and where he's going. He's got vision, he's got goals, and he's got gorgeous eyes.

He's the real deal.

He asks me about my last boyfriend, and I feel myself

tense up again, a different kind of tense. "Long story. We broke up back in June."

"Oh, wow, that's fresh."

"Yeah," I agree, reaching for the margarita.

"Was it serious?" he asks.

I sigh. This is unknowingly a complicated question, but I decide to answer it as honestly as I can. "I wanted it to be," I say, realizing this is the best way to put it into words.

"Sorry."

"Me too. But it's okay. I'm moving on, you know?" I smile wider now, and then take another gulp of margarita. I *am* moving on. I'm here, with Oliver, and I'm having a good time, even though that four-letter name keeps popping up.

I've got to take charge, though. Maren's right. I need to take charge and find my own happiness. I'm here with an amazing man who so many women would kill to be with. I just need to give him a chance, give us a chance, to be more than just friendly coworkers. I need to take that step.

So I decide to turn the conversation from the past and exes. The waiter brings our order—some dish I can't pronounce that Oliver insisted on ordering for us—and I poke around with my fork.

When Oliver takes a bite, I jump in. "So, it's crazy, but I don't think I've asked you, how many pets do you have?" This is much more comfortable territory, much more neutral than Luke, Melissa, and broken hearts.

He shakes his head, smirking. "None. I deal with enough pets all day, right?"

I grin, waiting for him to say *just kidding*. He doesn't. He just shrugs and keeps eating.

"You really don't have any?" I ask to verify. Most vets have loads of them. When I get my own place, I'm afraid to know how many I'll have.

"No. Like I said, we deal with so many animals a day. What's the point?"

"But don't you love animals?"

"I love the medicine behind it. I love the paychecks behind it, too," he says, grinning.

I try to muster up a laugh, too, truly confused. It's like I'm seeing Oliver for the first time. It's like I don't recognize him.

Stop trying to find the negatives, I remind myself. *He's not perfect. No one is. Your last guy sure as hell wasn't, and you overlooked his shortcomings. Oliver doesn't want to own a zoo. So what? It's not like you're getting married tomorrow.*

And even if you were, maybe it would be a good thing to have some balance, I reassure myself.

We continue eating, talking about favorite bands, holiday traditions, and Maren's wedding. As we're finishing up, a family with a small girl walks in, and the hostess ushers them to a booth near us. On the way, the little girl drops the doll she's carrying.

"Excuse me," Oliver says as he puts down his fork, leans out of our booth, and scoops up the doll. He ambles over to the family, offering a smile and holding out the raggedy toy.

"Did you drop this, sweetie?" he asks the little girl, who

has braids and huge brown eyes. She nods shyly.

"What's her name?" Oliver asks. The little girl looks to her mom as if seeing if it's okay to talk to the stranger. Her mom nods, and the little girl whispers in Oliver's ear.

"That's a beautiful name. I hope you have a great lunch, okay? See that pretty girl over there?"

The little girl in the booth looks at me. I wave and smile. "I'm on a date with her. I have to get back, okay?"

"Okay."

"What do you say?" the mom prods the little girl.

"Thank you," the tiny voice chirps.

"You're so welcome," he says, reaching out to shake the little girl's hand, who now blushes. He turns and heads back to our booth, and I almost melt from the adorableness of the encounter.

"You're good with kids," I say when he's returned.

"My older sister has triplets. I guess I just have always loved kids."

I smile. See, for every bad quality there's always a positive. So he doesn't want fifty cats. He's a charmer with kids. Looking at him and at his interaction, I know he'll be an amazing father someday.

We finish eating, and Oliver pays the bill. As he walks me to my car, he asks if I want to come by his place. "I would love to, but I have to help Maren finish up the wedding favors and verify some of the final checklists. I'm sorry. But I had a great time."

Oliver smiles. "I understand. I had a great time too. So I guess I'll see you tomorrow at work?"

"See you tomorrow. And thanks again."

I stand awkwardly by my car, again unsure of the protocol and hating this awkward feeling.

Oliver leans over and kisses me on the cheek, a slow, sweet kiss. I smile, get into my car, wave like a fifteen-year-old, and drive away, thinking about the gorgeous man who is going to be my date next weekend—and thinking about how many other amazing qualities he has.

Most of all, I'm thinking about how maybe with Oliver, moving on won't be so hard.

CHAPTER EIGHTEEN

LILA

"Grandma, you *cannot* wear that. Where is the dress we picked out for you?" I ask, standing in my maid of honor dress. It's a mermaid style, meaning it hugs every single curve and bump on my body way too snugly. I feel a little self-conscious.

It's nothing, though, compared to what Grandma Claire is wearing.

She's got on a hot pink dress that looks more like a bathing suit cover-up than an actual piece of clothing. The neckline plunges to quite an amazing depth, and the length of the dress leaves nothing to the imagination. It is something that would perhaps be uncomfortable-looking even on Heidi Klum.

"Hey, it's a wedding, a celebration. And I say while I've still got it, I may as well show it off!" Grandma lets out a scream that tells me Dad's tequila stock apparently isn't locked up like it should be, or she found out the combination again.

I exhale. "We have to leave in fifteen minutes to be at the church on time. Seriously, Grandma, go change."

I rush back to the hallway to Maren's bedroom where some of her high school friends, college roommates, and other girls from the wedding party are gathered to help her get it together.

They part ways when they see me. "Oh my, Maren, you look amazing!" I say, meaning it. I momentarily forget about the Grandma debacle as I lean in to hug my sister, who seriously looks like a model. "You look perfect."

"Thanks. Don't say anything gushy, though. I'm emotional, and I don't want to cry."

"Okay, you bitch. No problem," I say, and smile. Maren smacks me on the arm.

"Is everything okay? Everything going smoothly?" she asks.

"Of course," I lie effortlessly. I don't know how, but I've managed to take on the role of the wedding planner Maren insisted she didn't need to hire.

I don't have the heart to tell her that Grandma Claire is standing in the hallway in a stripper outfit, Mom is calling and screaming at the florist over the so-called lackluster boutonnieres, and the cake decorator I found on the fly is currently a no-show.

Details, details.

I rush to find Dad, who is out on the porch in his tux.

"Daddy, you look so handsome," I say, reaching to hug him.

"Thanks, Lila. I feel like a weirdo in this thing."

Dad's not much of a formal-attire-wearing man. "Well, it looks good. Now listen, I need some help and Mom's in a tizzy."

"Would you expect any less? What do you need?"

"Grandma's outfit isn't quite the approved outfit we picked. I think the actual dress we picked for her is in her closet, but she's, well, shall I say a bit drunk at the moment, I believe?"

"Dammit. She must have figured out the combination again. I swear that woman was a code breaker during WWII. Unbelievable!" He scowls, rushing inside to take care of the Grandma situation. At least one thing can be checked off my list.

Next, I call Oliver. "Hey, can you do me a huge favor? Can you stop by the reception hall and see if the cake showed up? I've tried calling a million times, but no one is answering. I think I may have been ripped off. If it's not there, we're going to have to wing it, maybe get some sheet cakes or cupcakes or something at one of the grocery stores?"

"Say no more," Oliver says, and I smile. "I'm on it. I'll figure it out."

"Thank you. You're a lifesaver."

"No worries. Oh, and Lila?"

"Yeah?"

"Calm down. It's going to be great. See you at the ceremony."

I hang up, grinning. It's so weird that a man I practically

just met is going to be my date to one of the biggest days in the family. It's odd having an almost stranger, a man who doesn't know the craziness that is my grandmother or the annoying helicopter tendencies of my mother, come join us. Still, Oliver's confidence and willingness to help eases my worries.

He's right. It's going to be great.

***

Somehow, it all comes together for the ceremony. I don't fall on my face walking down the aisle, even though I find myself staring at how handsome Oliver looks in his suit as I parade down the aisle runner. Grandma manages to sober up slightly and to get on the right outfit, thanks to Dad's intervention. The flowers look great, although Mom still insists the boutonnieres are the wrong color.

Most of all, Maren looks stunning in her slim, beaded red dress—she insisted white was boring, even for brides. When she walks down the aisle, Will appears to hold it together. Up on the altar, though, with a close-up view, I see his lip quiver and a single tear roll down his cheek.

Seeing the way he looks at her takes my breath away and jolts my heart. When my sister vows her life to my new brother-in-law, I find myself tearing up. There's just something about two people promising forever that gets me every time.

When they're pronounced husband and wife and Grandma lets out a "Yee-haw" loud enough for the entire church to hear, Will and Maren are all smiles. That's the only way I can describe it.

As I'm standing with the bridal party after the ceremony waiting for pictures, it hits me.

It's not about the wedding or the dress or the cake. It's not about the deejay or the invite list. Those things are nice, but that's not what's important.

It's about two people coming together and promising forever. It's about the way Will looked at Maren today, his eyes screaming he'd do anything for her. It's the way the thought of vowing forever to Will made Maren an emotional wreck.

It's the power of the love between them palpable without the wedding ceremony but even more apparent with it.

Seeing Maren and Will's big day, I realize without a doubt that I wasn't crazy for holding out for this. I want this, no, I need this. I need that kind of visible commitment, that symbol of forever love.

I can't settle for anything less.

* * *

After so many pictures that I permanently see dots in my vision, the bridal party and immediate family are loaded into the white limo the newlyweds rented to get us to the Oakwood Hall.

Champagne floats around and loud, obnoxious groomsmen make jokes about how much alcohol they can down. Oliver, still on the cake situation, gave me a kiss on the cheek and told me he'd meet me at the reception. Hence, I'm all alone in a sea of couples and rowdy single groomsmen who have already had way too much to drink.

"Excuse me," a voice says over the loudspeaker in the limo. I didn't know they even had those. "This is Paul, your driver. Yeah, turns out the last driver didn't fill up. We're going to need to stop for gas. Sorry for the inconvenience."

"Are you kidding me? Unbelievable, the incompetence," Mom mutters, throwing her hands up.

The groomsmen are excited, animatedly talking about running in to order some death dogs at the local gas station before we hit the reception. I just try to soothe the migraine building and pray Oliver found a decent solution to the cake situation.

As the limo pulls in to the gas pump, the groomsmen file out to go order some nachos and hot dogs—because that clearly makes sense. A few of the girls want to go pee, so the limo is basically vacant except for Maren, Will, and the immediate family. I actually soak in the silence for a moment.

Until it happens. Like a curse or the universe slapping me in the face, I'm sent flying back to the past; its sticky tentacles won't let me go.

"Lila, oh my God, look, it's Luke!" Grandma Claire screams with an excitement level so high, you'd think she just saw Alexander Skarsgard—her celebrity crush. She's seen *Tarzan* fifteen times just to ogle his abs.

We all turn to look out the window she's pointing out.

Sure enough, at the gas pump next to us, it is not Alexander Skarsgard but Luke. Luke stands, dressed in jeans and a flannel, filling up what I think is Evan's car, one his best friends. My heart does that little thing that's like a gasp for air. Before I can react, Grandma has the window down. "Luke! Hey, hot stuff! We miss you! Get in. We're going to Maren's reception, and Lila's in here alone."

"Grandma," I hiss, and Maren covers her mouth. I try to reach over to put up the window, but it's too late.

Luke steps over to the window to wave. "Hey, Grandma Claire. I miss you too," he says. Just hearing his voice does something to me. It's the first time I've heard it up close in a long time. It's almost like hearing a stranger's voice—yet there's a familiarity in it. It's the voice that used to say "I love you" and used to say my name in bed. It's a voice that's shared so many moments and secrets with me.

Yet, here we are, me on one side of the limo, and him on the other.

He makes eye contact with me. I offer a neutral smile. "Hi."

"Hey, Lila."

The whole family seems to take a collective breath, wondering what will happen next.

But nothing happens. Just a weird pause, an uncertainty of how to proceed.

"Well, congratulations, Maren and Will. Good luck to you," Luke says, and then he offers a weak smile, looks at me once more, and walks away.

"It's not too late," Grandma Claire yells out the window before Dad pounds the button to put the window up.

"Grandma, you can't say stuff like that," I chide, shaking my head.

"Of course I can. It's never too late. You kids are so dramatic. You like him. He likes you. Stop playing these games."

Suddenly, the limo door flies open and the groomsmen pile in along with the bridesmaids, talking about nachos and hot dogs. The moment is gone.

But Grandma Claire's words still resonate within. I think about them the whole time we're driving to the reception, and even once we're there.

I think about them until we get to the reception and I see Oliver standing by an improvised cupcake tree he's fashioned in oranges and whites.

"It looks, well, good under the circumstances," I say, eyeing the not-quite-wedding-worthy cupcake display. It'll do, though.

"I also got this little sheet cake for Maren and Will to cut," he says, pointing proudly to a cake on display beside the cupcakes.

It's an orange floral cake with "Happy Weddingday" scrawled on the top. It is pretty clear that Wedding used to say Birth. But maybe no one else will notice.

"It'll be great," I announce, meaning it, as someone hands me a drink. I gulp it greedily.

"You think you can save a dance for me, since I did such a good job and all?" he asks, pulling me in closer, his hand on my waist.

"I think I could manage to save you one or two." I look up into his blue eyes, my breath catching at the way he's looking at me.

He's gorgeous. He's sweet. He's perfect.

Dammit, I hate feeling stuck in limbo between my past and present. I hate the guilt I feel when I'm with Oliver thinking about Luke, but I also hate the guilt I feel when I see Luke and think about what used to be.

It is at this moment, though, by the sad excuse for a wedding cake as I'm internally arguing with myself, that Oliver clears it all away.

He leans in and, ever so gently, kisses me. His lips are warm and taste like cake—I'm guessing he taste-tested a cupcake. With that kiss, though, I feel all the swirling confusion melt away.

As the kiss intensifies and his tongue finds mine, swirling in an intricate pattern that makes my whole body glow with warmth, I am opened to the possibility yet again of what Oliver and I could be. I am opened to the possibility of a new story.

When the deejay calls for me to do my speech and I'm pulled away from the kiss, I realize there could be a new story in my life—if I could just close the last story with a sense of finality and stow the book away on a dusty shelf to be forgotten.

I just don't know how the hell I do that when Luke's claimed such a huge part of my heart.

* * *

"Lila, there's some sexy man here for you, and it's not Luke!" a shaky voice bellows from somewhere in the house. I roll over in my bed, smacking into the snoring Henry. Sunlight streams into my room, and my head is pounding.

Apparently I had a few too many whiskey sours last night.

I drag myself out of bed, trying to figure what the heck Grandma Claire is yelling about. Mom and Dad are delivering Maren's wedding presents this morning and then going to lunch. I vaguely remember Mom waking me and asking if I wanted to help, but hauling presents into Maren's house with a hangover sounds like torture—especially with Mom involved. Maren and Will are on their way to Aruba as we speak, so I'm sure I won't be missed. Plus, Mom will have more fun snooping in Maren and Will's apartment without me.

I stomp down the hallway, the sun way too bright.

"Lila, the young man brought you coffee. Did you hear me?" Grandma's voice is getting louder now. She catches me in the hallway. "Oh, dear. You're quite a mess. Here, let's get some lipstick on you. Lipstick always does the trick. The young man won't notice how horrible you look."

"Grandma, what are you talking about?" I ask, my voice raspy.

"That Oliver bloke you had at the wedding last night. For the life of me, I don't understand why you two didn't spend the night together. Weddings always make me pretty horny. But anyway, he's here. I let him in. He's got coffee for the two of you and everything."

I take a deep breath. I don't know whether to address Grandma Claire's over-the-top confession, my headache, or the fact Oliver is here and I look like shit.

"Do you want that lipstick?" she asks.

"No, Grandma. I just need a minute." And a miracle, in reality. I swing into the bathroom, glancing in the mirror.

Wow, I look rough.

I down a few Advil and slurp up some water from the bathroom sink. I take out the ponytail holder and try to fluff my hair. It's a lost cause, so back into a messy bun in goes.

I do my best to get it together, run back to my bedroom to rifle up a bra, and get myself back to the kitchen before Grandma can make Oliver too uncomfortable.

"So that's about the time I realized I was wearing the completely wrong cup size for three decades. Can you imagine?" Grandma is saying.

Oliver looks terrified. Horrified.

But he's graciously grinning and nodding. Grandma is drinking a cup of coffee. At the sight of me, Oliver leaps up, looking relieved.

"Hey, sorry to drop in. I just wanted to bring you a coffee and, well, see you."

He dashes across the kitchen, leaning in for a hug. I try not to think about how I probably smell, leaning into him. He looks like he's feeling fine, making me feel even worse.

"I'm a little rough this morning. How many whiskey sours did I have?"

"I think six. But it's fine. That's what weddings are for. Here, I brought you coffee. Figured you might be feeling a little rough."

He looks over to the table, realizing Grandma Claire is sipping what I assume was my coffee.

"Um, here," Oliver says, handing me what was clearly his. I wink at him.

"Very sweet. Thank you. Do you want to go out on the back porch?"

"Yeah, sounds good."

"You two go ahead. I don't want to intrude," Grandma Claire says, turning to wink at me.

"Grandma, you sure? You can come," I say, secretly hoping she decides to stay inside.

"No way, it's fine. That religious program I like is coming on in ten minutes. Figure it wouldn't hurt to get some extra heaven points today after the lewd thoughts I was having about the preacher at Maren's wedding."

Oliver and I pause, frozen by the shock of the woman's words. She never ceases to amaze, that's for sure.

"Okay, Grandma. Sounds like a plan," I say, shaking my head as I lead Oliver out the back door to the swing in the garden.

When we're alone, I look up at him as we sink into the swing. We sway languidly, the chill of the morning seeping through the sweatshirt I tossed on over my T-shirt. "Sorry about Grandma. She's a handful."

"It's fine. No apologies needed. Your family's great," he says.

I take a swig of the coffee. "I don't know if great is the word I'd use. They're… interesting, for sure."

"I had an amazing time last night," he says, putting an arm around my shoulder.

"I did too."

186

We swing for a long moment, not talking, just taking in the sight of the morning, the serenity of my mom's garden sharply contrasting with the chaos that is my family.

"I like spending time with you, Lila. A lot."

I turn and look up at the blue eyes that are becoming so familiar. "I like spending time with you, too," I say, and realize it's true.

Sitting here, swinging with Oliver, there's a deep-rooted serenity that isn't just because my family's not around. It's a peace I feel deep within. He makes me feel calm and rational. He makes me feel smart, like I'm doing the right thing.

Being with Oliver is easy because there's not much tension between us. There's just two people, heading in a similar direction, walking together.

I could get used to this.

And then the back door opens, Grandma Claire standing in her nightie. "Lila! Come quick! I seem to have clicked something on the television and there's something inappropriate on it."

I shake my head. "Grandma, I thought we told you to stop getting into the pay-per-view menu."

"What? I didn't. This newfangled television just does it on its own."

"Be right there," I yell, shaking my head but laughing.

"I take it Grandma Claire has had a few pay-per-view incidents?" Oliver asks, grinning.

"Oh, yes. Just to warn you, it's probably not going to be pretty. Grandma likes to click on the racier titles and then swear she didn't know they were dirty." I sigh, heading inside to see what new disaster awaits, the serenity wearing off a little bit.

When Oliver grabs my free hand, though, and holds it on the way into the living room, the peace is back, despite the horrifying, scream-inciting view we see when we get to the living room and see what Grandma Claire has ordered.

CHAPTER NINETEEN

Margot tosses back yet another beer, letting out a rebel yell when she does. The music is loud, and the fire is hot, the biting air slapping against my skin.

We're at Dean's house for his annual bonfire. All my old friends are here, most of them with wives or girlfriends. I thought it would be a good way for everyone to meet Margot.

And meet Margot they have.

Dressed to kill in her skintight black dress that is suctioned to her curves like a glove, she's been the star of the bonfire, to many of the guys' significant others' chagrin. Dancing wildly, drinking more alcohol than I thought possible, and singing karaoke are the highlights of Margot's bonfire experience.

"Well, you got yourself a wild one," Dean whispers to me as Margot tells Dean's wife, Sadie, about her trip to Cancun last summer.

"That I did," I admit, grinning before taking another gulp of beer.

"Nothing wrong with wild," Dean says. "I don't think you have to worry about her wanting to settle down anytime soon."

"No, I don't think so," I say, watching Margot dance her way over to me. "She claims to be allergic to diamond rings and commitment." Dean shakes his head and laughs.

"Stop being so boring. Dance with me," she demands, yanking me out to a secluded spot by the fire and interrupting our conversation.

"I'm not much of a dancer," I protest as she wraps her arms around my shoulders, her chest pressing against mine.

"Well, tonight you are," she says as a rock song comes on. We dance rather wildly in the middle of the yard, Margot laughing and having the time of her life. In truth, it really isn't my scene and I feel like I probably look like I'm having a stroke. Still, I dance with her, and it does feel kind of good, I tell myself.

The night continues to unfold, Margot encouraging round after round of shots. Back in my day, I could've given her a run for her money. Margot would've been no match for the Luke of before, the rebellious partier who was the master of beer pong.

Tonight, I'm doing my best to keep up.

When it's finally time to leave, Margot insists on going home with me. Who the hell am I to argue? Evan's out for the night with Anna, so the only one left behind is Floyd. I don't think he'll mind.

I call us a cab, and Margot is all over me in the back seat to the point the driver asks if she's going to be okay. He looks at me like I'm some skeevy weirdo, which pisses me off. Could also be the six beers I've had talking.

Margot sings so loudly on the way into my apartment that I think the neighbors are surely going to call the cops. She's walking unsteadily, and it's a chore to get her up the stairs.

Apparently she's overdone it, even for her alcohol-tolerant self.

"Come on, stud. Screw me," she says loudly once we're inside the door.

I grin and shake my head. She's absolutely gorgeous. Any guy would kill to have Margot Lane asking him to screw her, especially in that dress. I'd be lying to say I didn't fantasize about ripping it off her all night.

But even with my head a little hazy from all the drinking, I know I can't. I know I can't give in even if every part of my body is screaming at me to take her clothes off. It's not right, not even if she's begging.

I can't have sex with her like this. It's wrong.

"Come on, let's get you to bed," I say, leading her back up the hallway. She staggers and giggles.

"I like the sound of that."

I lead her towards my room, and she jumps on the bed. "Take off those clothes," she says.

I shake my head. "Not tonight, Margot. Let's get some sleep."

She gives me a pouty face that is sort of sad but sort

of sexy. I help her get her shoes off. "Sex tomorrow?" she asks.

I grin, shaking my head. "Sex tomorrow. But I have a feeling you're not going to be feeling like it."

"You don't know me very well then," she says, winking before plopping back on the pillow. I head to the bathroom to take a piss. By the time I'm back, also feeling like falling into bed, she's asleep, snoring lightly.

So I do exactly what I didn't imagine myself doing. I climb into bed beside Margot, her sexy skintight dress still showing off enough of her to make me crazy, and I go to sleep.

* * *

"That was an awesome night," Margot whispers in my ear. I groan, the sun shining in.

My head's pounding, and I feel like shit. I open an eye slightly to see Margot propped up over me, smiling.

She looks like she's had the best damn night of sleep of her life.

"How do you not feel like shit?" I ask, reaching to the nightstand for some Advil.

She shrugs. "Practice makes perfect," she says. "Maybe you're just getting old."

"Apparently."

"So anyway," she says, her voice way too chipper. She leans in to kiss my neck. "I'm guessing sex this morning is off the table?"

"Yeah, at least until this pounding in my head stops,"

I say. She treats sex so casually. I rarely hear a girl toss it around so easily.

"I figured. Anyway, my friend Miranda is having a party tonight. I promise I won't get so drunk. Just a few drinks. Then maybe we can go back to my place?"

Another party? I can't even think about getting out of bed right now. I can't imagine going out again tonight. "I don't know, Margot."

"Come on. You only live once."

"I'm not going to be alive at all, I have a feeling, once you're done with me."

She smiles, stroking my hair. "Just wait until you see what I can do in bed," she says, kissing my cheek.

I feel myself harden at the thought. Before I can pursue it, though, she's jumping out of bed. "Okay, I'm off. I have a manicure appointment in an hour. I'll pick you up at six if that's okay."

I just groan in response as Margot skips out the door.

Either Margot's right and I'm getting old, or this girl is just a rare breed. So much for an easy night of Netflix and songwriting. I feel like with Margot, there sure isn't a need for commitment… but the wild life does take a lot of energy.

CHAPTER TWENTY

LILA

"Well you look like sex on a stick," Grandma Claire proclaims.

"I agree, but I don't mean it as a compliment like she does," Mom says from her seat on the couch. The two are watching soap operas Mom DVR'd. I shake my head, trying to pretend to ignore them but now feeling paranoid.

I should've known this dress would be too much. The backless, supershort royal blue dress now seems foolish.

It's too late, though. Oliver's here.

I dash to the door before Grandma can even think of getting up. No need to scare Oliver away any more than he was at the wedding or the morning after. Seeing Grandma tango with all the groomsmen and twerk was something no one should have to witness, let alone the bra conversation and the pay-per-view debacle.

"Hey, Oliver!" Grandma shouts from the couch.

"Bye, Grandma and Mom! Love you."

I dash out and shut the door before anything embarrassing can happen.

"Hey, I got you these," Oliver says, handing me a dozen red roses. I smile and smell them.

"They're lovely." I head to Oliver's car.

"Aren't you going to put them in a vase?" he asks.

"Right, um, just wait here."

I dash inside and hand them to Mom, asking if she'll put them in a vase. Grandma insists she has a perfect vase. Yep, the flowers are gone.

I head back outside, Oliver already in the car waiting for me.

I climb in, all smiles, excited for a night out with Oliver, just the two of us, and even more excited for another kiss.

We drive to Chance's, a local Italian restaurant fancy enough to warrant dressy clothes. I haven't been there in ages. I'm more of a Panera bread, Chipotle, fast eats kind of girl. But the prospect of dressing up seemed fun when Oliver suggested it.

I turn on the radio, greeted by classical music. I kind of laugh, thinking maybe the radio is accidentally on the wrong channel. When I hit the autofind button, though, more classical greets me. I look over to see Oliver tapping his hands on the wheel.

"You like classical?" Oliver asks.

"Oh, yeah. It's lovely." *For a funeral or an elevator,* I think. Still, it hardly seems appropriate to tell him classical music makes me want to barf, especially when he seems to like it so much.

195

So I bite my tongue, listening to Oliver whistle along until we pull into the parking lot.

"Ready for some delicious Italian?" he asks as I leap out of the car.

"You bet." I walk into the restaurant on Oliver's arm, thinking how lucky I am and how glad I am to have opened my heart back up.

**

He's just nervous, I tell myself. You can't judge him from one dinner. The wedding was amazing. And that kiss rocked you. Just be polite.

I'm swirling the shrimp alfredo on my fork—which Oliver ordered for me, insisting he knew what I'd like. I hate seafood.

I smile and nod, acting like I have a clue what he's talking about with conservatives and liberals and something about natural resources.

Oliver's been animatedly talking politics now for at least a half hour. It's like an explosion of politics and government.

Which I admittedly am not very knowledgeable about.

But, in truth, I only know the zany intern from work, a few coffee dates, a few lunches, and the wedding. Maybe I don't know the real Oliver because I wasn't looking for him. Maybe I only know the pieces of Oliver I wanted to see.

The night continues, and he does mercifully turn the conversation to *Game of Thrones,* which I love, and the new video game that is out—which I also love. We also end up talking about baseball, though, which is one of Oliver's other loves. Another thing we don't have in common.

Still, when we start talking about the new heartworm vaccine that's in a trial period and about Panic at the Disco—our mutually favorite band—I breathe a sigh of relief, knowing we're back on track. We do have things in common. We do have a foundation of commonalities.

What, am I looking for perfection? No one's perfect. No one's going to be my one perfect match. Love's about giving and taking.

But Oliver and I are just starting out, and I can't help but get this nagging feeling that if there are already so many things I'm having to pretend to be okay with, what else is going to arise?

When I manage to gag down half the shrimp alfredo and ask for a box to take the rest home to Grandma, Oliver kind of shudders.

"Um, are you okay with leaving that behind? I have a no food in the car rule," he says.

"Oh, sure."

I think back to Maren and me eating Doritos Locos tacos in the car every Saturday or Luke and I wolfing down Big Macs on the way to the beach last summer.

No food in the car seems like a prison sentence.

Still, I remind myself that this is just one of those things that Oliver is serious about. I'm sure there's plenty about me he's not digging, either.

Does that mean I should discount him, discount us?

Classical music isn't so bad; maybe it wouldn't be such

a horrible thing to not eat in the car. These are things I can live with.

Because even though Oliver talks too much politics and is a bit serious in his music genres for my taste, he has plenty to offer. He's stable. He knows what he wants and where he's going.

He's crazy about kids, and he's super considerate.

And most of all, when he kisses me good night, I feel the electricity again.

Heading back home after our dinner and promising to go out with him again this weekend, I smile. The universe is all right again, and Oliver's sneaking into my heart.

Now I've just got to brush up on my politics and composers.

CHAPTER TWENTY-ONE

LUKE

"I still think we could be having way more fun back at your place or mine," Margot whispers, hanging on my arm as we stroll up the sidewalk. My heart is still beating from Margot almost crashing into Scarlet and John's mailbox.

"Come on, it's going to be great. You'll love my sister," I argue, hoping it's the truth.

"Not as much as I'd love to be doing all sorts of things to you," Margot whispers as we step onto the porch and John opens the door.

I paint on a smile and Margot ups the enthusiasm, hugging John and then Scarlet as she greets us.

In truth, I am happy to be here for dinner with my sister, mostly because it'll be a night away from the party scene— which Margot has been dragging me to quite a bit.

Scarlet invited us up a few days ago, insistent to meet the girl who has been stealing my time after I blew off family dinner for quite a few Sundays.

"I don't know, Scarlet," I'd said. "Margot's... different."

"I like different. Now come on. Bring her over," she argued.

So I'd agreed... mostly, like I said, to avoid another night out with Margot's friends.

Walking behind Margot, I take in the sight of her black dress hugging her curves. Dammit, the woman looks good no matter what she wears. Although scandalously tight seems to be her mantra when it comes to fashion—not that I have a problem with that.

We follow John and Scarlet into the dining room, where Scarlet's made a feast.

"You cooked all this?" I ask as we take our seats.

"Don't act so surprised."

"I mean, I just didn't know you were so Martha Stewart," I say, sitting down and eyeing a pot roast, mashed potatoes, green beans, and a whole other slew of items.

"Me neither," John pretends to whisper, and Scarlet hits him.

"Keep it up, and you two will be banned from my table. Don't let my brother fool you, Margot. I'm a damn good cook. Much better than him."

Margot just smiles, reaching for her wineglass and taking a hefty sip.

"Let's eat," Scarlet says, and we all start digging in.

I grab the dish of roast, passing it to Margot.

"Oh, sorry. I'm a vegetarian."

I pause, looking at her. "Oh, really? I'm sorry, I didn't know." And it's true. I didn't know. Then again, eating was never high on Margot's list of activities. Thinking about it, our only encounters usually involved making out, dancing, or drinking.

"I'm so sorry, Margot. Luke didn't tell me. Can I get you something else?"

"No, it's fine. I'll just have a few green beans. I'm dieting anyway."

Scarlet raises an eyebrow, but decides not to push the issue. I shrug, not sure what to say.

"You don't need to diet, baby. You look great," I try, deciding it's probably the best way to proceed. Plus it's the truth.

"I mean, I don't know how you would know. Not like you've ever seen all this naked," Margot says casually. There's a tiny edge to her voice, but not enough to show she's totally pissed. She makes the comment as if she's casually noting the weather or the date.

John chokes on his water, which he'd been sipping in the awkward moment.

"Okay, how about we say grace," Scarlet says, clasping her hands together.

"We never say grace," John interrupts. Scarlet shoots him a death glare.

"We do today. Lord, please help us all endure those things facing us, and help us all find the right path to happiness. Amen."

Scarlet spews the words so quickly we don't even have time to bow our heads. There is now deafening silence. The only sound filling the void is the sound of plates being scraped and passed.

I literally say nothing, pretending my plate of beef is the most engaging thing I've ever seen.

I mean, really, what am I supposed to say? My girlfriend just called me out for not having sex with her in front of my sister. Weird.

But perhaps the weird part is the fact that my girlfriend had to call me out for not having sex with her.

I mean, I'm no prude when it comes to sex, and before Lila, I had my share of fun. And Margot's freaking gorgeous.

But it's true. Every time there's an opening, a chance, I push back. I come up with an excuse. I tell her I'm not ready, like I'm some choirboy, a perfect symbol of innocence.

It's not a newfound religious fervor, though, or a born-again virgin pledge holding me back from ripping that tight dress off that even tighter body.

It's not because I'm waiting for commitment or trying to do the right thing.

It's Lila. Plain and simple.

Because any time I think about taking that dress off her or giving in, Lila's face, Lila's voice, Lila's everything comes flooding back.

Dammit. I'm never going to be over her, I think, as Scarlet mercifully turns the conversation to shoes and vegetarianism and who knows what else as I shamelessly shove food in my face, avoiding eye contact and reality.

***

"She's... nice enough," Scarlet says as we swing on the

back porch after dinner, a beer in my hand and a glass of wine in hers.

John has taken Margot to the garage to show her his motorcycle—upon Scarlet's prodding.

"But?" I ask before taking a sip.

"But she's not Lila."

"I kind of know that. That's kind of the point."

"I see," she says, and I can feel the weight of judgment in her words.

"What? Spit it out." I feel anger rising in my chest now.

"Nothing, big brother. It's just, she's not Lila. And I don't think that's as good of a thing as you would like to believe."

"Look, I'm moving on. Isn't that what you wanted for me?"

"No. I wanted you to be happy."

"Margot makes me happy." I say the words firmly as if that will make them have more weight.

"For now, maybe that's true. But you know what? Margot doesn't push you to be better or different. Margot doesn't challenge you. Margot is just... Margot. Just some girl on your arm. She isn't Lila. She doesn't light you up or make you come alive, Luke. I see it when you're sitting together. And clearly, you feel it too considering Margot's confession at dinner."

"I'm not talking about this anymore," I reply, getting pissed at Scarlet's observations.

"Well, I am. Look. You and Lila were so good because you pushed each other to be better, to be alive, to be vibrant."

"Margot pushes me to be bold and wild."

"Bold and wild isn't what I'm talking about. You're different with Margot, but not in a better way. Just in a different way. You know what I mean. I just think you need to think about that and think about what's holding you back with this girl. Because eventually, Luke, when the fun settles, what's going to be left?"

"Luke, oh my God, you need to get a motorcycle! It looks like so much fun," Margot shouts as she and John saunter up the steps on the porch, bringing a halt to the conversation at hand.

"Yeah, I always wanted one," I say, anxious to get up from the swing and head over to Margot, and more anxious to drop this conversation.

"What stopped you?" Margot asks, hanging on me as John walks over to take a seat on the swing beside his wife.

"Well, it wasn't practical."

"Screw practical. If you want one, get one."

I eye Margot, thinking about what Scarlet said. "So you don't think it's a bad idea?"

"No way. Do what you want, baby. I'm behind you no matter what."

I smile, but it feels forced.

Looking at Margot, I believe her. She would be okay with whatever I chose, whatever I did.

But is that truly what I'm looking for? A woman to be a "yes" woman, to let me run free without direction or challenging me to be better? A woman who is okay knowing my heart's not completely hers, not completely untangled from the woman I once loved?

After dessert when I drop Margot off—despite her pleading to come inside—I think about Scarlet's words the whole way home. I think about who I am without Lila. I think about who I am with Margot.

And I think about how truly fucked-up love is, more than I could've ever known at twelve.

* * *

The next morning, I trudge through the door, the familiar bell's tinkle a bit irritating. I push my sunglasses back on my head and, despite my grumpy mood, I feel myself smile when I see her behind the counter.

"It's about time you wandered in again, stranger," Dot says, rushing out from behind the doughnut display to give me a hug and plant a red lipstick kiss on my cheek.

"Sorry, Dot. I've been busy."

"Seems like it," she says. "Where's the new girlfriend?"

I'm taken aback. "How did you know?"

"Luke, I've lived in this town my whole life. I know everyone and everything that happens. Word gets around. Margot Lane, right? Pretty girl. A bit wild, though."

I grin, shaking my head. "Yeah, just a bit. But she's great. Really great."

Dot raises an eyebrow, shaking her head. "You're a terrible liar."

"Oh no, Dot, not you, too."

"I'm guessing your sister isn't a fan?"

She leads me toward the table in the corner. I hold back. "Maybe a different table?" I ask.

"Nonsense. You and Lila are over, right? You've moved on. So there can't be any harm in sitting at your old table. That part of your life is over, huh?"

I stare at Dot, her eyes challenging me to state otherwise. I sit down, and she seems a little disappointed.

Dot sits down across from me after shouting to Nicholas to bring over the Luke and Lila special. Yes, our order has a name. And yes, Dot just used it.

"No, Scarlet isn't crazy about Margot. She's just hung up on the fact she's not Lila."

"And she isn't. Far from it. But how do you feel?"

"I didn't know I was getting free counseling," I tease.

Dot smacks my hand, smiling. "If you weren't so cute, you couldn't get away with being such a wisecracker."

"If you say so. But I feel... good. You know? I have to move on, and Margot's definitely helping."

"Interesting."

"What?" I ask, afraid to see where Dot will take this.

"Nothing, it's just, for moving on and Margot being so helpful, you're in an awfully morose mood. No usual Luke smile."

"Just tired."

"Oh, I see. Margot Lane is wild in all kinds of ways, huh?"

I feel my cheeks redden. "Not tired from... um... that."

"Also interesting."

"Dot, can we not go there?"

"Of course, of course, whatever you want," she says as Nicholas brings over a tray of three peanut-butter doughnuts.

Nostalgia stirs in me.

An unwelcome nostalgia.

I try not to think about it as I grab a doughnut and scarf it down. Dot helps herself to one of the doughnuts, too, still sitting across from me in Lila's seat.

"All I'm going to say," Dot utters around a mouthful of crumbs, "is that if Margot is really the one you want, the one you should be moving on with, then why isn't she sitting here instead of some washed-up old baker?"

I open my mouth to argue, but Dot just shakes her head, pats my hand, and heads off to return to work, leaving me alone at a table with too many memories and too much doughnut left for just one lonely, confused man.

CHAPTER TWENTY-TWO

LUKE

I can't believe it's happening. This could be my big break. Despite all that's going on in my messed-up life, this could be the moment I've been waiting for.

I've got an invite to a big music festival in Ohio. They were looking for an opener, and someone apparently heard my song at the Oakwood Music Festival. Thanks to a cancellation and desperation, Luke Bowman got the gig.

Which means I have exactly twenty-four hours to get my ass to Ohio and be ready to play for a crowd of thousands. This is it, though. This could put me on the map.

As I'm getting my bag packed and leaving instructions for Evan about Floyd, there's a knock at my door.

I dash to answer it, flinging it open to see a surprising sight.

It's Margot. With a suitcase.

"Surprise!" she yells, jumping into my arms. "Cleveland, here we come!"

"Margot?" I'm still confused, staring at her, at the suitcase.

"What, silly? Did you really think I was letting you go to Ohio for your first big gig alone? No way, mister. I know how girls look at musicians. And if you haven't slept with me yet, there's no way I'm letting some groupie get her hands on you."

"What about work?"

"My boss let me off."

"I just called you a few hours ago," I say, stunned. It's true. I'd only found out about the gig myself this morning and had called to share the good news with Margot. I didn't think she'd be dropping everything to come along.

"I know, but this is huge. I didn't want to miss it. And now you won't be so lonely on the drive."

I don't have time to ponder Margot's self-invitation, although I am thrilled at the prospect I won't have to drive by myself. It might be good to have some company for the drive to keep me from freaking myself out the whole way there. Plus, it will be good to have a friendly face in the crowd, to have someone there for my big moment.

I smile, thinking about how lucky I am to have her. What a selfless move. Clearly, she does care.

I wrap her in my arms. "Thank you. You're amazing," I say, meaning it. She pulls back enough to plant a kiss on my lips, her hands wandering.

"Babe, we have to hit the road in twenty minutes," I say.

"Oh, I can do a lot with twenty minutes," she says, and I shake my head, knowing she isn't lying.

"I have to finish packing."

"Okay, but don't say I didn't try to do you when you were still just Luke Bowman and not yet a star, okay?"

"Deal," I say, rushing back down the hallway to throw the final things in my suitcase and hit the road to my potential future.

***

"You sure you don't need anything?" Margot asks before rushing into the gas station to freshen up. She insists she doesn't want to roll into town with bad eyeliner or hair.

"I'm fine," I say, leaning back in my seat, staring at the lyrics I was working on during the drive.

As I watch her slink into the gas station, I pull out my cell phone, glancing at the blinking screen.

My fingers unlock the screen, and I head to the contacts list, not sure what I'm doing yet completely sure.

I scroll until I find the name, the familiar number.

I shouldn't be doing this. It's been so long since we've talked. It's weird. It's not appropriate. She's not my go-to anymore.

But it feels inappropriate to not call. She was there through all those dreams and all those shows. She was there to push me. She would be the one here if things hadn't ended up like they had.

She'd be in the seat beside me, pumping me up and jumping up and down that my dream, that our dream, was coming true.

Without another thought and knowing I don't have much

time, I guiltily hit Call.

It rings. And rings. And rings.

And then voice mail. She's probably working. I should just hang up, leave it go.

But then I hear the familiar message, her voice sending a shudder through me.

"Hey," I say, deciding I am already calling so I might as well lay it all out there. "It's me, Luke. I just wanted to tell you that I'm heading to Cleveland to a music festival. Someone saw me play around town and asked me to open for the festival. I'm going to be on stage and everything, a few thousand. I just… well, I don't know why I'm calling. I just wanted you to know I guess. You're the one who helped me do this, Lila, so I wanted you to know. I hope everything is going well for you. I'm sure it is. But, um, okay. Bye now."

I hang up, and then slam my fist on the dashboard. "Shit."

I sounded like a muttering idiot. I *am* a muttering idiot.

I hate how we've been degraded to this, two people uncertain whether or not to leave an awkward voice mail. I hate what we've become.

As I watch Margot sauntering back toward the car, I realize I hate how I'm caught in the middle, how I'm stuck between the safe, commitment-free life with Margot… and the life I wanted with Lila but am too afraid to grab.

It sucks not being good enough.

* * *

I rarely get nervous at gigs—probably because I've barely

had anything that could qualify as an actual gig. My haunts are usually dusty bars, small stages, and sparse crowds.

This is different, though.

On stage looking out into a skeptical crowd of thousands who feel ready to boo any second, my hands tremble as I grip the mic. I'm terrified.

But it's now or never.

I look directly in front of the stage at the VIP seats. I was allotted one for a guest, so of course Margot got it. As I shakily introduce myself to the crowd as they go from a loud roar to a dull murmur, I look to the seat for confidence, needing a boost. I desperately need a friendly face.

Margot lets out a loud scream, jumping and waving at the crowd after I've said my name.

"I'm his girlfriend," she shrieks for all to hear, jumping and waving like a raucous schoolgirl.

There's no reassuring thumbs-up for me or a nod. There's no sweet smile telling me I've got this.

There's just Margot in her flashy red, waving and smiling at some guys in the second row as they catcall her.

I don't have time to analyze it. The music starts, and it's now or never. So I sing my heart out and try to ignore the fact that the entire time I'm singing, Margot's taking selfies and not even listening to a word I sing, not hearing me at all.

Regardless, I don't get booed offstage and I even get some congratulations backstage from some bigger newcomers to the music scene. I should feel elated. This could be the start of something bigger.

But backstage, I pull out my phone, realizing I'm looking

for a message, a voice mail, a text that isn't there.

"You were great, baby," Margot says, rushing me before I can even take a breath. "Let's get some pics for Instagram, okay?"

I smile for the camera, listening to Margot babble on and on about fame, fortune, and Instagram-worthy pics.

"What did you think of the new song I played? Did you like the chorus?" I ask.

"Oh, yeah, yeah, it was great," she says, waving a hand as she types on her phone, presumably posting all over Instagram about her newfound "fame."

We drive home after the festival, Margot having work in the morning. It's a chatty ride, Margot insistently talking about next steps and VIP suites and all sorts of things I try to focus on.

As we're nearing home, she turns to me. "You're in a mood. What's wrong?" There's no edge to her voice, which irritates me further. It's like she's commenting on the weather, not on my feelings.

"It's just, I feel like you didn't even hear me up there. This isn't about fame and money for me, Margot. It's so much more. I don't think you get that."

She blinks, looking at me as we're stopped at the red light. "So you don't want to be famous?"

"I didn't say that. But you act like that's what it's all about. It's about the music. It's about doing what I love."

"And it's also about getting bigger. Think of the money. Think about what it would be like to hear everyone shouting your name. Think of what this could be for us."

I stare at Margot Lane, seeing her for maybe the first time. I see that behind the wild and fun, carefree Margot is something else. I glance back at the light, noticing it has changed to green. I step on the gas.

"You don't get it."

"Well, how could I? You don't talk to me about it." The edge in her voice tells me she's really getting frustrated with me.

I stew, staring out the window, wondering how I got here. Wondering where exactly I'm going.

"I know I'm not her, you know," Margot says quietly as we drive on. "I know that. But I'm trying here."

I turn to Margot. "What are you talking about?"

"You told me from the beginning your heart was somewhere else. It's not a secret, and I'm okay with that because sometimes my heart is somewhere else too. But, Luke, you can't have it all. You can't agree to be fun and free with me but then get pissed when I'm not her. I'm not Lila. I never will be. It's not fair to keep comparing me to her. You can't be okay with the fact I'm different but then hold it against me when I'm not acting like her."

I stare at this beautiful girl beside me. She's right. It's not fair.

"You're right. I'm an idiot, Margot. It's never been fair. I'm sorry. I just… I'm too broken to be with someone new. I'm not over her. I don't think I ever will be. I should've never let this progress to where it is. I should've never pretended I could make this work. I'm sorry. I really am."

Margot doesn't scream or cry. She doesn't act surprised

or yell. She simply pats my leg with her hand. "I know, Luke. I know. But maybe you need to find a way to be over her. Because even apart, this girl is killing you."

We drive home in silence, and when we get to my place, Margot simply kisses my cheek and smiles. "You're a good guy, Luke. Really. Call me sometime, okay?"

And just like that, another girl is driving away, presumably gone.

The familiar anger and sadness creeps in… but it's not for Margot Lane. It's for someone else I don't even know anymore.

CHAPTER TWENTY-THREE

LILA

I aimlessly scroll through Facebook, telling myself I did the right thing by deleting that voice mail. I'm moving on. I can't let him pull me back in.

I'd been shocked after all these months to hear from him. When I saw the familiar number under missed calls and the voice mail, though, my heart instantly stopped. Was something wrong? Surely there was a major emergency if he was calling.

But when I listened to the message, that familiar voice sending a shiver through me, I'd smiled. His dreams were coming true. In a way, the dreams we had together were coming true. We'd spent so many nights talking, fantasizing about Luke's career, about what he wanted, about how music could be his day job. I was his number-one fan and his cheerleader, keeping him going when he wanted to quit. His voice is truly special, and he has this charm about him that comes alive onstage. It's like he was born to be there.

When Luke couldn't see that, I helped him. I was there in the front row at every gig, from basement-like bars to small fairs, listening to every word he sang, feeling like he was always singing to just me.

But not now. Now, there is a new girl in my seat. There are new eyes he stares into as he sings. There are probably new words, new songs for a new life he's built without me.

It hurts, even if I don't want it to. It kills me to think about that girl in my seat, where I'd always been.

And it's not because I want the fame and the glory. It's not because I'm afraid he's going to write killer breakup songs about me that hit the radio. It's because... well, I don't know the answer to the because.

I just know it hurts not being the one there with Luke.

I snap out of it, shoving it aside. It's over. We're over. We walked away.

Now I'm finding new happiness, the happiness with a safe, secure man who can lead me to my goals, who can maybe someday give me my dream life.

The horn honks outside. Oliver is apparently waiting in his car. I don't completely blame him—Grandma Claire is quite the handful. Still, I look over on the sofa where Grandma Claire is watching the evening news with Cookie and Trixie on her lap and I see a frown.

"You know, in my day, it was rude to just wait outside when you were picking up your date," Grandma Claire says huffily.

"Oh, stop. Oliver is an amazing guy. He's probably just in a hurry." Mom hands Grandma Claire a cup of tea as she waves at me. "Don't you think…," she begins, eyeing my outfit.

"Goodbye, Mother," I say, rushing out the door before I can hear about how if I want a proposal someday, I need to start taking my time with Oliver seriously.

Mom is, of course, Oliver Waynesboro's biggest fan these days. A prominent family, a solid career, good looks, and just the right amount of charm equates to a perfect match for her daughter, at least in Lucy Morrow's book. Oliver, at least in Mom's eyes, is everything Luke wasn't. He's dedicated and rational. He's a planner and a go-getter.

He's serious about family, about marriage, about life.

So naturally, Mom has been pushing nuptials since Maren's wedding.

He is an amazing guy, I think as I head to the Mustang and Oliver waves. And he is serious about family, about marriage, and about everything. He's the perfect fit, the perfect, stable guy to give me the life I've so desperately been wanting for the past few years. Looking at Oliver, I can see this life set out before us of the white picket fence, two kids, and a steady, planned-out way of living.

I get into the car, and Oliver leans over, kissing me gently. "You look gorgeous," he says, and I smile, buckling up as we pull out.

"Where are we going?" I ask.

"Well, I have to be back to Park Lane in an hour, so I thought we'd make a quick stop at that doughnut place we tried before."

"Oh, yeah, great," I say, trying my hardest to make the

smile on my face genuine. "Do you mind if I grab Henry, then? Dot loves him and we can grab a table outside." We're backing down the driveway, but there's still time. I reach to unbuckle my belt.

Oliver puts a hand on mine to stop me. "We don't have a lot of time, and it'll just be easier without him, don't you think?"

I stare into those gorgeous blue eyes I've been getting to know.

I paint back on the smile. "Sure," I say, thinking about how things with Oliver are easier.

Easier and simpler.

My mind threatens to wander back to all those times Luke and I walked Henry up for doughnuts, his favorite being the vanilla birthday cake supreme doughnut, which Dot would decorate with a biscuit when Henry was in tow. It threatens to think about all the laughs and the questions we'd get as Henry slobbered underneath our tiny table out in front of Dot's, as we'd talk about our favorite shows and what we were doing tomorrow.

Just like the voice mail, though, I hit delete. I throw those thoughts away because they're useless now. Luke was my past.

Looking over at Oliver, who is animatedly chatting about his sister's pregnancy announcement and how he can't wait to be an uncle again and how we should go visit his family in Maine sometime soon, I smile.

"What is it?" he asks.

"You're a great guy," I say, meaning it, hanging on

every word.

"And you're pretty amazing yourself, Lila. I'm lucky to have you in my life. You make me happy."

And with that, the past is tossed aside, talks of the future, of my future, settling in.

* * *

Dot hugs me as Oliver and I settle into a table—a new table, our table—after Oliver orders for us. When Nicholas brings us our plate, there aren't peanut-butter doughnuts.

There is one chocolate toffee doughnut and one plain, glazed doughnut.

"Oh, they both look good," I say, meaning it. "Want to split them?"

Oliver looks at me. "Um, why don't you just pick one?" he asks.

I nod, a little disappointed, which is crazy because it's just a damn doughnut. I grab for the chocolate toffee doughnut, and Oliver picks up the glazed.

We talk about the recent patients at Park Lane and about plans for the holidays. Oliver tells me he bought us two tickets to the symphony for next weekend, and I graciously thank him, telling him it will be my first time. We chat about the weather and about the new restaurant in town.

In short, we chat away the time together. All the while, I notice Dot studying us from behind the counter as she's wiping down surfaces and talking to other customers.

When we're just finishing up, she wanders over. "How is everything?" Dot asks, and I know she isn't just talking about the doughnuts.

But Oliver is none the wiser. "Everything was great. This glazed doughnut was perfect. I know people like a lot of fancy frills, but why mess with simple when it's good, right?"

Dot rests a hand on the back of my chair, leaning over my shoulder. I can smell her flowery perfume. "Agreed, young man. Agreed. Sometimes in life we're looking for something new and exciting and frilly, but what we had right in front of us was just simply good, you know? Being adventurous and bold and trying new things sounds great, but not if it isn't what you really want. That plain glazed doughnut, if you eat it every single day, can get dull and less exciting. You might be tempted to move on to something better, to something that seems better for your life. They say variety is the spice of life, but I disagree. I think once you find something that works, it's worth sticking with it, even if it seems like life is just passing by."

I feel my chest tighten. I don't think we're talking about doughnuts anymore. Dot gives my shoulder a squeeze, but I don't turn around. I can't turn around.

"Wow, that lady really is passionate about doughnuts," Oliver says, shaking his head, but none the wiser.

I smile. "Yeah, she really is." I feel myself getting misty-eyed, but I try to shrug it off, clapping my hands and talking about how that chocolate toffee doughnut was amazing and how happy I am that I got to try something new.

But Dot's words stick in my head. Was that really what I'd done? Had I convinced myself I couldn't be with Luke anymore because it wasn't what I wanted in life when the truth was I just felt like I needed a change? Had monotony and fear just overthrown the best damn thing that happened to me?

And did my three peanut-butter doughnut life really get better when I went to a glazed and a chocolate toffee doughnut?

Was letting Luke go for a chance at a life I thought I wanted, a life of commitment and stability, really making me happy?

I get what Dot was saying. I do. As Oliver grabs my hand and leads me to the car, kissing me on my cheek, I settle against him, thinking that I'm just in my head too much.

Dot's words might ring true, I don't know. Regardless, I don't think I'm brave enough to give her words a go.

CHAPTER TWENTY-FOUR

LILA

"Good? That's all you're going to give me? Really? I thought we were sisters slash best friends," Maren complains as she sashays up the walkway to the apartment we're looking at.

We're in a pretty run-down area of town, and the apartment building is no exception. The red paint is peeling in huge chunks on the front, and the "shutters" on the windows out front are crooked and ready to make their downward descent to the ground.

But when I look at the building I called last week after finding it in a newspaper ad, I see one thing: Freedom.

Freedom from Mom that is, who won't get off my back about Oliver, my hair, student loans, my job, and my eating habits.

"Maren, we've only been... dating, I guess you could call it, for a little over a month."

"Yes, when two people go out a few times a week making googly eyes at each other, we call that dating."

"Not to mention their hot lunch dates at work every day and their flirtatious smiles over rabies vaccines," Zoey chimes in from behind me.

"Honestly, I don't know why I go anywhere with both of you."

"Because you love us. And you need our opinions on your life to make sure you're making good decisions," Zoey says, squeezing me.

"Well, what are your opinions of Willow Estates so far?" I ask, appraising the building in front of us.

"I don't think I'd use the word estates, is what I think," Zoey says as we eye the building in all its glory. We can hear two angry voices yelling from up above, and one of the third story windows has a beach towel billowing in the breeze—out the window.

Not quite my dream home.

"I think even if there are dirt floors and no doors, it's still got to be heaven compared to living with Mom. I honestly don't know how you've survived this long."

"With lots of tequila from Dad's stash," I say, meaning it. It's been a long road.

Maren opens the door, the handle almost coming clean off. We scuttle toward the crudely hung "office" sign on the first door, which is written on lined paper and taped up with duct tape. This isn't looking promising.

"Hi, I'm Lila Morrow. I called about looking at your open apartment?" I ask the elderly woman at the desk. She coughs dramatically for a solid ten seconds, eyes us all suspiciously, and then wordlessly walks out from behind the desk.

She trudges past us and down the hallway. We stand, staring at each other in the hallway.

"Are you coming?" she asks.

"Right, yes," I say, scurrying to the front of the group as she leads us down the hallway to 104A.

"Feels like a mildew-ridden hotel," Maren whispers.

The lady coughs again as she opens up the door.

"Home sweet home," she says. I would think she's being sarcastic, but there isn't an ounce of emotion in her voice.

I step inside the apartment—which does look like a mildewy hotel room from a bad horror film. The carpet is a terrible brown color, and it appears to be in every room. I walk down the entranceway to the living room, a bare box of a room with no character to speak of. There's a tiny kitchen with the essentials—also carpeted, I might add— and a bathroom big enough for maybe just me.

Still, there is a balcony off the living room and there's a large backyard for the entire complex—and it's fenced in.

Plus, this place accepts dogs. Which isn't surprising because it smells a little like a damp dog.

It is not the home of my dreams. But it's a start. It fits my budget.

And there's no grating voice of my mother here.

"What do you think?" Maren asks, her face clearly saying it's not a good idea.

"It smells a little funky, but we could always get some air fresheners, you know?" Zoey says, being a good sport.

"It doesn't quite look like a place that would get a Lila

Morrow stamp of approval," Maren says, then remembering the landlady is here, adds, "No offense."

The landlady is biting her fingernails, not out of nervousness, but out of boredom. She doesn't respond.

"It doesn't. This is not a place I would have on my life plan in a million years."

"Well, I guess you could deal with Mom another few weeks, right?" Maren says, strutting out.

"Which is why I'll take it," I declare, smiling, despite the ugly carpet and weird smell. "It's going to be fine. And it'll be a step in the right direction."

"I'll get the paperwork," the lady says, unimpressed by my life decision.

"Lila, are you sure?" Zoey asks. Zoey currently lives with her brother in a super nice townhouse on the outskirts of town, so I'm sure this looks like a dump to her.

"Positive." And I am. I need to get my life going in the right direction. I need to do something.

I sign the papers and agree to move in the first of next month, which will give me time to usher in the new year in my new home and my new life.

"Mom's going to hate, hate, hate this place," Maren says as we stroll out. "She'll probably hate it so much, she won't even visit you here."

"Which means she'll have to use her visiting time at your place," I say, smiling.

"Oh, hell no. Newlyweds excuse, remember?"

Maren has been telling us all no company allowed because she and Will are still newlyweds and enjoying their time—wink, wink.

"You know, that excuse is going to wear off soon enough," I argue.

"I will renew our vows every month if I have to in order to keep that excuse in play."

"You two are so mean to your mom," Zoey teases, getting in the back seat. Maren drives off.

I turn to eye Zoey. "Really?"

"No. Trust me, I've felt Lucy Morrow's wrath. I think you deserve a medal for living there as long as you did. And Grandma Claire, too."

"Grandma Claire is too drunk most of the time to care. Plus, I think she enjoys pissing Mom off."

"Who doesn't?" Maren asks. "Now, where are we going to celebrate?"

"Big Dippers!" Zoey and I scream like children, which is our favorite ice cream stand in town.

"Honestly, you two are both so juvenile. But ice cream sounds about right. So when are you breaking the news to Mom?"

"Next week, I think. Give her time to get her griping out and plus, I'll have to start packing soon."

"You're going to tell her over Thanksgiving dinner?"

"It's already chaotic, so why not?"

"Oh, dear. This will be quite the Thanksgiving then," Maren says, looking over at me. It seems like she wants to tell me something, but then she must think better of it because she turns the radio up.

Something's going on with her. I can sense it. But I don't

push her, singing along to the new song by Bruno Mars as we pull into the Big Dipper parking lot, all three of us anxious for the Big Dipper Sundae Special.

We eat our ice cream, chatting about home improvements I already need to make and taking bets on how many guilt trips Mom will play about me moving out.

CHAPTER TWENTY-FIVE

LILA

"Oh, please, let's watch *Pretty Woman*. I do love that one," Grandma Claire begs from her perch on the sofa, Trixie on her lap. I'm a little worried the cat isn't even breathing because it hasn't moved in hours.

"Grandma, no. We've seen that one so many times," Maren says from her seat on the other sofa, leaning on Will.

It's our Morrow family pre-Thanksgiving Moviefest. Every year, we all pile into the living room and eat homemade pizza—thanks to Dad—and watch movies to welcome in the holiday season. Tomorrow night, as scheduled by Mom, we will put in a Christmas movie after the Thanksgiving dinner has been finished, and decorate the tree.

We get pretty serious about the holidays around here, thanks to Mom.

"Let's let the guest of honor pick," Mom says, shooting a smile to Oliver, who is cuddled up next to me on the love seat. Henry is snoring at our feet.

I was pretty nervous about Oliver coming over tonight. Not that he hasn't seen the Morrow family in their shining, blaring glory—but still, it's one thing getting a taste of them, and it's another to spend an entire holiday with them. Oliver's staying in town for the holiday, even though his parents in Maine are a little upset.

Mom swears this is a good sign Oliver's going to propose—even though we haven't even said the "L" word yet. Mom chocks this up to "details."

"Yes, let's let Lila's *boyfriend* pick," Maren says. She's been using that word every chance she can, to my chagrin. Although obviously it's true. We're far past the friends stage now. I think spending Thanksgiving with someone's family pretty much seals that.

"*Star Wars?*" he suggests, prompting a groan from me, Maren, and Grandma Claire, but a "Hell yes" from Dad.

"You're not *a Star Wars* fan?" he asks me.

"God no," I say, which prompts him to open his mouth in mock horror.

"Well this might be off then," he says, and I nudge him in the ribs.

"All right, let's just go with *Pretty Woman* and be done with it," Mom finally says, rolling her eyes.

Grandma Claire practically leaps out of her seat, sending Trixie flying off her lap. Dad, Will, and Oliver groan. Maren begins quoting from the movie, and I just shake my head.

I don't know why we even pretend anymore. For the past ten years since Grandma Claire moved in with Mom and Dad, this has been the routine.

Mom passes around glasses of champagne as the movie begins, and we all tuck in, getting ready for what apparently is going to be the Morrow Pre-Thanksgiving Movie pick— because I guess, when it comes down to it, we're not ones for change.

I snuggle against Oliver, who is a remarkably good sport about Grandma Claire's lascivious comments about Richard Gere, and think that some things do change in life—but some things just clearly don't.

Like Grandma's desire to trade places with Julia Roberts.

CHAPTER TWENTY-SIX

LILA

"Mom, I love you, but for Christ's sake, could you please not use your hands to serve yourself mashed potatoes?" Dad shouts as Maren and Will argue over whose half of the wishbone is actually bigger.

"Do not use that term at the Thanksgiving table," Mom now yells at Dad, while Grandma continues scooping potatoes onto her plate—with her hand.

Cookie is barking under the table, and Trixie is lapping up milk from a saucer at the dining room table. Grandma Claire had a meltdown when Mom suggested the elderly cat should not be given a seat at the table. Grandma is convinced it may be Trixie's last Thanksgiving—as we all are—so she demanded the cat have a seat at the table.

Oliver holds my hand, giving it a squeeze, as Mom and Dad continue to fight about religion and Will and Maren continue to argue about the damn wishbone. It's chaos, sheer chaos, and I know any second Oliver's going to get in his Mustang and hightail it to Maine, to a probably normal, quiet holiday.

"I'm sorry," I say.

"For what?" Oliver asks, squeezing my hand again.

"This," I reply, gesturing to the chaos that is the family.

In the middle of the table, the turkey, scorched to a crisp, sits waiting to be served. I'm suddenly feeling very vegan. There's also a pie on the table that is clearly the kind you buy in the freezer section, as evidenced by its flimsy pan and the fact it still looks frosty.

At least Mom tried, just like she does every year.

When the fighting calms down to a mere murmur, I speak up. "Guys, can we please just eat?"

Everyone turns to me, seemingly remembering that we have a new guest, Oliver. When Luke was around, he was used to all this. Now, though, Maren smooths out her shirt and Mom plasters on her company smile, remembering Oliver isn't completely used to the Morrow family chaos.

"Who wants mashed potatoes?" Grandma Claire asks, holding up a palmful. We all stare, not sure how to handle it.

Then Oliver does the unthinkable. He shrugs and passes Grandma his plate. She proceeds to plop a glob on his plate with her hands. Maren starts laughing, and I shake my head, taking a huge gulp of wine, knowing I'll need it.

"Shouldn't we like, say what we're thankful for or something?" Maren asks, apparently trying to keep up the appearance that we're somewhat normal for Oliver.

I think that boat sank a long time ago.

"I'm thankful for hot pizza men and that Lila found a

new man." Grandma Claire winks at me, and I feel my face redden. I guess it could've been worse.

"Although," Grandma Claire begins, and I know something awful is coming. "I do miss Luke. He had nice curls. They were so scrumptious."

I look across the table, blinking. This is a disaster.

But thankfully, Maren turns the conversation as Oliver awkwardly takes a sip of wine.

"Well, I think we have a lot to be thankful for. Our family is growing, and we're all finding happiness. And we've got some big news to share. Lila?"

Oh shit. The moving out part. Well, things are already messy, so…

"I have a new apartment. I'm moving in the first of December."

Mom stares at me. "I didn't know you two were moving in already. That was fast." She smiles as if to say "gotcha."

"Oh no, we're not… it's just me," I fumble.

"Congratulations," Oliver says, kissing me on the cheek. He leans in, "Although moving in isn't something I'd be opposed to, just so you know."

My cheeks are definitely burning now.

"Oh, good. Can I come with you, Lila? Your mom is such a stick-in-the-mud. Plus, it'll be easier for us to get to the casino on Thursdays."

"What casino?" Mom asks.

"Nothing, Mom. It's all good," I say, biting my lip.

"Well, anyway, we're happy for you, Lila. It's going to be great," Maren says, raising her glass of water in cheers.

"I don't know why you're in a hurry to move out. It's not like you have it so bad here," Mom argues, her anger making itself known. I practically choke.

"Anyway, that's not the only announcement. Will and I have an announcement of our own."

I look up now, giving my sister a glance. I knew something was up. I knew it. I feel a grin forming, but I wait to hear the words.

"We're having a baby," Will says. "We just found out."

"I'm pregnant!" Maren says, and I scream, leaping to my feet and racing around the table to give her a hug.

"That was fast," Mom says. "You've only been married...."

"Mom, really? We were living together, for Christ's sake. Do you think we were chaste that whole time?"

"Do not use the Lord's name in vain," Mom argues as she, too, rises to give Maren a hug after scowling a bit.

"A baby. A grandchild. This is great," Dad says, heading over to shake Will's hand. The table erupts into sheer chaos again, only Oliver and Grandma Claire in their seats.

There's discussion of due dates and baby showers and sheer joy. This is amazing news.

"Wow, this guy here must be pretty fertile," Grandma Claire says, nudging Will when he passes her. Of course, she knows how to make a moment awkward.

"Well, now that the food is probably cold, I suppose we should eat. Looks like it's going to be a big year of changes again for the Morrow family," Mom says, and for once, I don't hear a tinge of judgment or regret or anything but... love. Just love.

We all raise our glasses in a final toast before we dig into the burnt turkey and fondled mashed potatoes.

It's not quite the perfect Thanksgiving dinner of the movies, but I don't think anything in this family is.

After we've eaten dinner and cleared the table, I'm on the front porch seeking a moment of quiet with Oliver, staring at the stars in the chilly autumn wind.

"It was a great night," Oliver says.

I smile, looking at him, glancing back through the window at my family. They're gathered around in the living room now, arguing over who should venture to the attic to get the tree and bring it down. I'm glad I've escaped that argument.

"It was," I agree. Oliver takes a step toward me, pulling me to him. His lips find mine, and we kiss under the stars. I feel the electricity between us, the mutual attraction.

I'm glad he's here, I really am.

"I'm sorry for what my grandma said," I say when he pulls back, hoping I don't blow the moment but feeling like I need to acknowledge it.

"It's okay," Oliver says, sounding like he means it. "I know he was a huge part of your life. I get that. But I also know he's your past. And I know I'd like to continue being your future. I know this might have started as a rebound," he says.

I open my mouth to protest, but he shushes me. "It's okay. I get it. But the thing is, Lila, I think we've grown into something more. I know we need to take it slow and see where this goes. But being here tonight with your family, with you, it just felt… right. You know?"

"I do," I say, smiling up at him. He pulls me into a tight hug, and for the first time in a long time, I feel content. I feel safe in his arms.

I look back through the window, where Will is trudging up the stairs, apparently nominated to go digging in the attic for the tree. Mom is yelling at Grandma about something with Trixie, and Cookie is nipping at Maren. Dad is holding his head in the recliner, probably asking God for a little sanity.

They're a crazy crew, an exhausting family unit. But they're mine.

And looking at them, standing here in Oliver's arms, I'm glad.

Standing here, I know now that this is what I want. I want the whole lot—the crazy family, the love that Maren and Will have, the excitement of a son or daughter coming my way. I want big family dinners and burnt turkeys at Thanksgiving and exciting news being shared.

Standing here in Oliver's arms looking in from a different vantage point, I realize that maybe it's all been in reach all along.

My family, the love, the connection—it's been here this whole time. I thought I had to get a promise and a ring to have that feeling, to experience that love. Standing here tonight, though, watching Will and Maren smile over their unexpected miracle on his or her way, I realize you just can't plan life.

This is not the future I imagined for myself last year at

this time.

Last year, I stood here, in this spot, looking in as Luke held me, talking about pumpkin pies and the thrill of Christmas coming up. We stood here with no real plan for the future, with no certainty about where we were going or the next step.

Last year, Maren stood here, not knowing what was coming up around the bend, that in one year, she'd be expecting her first baby with her new husband.

Life is a constant, changing road—and as much as I want to plan for every second of it, I can't. I can't predict where it's going to go, and I can't expect to make time stipulations for what is going to happen next.

Life's about rolling with the changes and learning to find simple joy in every stage, in every unexpected turn, and in every moment.

Standing here tonight, I'm the same Lila I was last year— but I'm also a little bit different. We're all a little different.

And it feels... okay. It all feels okay.

CHAPTER TWENTY-SEVEN

LUKE

"Bowser, get down!" Charley's voice booms as I scamper through the screen door. Despite the chill in the air, the door is wide open so Charley can get from the kitchen to the grill.

Carrying a plate of steaks, Charley doesn't have time—or, thanks to his huge Santa belly he's worked hard on for the past few months, energy—to get Bowser in time. The dog pisses all over my shoes.

And I don't even flinch. This feels just about right, these days.

"Wow, you look worse than before," Scarlet says, kissing me on the cheek. I mindlessly run a hand through the scruffy beard I've grown out.

"Oh my, Luke, are you homeless? Because you look kind of homeless. Here, have a brownie," Mom says, fluttering about, setting the table as if she's using fine china. In reality, there are foam plates and sporks on the table. Not quite the Thanksgiving feast of the movies—but a typical Bowman

Thanksgiving feast.

With one change.

Mom's managed to keep a man around through the holidays.

The man of the month theme in Mom's life has apparently been changed up. Charley's managed to stick around, and although it's hard for me to admit it looking at the goofy but nice Santa Claus stand-in, I have to admit Mom looks happy.

It could, of course, be the brownies.

Thanksgiving's never, as you can imagine, been a good holiday in the Bowman household. Once Dad left, we tossed aside the turkey and stuffing, Macy's Day parade kind of Thanksgiving traditions. Typically, we just treated it as another day, ordering a pizza from one lonely shop still open or grabbing some McDonald's.

This year's a little different. Mom's decided to celebrate.

Still no turkey, mind you—that would be way too traditional.

Instead, Charley's throwing steaks on the grill, despite the chilly air, and Scarlet and John brought over some pasta salad and rolls. Mom took care of dessert, which is good because a pot brownie sounds about perfect right now.

Despite the homeless comment and the dog piss, I'm glad to be here this Thanksgiving. It's been quite a few years since I've spent the day with my family—this was always Lila's family's holiday.

But things change, and there's no use dwelling on it. Although, in truth, it feels like that's all I do.

"Have you talked to Margot?" Scarlet asks, as if she can read my mind.

"Just a few texts. Things ended… amicably, all things considered. She really is a good woman."

Scarlet gives me a squeeze. "Love you, big brother. Glad you're here."

"And I'm glad you're here too," Mom says, putting her arms around me, too, in a mushy, group hug.

"Okay, everyone needs to slow down on the brownies. Everyone is being way too sentimental," I say, shaking my head.

"They're just brownies, for real," Mom says as everyone pulls back.

I raise an eyebrow suspiciously.

"What? I'm serious. I'm just actually happy. Things are good. Well, mostly good."

"Oh yeah?" I ask. I knew Mom was happy with Charley, but looking at her now, I see a glow I haven't seen—well, forever.

At this moment, Charley comes strolling in, putting an arm around my mother's shoulders. "Should we tell them?"

I eye Scarlet, not sure what the hell is happening. Mom practically busts out of her skin. She dashes across the tiny kitchen, opens up what has always been the junk drawer in our home, and pulls something out. She dashes back to us, flashing her left hand.

"We're getting married! For real!"

I freeze, staring at the scene. Santa Claus is holding on to my mom, and they're both grinning wildly. Scarlet coughs, and then dashes over to Mom.

"Congratulations," she says. "I'm happy for you guys."

I follow suit after a moment of being frozen, giving them both my congratulations.

In truth, though, as we sit down to dinner, Mom and Charley talking about wedding dates and giving details of the proposal—which involved a nude sculpture of some sort, I tried to block it out—I'm lost in my thoughts.

I can't believe it. I can't believe after everything, Mom's biting the bullet again.

"You okay, honey?" Mom asks when we're clearing dishes.

"I'm good. I'm just... surprised is all."

She squeezes me into her. "I know that my life, your father, it probably gave you such a jaded view of love. And to be honest, before Charley, I believed love was a nightmare. But sometimes people can change your mind if you let them, you know? Sometimes if you let yourself be vulnerable and open up, you realize commitment doesn't have to be a bad thing."

"But what if it doesn't work out?" I ask, the question that's been plaguing me for way too long.

"But what if it does?" she counters before slipping out of the kitchen and into the living room, where Charley is setting up a game of Taboo for the family to play.

"You coming, big brother?" Scarlet asks, slinking up beside me.

"In a minute. I'm just going to step out for a while, clear my head."

"Luke?" Scarlet says as I head out the door, the damn dog following me. I stop and turn. "Have you called Lila?"

"Of course not." I lean on the shoddy railing on the porch, looking up at the night sky.

"Maybe you should." Her words are uncharacteristically soft and serious.

"Scarlet, I—"

"Luke, listen. I know you're not over her, no matter what you say. And you know what else? I don't think she's over you either, if I know Lila. You two were good together. You can still work this out. Just think about it."

I shake my head.

"One more thing," she says when my hand is on the door.

I turn again, rolling my eyes. "What now?"

"Shave the damn beard. You really do look scruffy, and not in a sexy way, okay? Sisterly advice."

I let the screen door slam behind me as I wander over to the wicker chair on the front porch, the air biting into my skin as I stare at the night sky, thinking about a whole lot of things.

Mostly, thinking about the goodbye that sealed my view of love in the present day.

***

I paused my game, closed the bag of popcorn so she wouldn't complain it was stale, and dusted some crumbs off myself as the door below slammed shut. Even though it was staying lighter out longer now, it was pitch black, her hectic schedule keeping her out.

Her feet stomped up the stairs to our trustworthy one-bedroom that had long since overfilled with mindless things, more shoes, and enough tension to make me think that first day when we moved in was just a dream.

Keys slammed on the counter. Fridge opened for a water. The wordless, icy tension in the air.

She was home.

I stood, slinking out to the kitchen, feeling the tension in my chest.

Where had things gone so damn wrong? When had they fallen apart?

When did this crack in our relationship creep in, and how didn't we notice?

If I had to pinpoint it, perhaps it was Christmas, when the tears had flowed over the disappointment exploding out of her chest.

Maybe, though, it had seeped in, day in and day out, as she worked toward her goals and I sat here, a roofer with a failing singing career and no idea what the hell I wanted out of life.

Maybe it happened as I sat still, as usual, and she kept moving, dreaming, hoping. Maybe we were doomed from the start, two very different people. In the beginning, it had been charming. Maybe, though, in the long haul it wouldn't work, it couldn't work. We were too different.

And maybe I was lying to myself, feeding myself this horseshit about fate and circumstances because I didn't want to face the facts.

I was doing this to us. This had started with that twelve-

year-old boy who decided love and marriage fucked you over. It started with this twentysomething who was too much of a coward to let go of that fear—the fear of failure, of falling apart.

Most of all, the fear that I'd be my father's son and do him proud, that when things got tough, I wouldn't be man enough for Lila.

That I would hurt her.

I'd tried to explain it, over and over, in the best way I could. But how did you explain to a girl like Lila, a girl who believed in forever and who had two mostly happily married parents as role models, that forever was a frightening prospect? How did you explain that it really was you and not her? How did you explain that you wanted, you needed to give her forever, give her that commitment she needed, but that you just couldn't... because you loved her too much?

How did you put your reservations and fears out there for her to sift through and understand?

How did you ask her to let go of her dreams of a marriage, of a house, of a real family, because you were too fucked-up to just get over yourself?

You didn't. You couldn't. And as that knowledge seeped in over the past year, as we fought and scuffled like couples do but with the underlying knowledge that forever was always off the table, I think it cracked us.

I think resentment leaked in. I think frustration, more frustration than the average couple feels, crept in when we weren't looking.

Suddenly, her long hours made me lonely, and my short

hours made her pissed. Her need to schedule out our lives felt constraining, and I'm sure my desire to just go with it made her insane. Where once we had been the yin to each other's yang, we now became the detriment of each other, the destructive bomb in our identities.

We didn't fit anymore. We couldn't see the soul mates aspect anymore, and even if we did, I wasn't ready to seal that soul mate bond with the ring she needed.

I know she tried to get over it. She told me she didn't need a ring, didn't need that promise. And I almost believed her.

But Christmas had revealed the truth. And I didn't fault her for that. I didn't blame her. The heart wants what it wants in life. I just hated myself for not helping her get that picture.

I tiptoed out to the kitchen, feeling like I was walking on literal eggshells and not the metaphorical ones that now littered our relationship.

"How was work?" I asked, an icy quality to my voice.

"Fine," she said and then sipped her water, not bothering to look at me.

We didn't look at each other anymore. We didn't smile or talk or laugh.

We just existed.

And standing there, staring at Lila Morrow, the woman who stole my heart over a dying cat, it hit me.

We couldn't do this. We'd tried to reclaim what we had. We tried to move past the Christmas debacle. We'd painted on those smiles and assured ourselves we weren't breaking.

But, when we weren't looking, we didn't see that the break was already unfixable. It was already a devastating crack that couldn't be patched or smoothed over.

Lila and I, no matter how much I didn't want it to be true, were done.

So, I rustled up the courage I couldn't find when it came to us.

I would hate myself for that for days, weeks, and months afterward.

"We can't do this anymore," I said, a quiet solemnity filling the room. Lila put the glass on the counter, still not making eye contact.

"I know."

Two words, two simple, soft-spoken words that sealed our fate, that sealed what I already knew to be true.

We'd both known, in honesty, since Christmas. We'd both known maybe even longer.

We'd known what we didn't want to know. We were broken. We were over.

Luke and Lila as we knew us couldn't exist.

A piece of me wanted her to fight me, to say it would be okay. But she didn't.

Slowly, painfully, she seemed to force herself to look at me, those eyes staring into mine, the tears welling.

"I loved you, Luke."

Loved. Past tense.

I nodded, wondering what I should do. I wanted to cross the room, to pull her into my arms, to tell her I would make this better. But looking into her face then, I knew I couldn't.

I couldn't give her what she wanted, not here.

I also saw something else, though—I saw a hope of freedom. I saw the Lila Morrow who knew her plans for her life didn't have to end here, with me, this curly-haired singing failure. I knew she could go out and find someone who deserved her, who could give her the ring and the promises and forever. I knew she could find someone who wasn't already broken, already screwed-up when it came to love.

She could find someone who hadn't fooled himself into believing he was healed and capable of overcoming his past, his demons.

I wanted to run across the room and beg her to stay. I wanted to force down my fears and promise her what she wanted to hear.

But at that moment, I saw in her eyes resignation. So I resigned myself to the fate of losing Lila.

I told myself it was the selfless thing to do, the best thing to do. In that moment, I convinced myself we'd already both checked out and that we didn't fit. I convinced myself the fates weren't in our favor.

But that night, when I slept on the couch, I knew the truth.

I'd chosen this. I'd chosen it from the second I saw her, the second I knew a girl like Lila deserved so much better than me.

I knew from the second I kissed her that she would be my undoing, and that I wouldn't be able to stop it.

Lying on the couch, there was just bone-chilling silence.

There were no screaming fights or swearing arguments—we were both too tired, too done for that.

There was just the silence of broken hearts, of shattered dreams, and of painful tomorrows we knew were coming.

In the coming weeks, we divided our things and prepared for the disentanglement of our lives. We let the iciness creep in and take over, broadening the gap that had already been growing between us. We didn't get out our ice picks and try to chip it away. We'd given up now, resigned ourselves to going our separate ways.

Over the next few weeks, I wrestled with myself. So many times, I wanted to cross that icy sea and grab her, throw her a life ring, toss her a straw of hope. I wanted to tell her I'd change, that I would be the man who deserved her. I wanted to promise her the forever I knew would be shaky.

But looking at Lila Morrow from a newfound distance, I realized what I'd known all along. I couldn't be the man for her. I couldn't be what she needed. Lila was a go-getter, a planner, and a woman on a mission in life.

And I was me. Luke Bowman, the abandoned son of an asshole, the man who believed marriage was fucked from the start.

I wanted Lila to be the woman to change my mind. I wanted to believe our love was strong enough to change me.

But maybe I had just been as naïve as my twelve-year-old self who thought my dad was coming back. Maybe I'd let the feelings I had with Lila overpower my brain.

So, as I watched her pack up her now ninety-one pairs of shoes in boxes, labeling them carefully, and make arrangements to move back in with her mom, I sat by and watched. I watched as she sorted herself out in the orderly way she did, compartmentalizing all the pieces of herself and gluing the Lila she was without Luke back together. I watched her rip all shreds of us out of her life, watched her piecemeal together a semblance of normalcy. I watched her march forward to a carefully planned path that now just erased me from it.

I watched her walk into the unknown with a sense of purpose I'd never had.

I watched her walk away with a huge piece of my heart and the painful knowledge that I never deserved her and that I'd never have her again.

Most of all, when we said our final goodbye, I watched the best damn thing that ever happened to me walk away, knowing the whole time I was making the biggest mistake ever—but not knowing how to find the courage to stop it all.

* * *

"This is a terrible idea," I say out loud to myself as I'm driving the familiar road. And it is, in fact, probably the worst idea I've had in forever.

I haven't talked to her in months. I haven't seen or heard from her. And what if her new boyfriend's there? What am I going to say anyway? What do I hope will come out of this?

Maybe Mom did put some pot in the brownies because I'm clearly not thinking straight.

I can't manage to force my foot to the brake, though. It's like I'm on autopilot, unable to stop the train that is my heart.

When I get to the familiar street, I park a few houses down, shut the truck off, and take a deep breath. I have no idea what I'm doing.

But maybe I do.

I get out of the truck and shut the door as quietly as I can, almost as if in reverence for what I'm about to do.

Dammit, I miss her.

And if Mom can get over her fears and her qualms about love, what's stopping me? What's stopping me from being the man Lila needs?

I tiptoe up the familiar sidewalk, up the driveway that holds so many memories. I step onto the porch, my heart thudding so hard I can hear it pounding in my head. I'm reaching my fist up to knock when I glance through the front window and see it.

Lila.

She's smiling, beaming by the tree, the Morrow family tradition I was once a part of on Thanksgiving. She's hanging an ornament on the side.

She isn't alone, though.

His arms are wrapped around her. He's kissing her neck, and she's giggling, the lights from the tree making the glow of her skin even more palpable, even through the window.

She looks… happy. Peaceful. Joyous.

Who the hell am I to come crashing into that?

She's moved on. She's found what she was looking for.

It just isn't me.

I slink away from the door, rushing back to my truck before someone can see me. I walk away from the home that used to house who I considered family. I walk away from the traditions and the love.

I get back in my cold, empty truck and drive away, having no clue where I'm truly going.

* * *

"Here," a familiar, kind voice says behind me, and I stop strumming on my guitar for a minute. I'm singing to an empty street, the light above me the only thing keeping me company. With every word I sing, my breath comes out as a cloud, the chilly November air biting into me. My fingers are practically numb, but I needed to be here.

I needed to sing, to mourn, and to work out what I saw tonight in the only way I can.

I turn to see Dot, wrapped in a red parka and a scarf. She hands me a plate with a doughnut on it.

"It's my pumpkin tarte doughnut, since its Thanksgiving and all."

"I thought you would be closed," I say, taking the plate and the heavenly looking doughnut.

"I was. But I was driving by and saw a lonely friend on the street corner, and thought he could use a doughnut."

"Thanks, Dot."

"Now why don't you come inside for a few minutes? I have some organizing to get done, and it's too damn cold to stand out here. Come on with me, tell me what has you here alone on Thanksgiving of all days."

I oblige, pack up my guitar in its case, and follow her inside. She flips on the light before taking off her parka and tossing it on the nearby table.

I do the same, slinking into a chair.

Dot heads behind the counter. She busies her hands as she always does. "So tell me, Luke Bowman, what are you doing?"

"To tell you the truth, Dot? I have no idea."

Dot sighs, stopping her work to walk over to me. She sits across from me.

"Tell me all about it."

I do. I tell her about my Mom and Charley. I tell her about Margot. I tell her about Scarlet's words and the visit to Lila's and the sight in the window.

I tell her how I miss Lila but how I know I'm not what she needs. I bare it all to her, the things I've been too cowardly to say to anyone else, most of all to the woman who really should be hearing it.

Dot just shakes her head when I'm all done. "Luke Bowman, you're an idiot, you know that?"

"Thanks, Dot," I say, shaking my head too.

"I mean it. All this not good enough talk. Snap out of it. That girl was head over heels for you, you know? And she still is."

"She has a new boyfriend."

Dot just laughs. "He may be her boyfriend, but he's not you. Not even close. Lila might have on a smile with him, but I see the cracks. I see how her eyes look off into the distance when he's talking. I see how she's thinking exactly what you are—that he's not you and never will be. I wish you two would stop playing this damn dance. Life's too short. Sure, you weren't perfect together. But guess what? Nobody is. Love is hard work, married or not. And when you find someone who fits you, someone who makes you happy, you hang on to it like it's a one-of-a-kind flavor of doughnut. And when it crumbles, you pick up the crumbs and put it back together. That's what you two need to do. Pick up the crumbs, Luke. Stop being a coward. Tell her how you feel. Be honest about what you're afraid of. Find a way to work it out. Because if you don't, you two are going to live these fake, ingenuine lives forever. And that, my friend, would be a real shame."

"I can't, Dot. I can't ruin her happiness."

"Well, then, I guess you better get used to singing sad songs under the streetlight," she says, clearly disappointed. At that, Dot wipes off her hands, stands, and goes back to her work, humming to herself as she tidies up. I sit for a long while, taking in Dot's words.

I wish I could take her advice. I wish I could find a way to go back, to choose differently. But I can't. And I can't expect Lila to drop everything for me. We've been there. What's changed?

Nothing. I'm no different than the man she walked away from. So why should I threaten what she has now? She's moved on. I need to let go.

"Thanks, Dot," I say after a long while, getting up and hugging her. "Do you want me to walk you to your car?"

"I'm good, honey. You go on home. You've got a lot of thinking to do."

"You sure?"

"I'm positive. See you soon," she says, winking at me. I smile, heading out of Dot's not really feeling any better, but happy to have everything out in the universe and off my chest.

And happy to know despite what Dot thinks, I at least feel like I'm doing the right thing.

CHAPTER TWENTY-EIGHT

LILA

As usual, the weeks between Thanksgiving and Christmas are a blur. Oliver and I spend more time together, going ice skating for the first time and having way too much coffee. I also spend a lot of time tediously packing up yet again and moving into my new place, to Mom's utter disdain. Her first visit is filled with scowls and snarky comments. But thanks to Maren and Zoey, we get the place looking pretty okay, buying lots and lots of area rugs and cute decorations.

And air fresheners.

So by Christmas Eve, when my family gathers in the living room of Mom and Dad's to watch the Griswolds' Christmas, as is our custom, I'm feeling pretty content if not a little lonely.

Oliver's understandably gone to Maine for the holiday to spend time with his parents and, despite his invite, I wanted to stay put. There've been so many changes. Even though they drive me up a wall and fifteen minutes into our

Christmas Eve celebration I want to drink the entire pitcher of eggnog, I wasn't quite ready to change this tradition.

Maybe it's Maren's pregnancy. Maybe it's because so much has changed this year that I don't have sure footing. Whatever it is, I'm feeling sentimental.

Cuddling up with Henry and Trixie on the love seat alone, the only hint of Oliver the perfume he bought me— expensive perfume, I must say—I'm cozy, content even.

And then my phone buzzes.

"Oh, is that your hot boyfriend?" Maren sings like I'm fifteen, and I roll my eyes.

"Hush, the good part's coming up," Grandma yells. Who knows what part she thinks is good, but I dare not ask.

I look down to see a text, but it isn't from Oliver.

It's from Luke.

And it says **Emergency**.

With that, I'm off the couch and into the kitchen, panic setting in.

* * *

I'm barely inside the vet office, flicking on the lights, when Luke follows, rushing in with Floyd.

Doctor mode sets in. "Bring him back to room one," I say, rushing back to get the equipment I need.

Floyd is in Luke's arms, not looking very well. He's clearly in distress, not his usual, wily self.

I rush him back, examining and checking for obvious traumas. "You said he hasn't been eating?" I ask.

"It's been a few days. I thought he was just under the weather."

"Has he been vomiting?"

"Yes, and today, it's been a lot. He's just not himself, Lila. I don't know what to do. I'm sorry, I know it's Christmas Eve, but I didn't know what to do." Luke's voice is shaking with panic. I've only seen him this worried one other time.

Luke's clearly beside himself, worried about Floyd—and for good reason. The cat's clearly in need of medical attention.

"Stay here, Luke. I'm going to x-ray him. I think he's got something lodged. Did he eat anything weird?"

"Not that I know of."

I rush Floyd back to the X-ray machine and, within a few minutes, it's confirmed.

Floyd needs surgery, and it looks like I'm the only one who can save him now.

***

"Thank you again. I'm so sorry," Luke says hours later when we're sitting in the back room, Floyd coming out of surgery just fine. I'll have to stay and keep an eye on him, so we're back in the room Floyd is no stranger to. The poor guy is sleeping now, and we're on the sofa, taking a breath for the first time all night.

"It's okay. It's not your fault. I'm glad I could help," I say, meaning it. I'm exhausted and worn out, the surgery taking its toll on me.

"I still can't believe he ate a damn piece of his cat scratcher."

"It happens a lot, actually. And if the cardboard wedges

just right, well, you get this kind of situation. It's a good thing you brought him in when you did."

"It's a good thing you're such a kind person. Thank you. But I'm sure you have somewhere you need to be. I don't want to ruin the rest of your holiday."

I turn and look at him, the curly-haired man from my past who still feels so familiar. Despite the harrowing situation and the exhaustion, I smile, sitting here beside him. "You didn't. It's fine. Like I said, I'm glad I could help."

We settle into the quiet silence. All around, families are tucking in little ones, getting ready for Santa Claus. Christmas carols are being sung and holiday food is being stowed away.

And here we are, a guy and a girl who not long ago shared a life, sitting on a smelly sofa in the hospital wing of the veterinarian's office, nursing a saved cat back to life.

"Merry Christmas," Luke whispers now. I turn and grin.

"Merry Christmas."

We sit in another string of silence for a long time, both weighing the oddness of the situation, both not sure what to say. There's a familiarity lingering between us, but the tension of the past six months is also lingering.

You can't tear apart a relationship and then expect things to be the same. You just can't.

"It seems like Floyd is just trying to bring us together. First, the car, and now this. Crazy cat," Luke mutters.

I smile. "It is rather weird how we've ended up here twice now."

"Things are a bit different this time, though," he says,

and there's a seriousness in his voice.

"Yeah, they are. How are things with your singing, by the way?" I ask, wanting to change the subject and genuinely curious.

"Good. I mean, I went back to roofing once my leg healed, so it's not like I've quit my day job. But I have a few more gigs around. I'm booked for a gig in New York in February."

My face lights up. "Really? That's amazing! Your girlfriend must be so excited." Oops. I've just admitted to Facebook stalking Luke, because how else would I have known that? Too late to back out now, though.

Luckily, Luke doesn't question me.

"Oh, we're not…. Not anymore."

I feel my cheeks warm. I don't know why I brought it up. It was completely out of place and inappropriate. I guess I just felt the need to.

"What about you? How are things going?"

"Good. I got my own apartment."

Luke grins. "Couldn't stand Lucy?"

"You have no idea," I say.

"Oh, but I do."

And it hits me. He does. He has a complete idea. He knows exactly where I'm coming from.

I wait for him to ask about Oliver, but he doesn't. I mean, it doesn't matter. It shouldn't matter anyway.

Another silence creeps in, which is odd because when Luke and I were together, we were never silent. There was always too much talking and laughter. Now there's just… quiet.

We stare at Floyd, both lost in our individual thoughts. There's so much I want to say to him, the man who still, in truth, has his fingers wrapped around my heart. I've loosened them in these past months, but looking at him, sitting by him, I know they're still grasping a little bit, even if he doesn't want them to be.

I sit and I think about everything that's happened to bring us here. I think about everything that hasn't happened.

As we sit, staring at Floyd, I think about last year at this time and how, in many ways, Christmas day was the first tear in what would become a huge, gaping shred in the page of us.

***

It had started with a dying guinea pig, in all reality.

The little girl had rushed into Park Lane, clutching the cage with big, streaming tears falling down. Her mother ushered the little girl into my room as I leaned down to examine the emergency patient.

"And who do we have here?" I asked.

"Sparkles," the small, wavering voice said. "He's sick. Please help him."

"Well, let's just see what we can do for Sparkles here," I said, my gut clenching. Looking at the love the little girl clearly had for Sparkles and comparing it to the listlessness of the creature, my heart broke. Please God, let me be able to help Sparkles. I don't want to crush this little girl's hopes today.

I examined Sparkles, running through the regular

procedures and running some tests. After the little girl paced around the room, staring worriedly at me, I smiled.

"What's your name, sweetie?" I asked.

"Gina," she said.

"Well, Gina, good news. Sparkles is going to be just fine. He just has a little cold. Have you ever had a cold?" I asked.

The little girl nodded, very seriously.

"Then you know he's going to be just fine. Your mommy just needs to put a few drops of medicine in his water, and then in a few days, if you give him lots of love, he'll be just fine. Okay?"

She nodded, the biggest smile on her face.

I stood up to talk to Gina's mom. "Sparkles just needs two doses of antibiotic a day. Keep an eye on him. If he gets any worse, bring him in right away, okay?"

"Thank you so much, Dr. Morrow. You're amazing."

"No problem," I said, handing the cage over.

"Do you have any little ones?" the mom asked.

I shook my head. "Not yet."

"Well, you're great with kids. You'll be a great mom someday," she said before leading Gina and Sparkles out to the checkout.

When they were gone, I leaned on the counter.

They were the kind, simple words of an unknowing stranger. They were nothing, really, just a few appreciative words. But they stabbed right into my core.

Because in truth, I'd been starting to hear the ticking of the biological clock. I'd been trying to quiet it, trying to convince myself it was all fine. We had time.

But it wasn't time I was worried about, really.

It was Luke.

I loved that man with all my heart, loved the life we'd built. He was an amazing companion, the only person who could make me smile when I felt like crying. He was fun and loving. He had a tight hold on my heart.

I knew he'd had a rough upbringing and a negative view of marriage and love. He was straightforward in the beginning.

But being the girl who thought she could save anything, I apparently thought I could save him too. I thought I could save him from his dark views of love, of marriage, of parenthood. I thought I could be the woman to change his mind. I thought he'd get over it.

There we were, though, years later, still unchanged. He still was terrified of the prospect of having kids, still adamant he never wanted to be a father.

He was still adamant we didn't need a forever commitment or a family to be happy.

"We're good just the way we are," he always said, despite my prodding.

And I thought it would be enough. I thought if I couldn't save him from his views, I could change mine. I should be appreciative of what we had.

I was. Mostly. And then little reminders happened, like that day, reminders of what I was missing.

Reminders of the hole I felt growing inside, the yearning for a child, a family, and for the life I'd always envisioned.

***

"Congratulations!" I said, two weeks after the Sparkles incident when we were sitting around my mom's dinner table on Christmas day.

Maren had just shared the amazing news. She and Will were getting married.

And I meant the congratulations. I was happy to see Maren getting what she wanted.

It's not a race, *I reminded myself.* It's not a competition. It's okay that we're on a different page.

Staring at her ring, though, the wound spread a little deeper and wider. I tried not to look at Luke, tried to keep the smile on my face. I told myself it was fine, that I was happy.

But a few hours later when everyone was grouped off around the house, I came back from the bathroom and overheard the damning words that put the final nail in the coffin.

Because what I hadn't realized up until that moment was despite my internal arguing and Luke's words, despite everything, I'd still had hope.

I still was holding out that Luke would change his mind, that we'd get our happily ever after.

A few overheard words decimated that hope and began the ending of our story.

* * *

"Hey," his soft voice says, a hand shaking me. I open my eyes, looking up into Luke's face.

I was asleep on his shoulder. The drool puddle is there again.

"Shit, I'm sorry," I say, jumping up from his shoulder, trying to smooth my shirt. "What time is it?"

"Six in the morning. It's okay. I kept an eye on Floyd. He seems like he's doing just fine."

I scamper over to the cage, trying to ignore the fact I just fell asleep on my ex's shoulder on Christmas. I examine Floyd, who is looking so much better. He's actually sitting up, looking at me with those beautiful green eyes.

"He's doing well," I say. "I think you can take him home today, as long as you keep a careful watch of him and promise to call if there is anything wrong at all."

"Of course," he says. "You know I will."

I smile, turning to look at Luke, thinking about how much has happened between us, thinking about all that's changed.

And looking at him, I think about all that hasn't. I think about the way he still makes me feel at ease, makes me feel comfortable in my skin.

I think about the way his gaze looking at me makes me shiver.

I think about the chemistry that's still there, the longing, and the love.

I still love him.

I shove the thought aside as quickly as it comes. That part of my life is over. We're over.

"Thank you," Luke says, standing, taking a few steps across the room, never taking his eyes off me.

For a moment, I think he's going to kiss me. I think he's going to say he's sorry, he's crazy, that he misses me.

For a long moment, we just stand, waiting to see who is going to make the next move.

Slowly, cautiously, I step out of the room, the moment clearly gone. "I'll get his meds ready," I say.

"Okay," Luke replies.

And with one word, the hope is lost again.

* * *

"I've been worried sick," Maren screams into the phone when I call her after Luke and Floyd are carefully loaded up.

I'm perched on the sofa in the hospital area, too tired emotionally and physically to get in my car and drive home, too tired to answer questions.

But I needed to talk to someone.

"I'm okay. Floyd's okay."

"So you spent the night there with him?"

"Yeah. I had to perform surgery, but he's all better."

"Not Floyd him," she says. "Luke him."

"Yes," I say.

"And?" she asks.

"And nothing. Nothing happened. It's over."

Maren breathes into the phone. "But?" she asks. "I can tell there's a but."

I slump back on the sofa, staring at the ceiling. "But, it's so damn complicated. I don't know why it has to be. I closed that door. I'm happy with Oliver, I am. But...."

"But you're not over him. But when you're with him, you still feel those feelings. You still wonder what could still be."

"How'd you know?"

"Because it's written all over your face. Because when you're with Oliver, you're happy, sure, but it's a different happy. It's a surface-level happy," she says. I sigh.

"Luke didn't exactly make me deep happy."

"Not all the time, no. You had your rocks. You had your issues. But, I don't know, Lila, it's like you cared about those issues because he made you so happy, you know? When you were good, you were really, really good. He rounded you out. I don't think you can just let that go."

"I don't know what to do, Maren. When we broke up, I thought it was right. Everyone thought it was right. Even you said so yourself. But now I don't know."

"Love isn't easy, Lila. You know that. No matter what you choose, there'll be a struggle and sadness. So I guess you just need to think about what pathway has the best chance of making you happy, which path is worth the sadness for the end game, whatever that might be."

"What should I do?"

"I don't know, sis. I do know you need to make up your mind. You need to think about what you want and who makes you happy. And then, you need to go after it no matter what, no holding back."

"I love you. Merry Christmas," I say, meaning it.

"Love you, too. Now get your butt over here. Mom's having a fit about you not being here, and I truly can't stand another second of it."

I grin. "I'll be there in a few."

I hang up, still staring at the ceiling, still confused as hell.

Because for every hard moment with Luke, for every crack in our relationship, there was an equally good one.

I drift through memories, thinking about all the sweet, passionate moments, the thoughtful gifts, the tender embraces. I think about our walks for breakfast around town on our days off and our trips to see all my chick flick movies. I think about our Valentine's Day when we snuggled on the sofa, ordered two pizzas and drank vodka until we were so drunk, we thought *Finding Nemo* was hilarious. I think about how he knew every detail of me, knew when I was ready to break before I knew it myself.

I swirl in the magic that was us, that could still be us, if we'd just find a way to put down our pride, to settle our differences, and to find a way to make this work.

But it all feels exhausting, unsteady, unsure.

And just when I'm thinking about how messed up life truly is, my phone lights up.

It's Oliver.

I'm tossed back into limbo, a hellish state of feeling guilty for being stuck between two men—and wondering how I ever let this happen.

CHAPTER TWENTY-NINE

LUKE

"Merry Christmas, sweetie," Mom says when I open the door back at the apartment. Floyd is sleeping on my bed, and since I've been keeping an eye on him—as in, not leaving my room where he's sleeping—I'm pretty exhausted. I didn't get much sleep last night, the feel of Lila on my arm stirring all kinds of thoughts, good and bad.

"Thanks, Mom. Sorry I didn't get to stay," I say.

"How's Floyd?" she asks as she scurries inside my apartment, a stack of gifts in her arms.

"Better."

"Thanks to Lila, of course," she says, winking.

"Where's Charley?"

"Last minute gig at the hospital. The Santa Claus working pediatrics apparently got a cold and couldn't go, so Charley's filling in."

"That's nice," I say, leading Mom to our sad excuse for a kitchen, hurrying to make coffee.

"Sit, I'll get it," Mom says, and I oblige, feeling like hell. As she starts the coffeepot, she turns to me and asks, "How did it go? With Lila?"

I lean my head into my hands. "Good. Confusing. A mess."

Mom sighs. "I don't know why you two insist on playing this game. You know you're both not over each other. Why not tell her how you feel? It's childish, you know. Just man up."

"Because nothing's changed," I say. "We're still us."

"Exactly. You're still you. You're still the Luke and Lila who radiate sickening happiness around each other. You're the Luke who makes the rational Lila a little bit wilder and a little bit more fun. She's the Lila who saved your cat twice now, who makes you settle a bit, who makes you plan for the future. You balance each other. You're amazing together. And sure, you didn't have it all figured out. But that doesn't mean you still can't."

"You know why things fell apart."

"Because you were being a wimp when it came to commitment. So what?"

"You know what she heard last Christmas. I can't take that back."

"But you can make it better. Stop making excuses, Luke. Take ownership of your life or someone else will."

"She's with someone."

"He's not you."

I groan. "Can we just open some Christmas gifts now?" I ask as she hands me a cup of coffee.

"You can change the subject all you want, but you know your mom's never wrong."

"Never? Like when you thought the waiter at Chili's was the love of your life and he turned out to be gay? Or the time you swore the engine light always came on in your old Camaro and it was no big deal on the way to Ohio? Or—"

"Okay," Mom says, putting up a hand. "I get it. But I'm not wrong about this. Now, come on. Give your mom the amazing presents you got her and then get your ass together. Aren't you going on tour soon?"

"It's not a tour, Mom. It's a few gigs."

"Well, it's going to be a tour soon enough, so you better get things figured out here."

I sigh, shaking my head. "Merry Christmas, Mom. I love you," I say, leaning in to hug her before heading to my room to get her gifts.

"Love you, too, foolish son of mine."

Later, when the gifts have been opened and our farewells said, I cuddle in beside Floyd, who is still doing well.

I think about where it all went wrong. I think about those words I can't take back. I think about how tonight just solidified for me what I already know: I'm still madly in love with a woman I can't have.

And it's all my damn fault.

* * *

"Congratulations, man. What awesome news," I said again as Will and I stood in the corner of the Morrow living room. Grandma Claire giggled wildly at the gift she'd just

handed to Lila's mom—I averted my eyes because knowing Grandma as I did, I was sure it was something terrifying, something I wouldn't want to associate with her later.

"Thanks," Will said, taking another swig of his beer. "I'm excited to be part of the family."

Maren and Will had just announced their engagement at the Morrow family Christmas celebration. It wasn't a shock. We'd all seen it coming, the way those two couldn't get enough of each other, the hints about weddings and forevers.

"When is it your turn? You and Lila have been together as long as us. When are you going to pop the question?" Will asked. I knew he meant no harm. It was a logical question and a logical observation.

Marriage was the logical next step.

But not for us. Not for me. Not after my past.

"Oh, no. Lila and I aren't that kind of couple," I said, smirking, trying to play it off.

"So no wedding plans?" Will asked for clarity.

"None. Ever. Not in this lifetime."

I took a swig from my beer, ignoring Will's questioning face. I turned the conversation, wanting to get out of this already uncomfortable circle of words.

I knew Maren's ring would stir questions, would stir new conversations with Lila. I knew she said she was okay with where we stood, where I stood, with marriage.

I just didn't expect how uncomfortable it would be. I didn't realize how Maren and Will's relationship was a tracking mechanism for our own and that this could change everything.

A few minutes later, Lila came strolling down the hall, the Christmas spirit gone.

"Hey, baby," I said, wondering what had shifted in her.

"Hey," she said, lackluster, no emotion. The typical Lila smile was gone.

There was a palpable coldness the rest of the evening. She smiled through, laughing at Grandma Claire's wild comments and fighting with her mom. To everyone else, everything with Lila was fine.

I could see the truth. I could see that the smile she wore was her fake smile and that something was off.

It was only later on that night that I found out why.

It was later, when I found out she'd heard every damning word I'd said, that I realized we were coming undone, like it or not. And I was too cowardly to stop it, despite how much I loved that woman.

***

That night was the beginning of the end. I doubt Maren and Will realized that with their yes to forever, the no to mine and Lila's was sealed.

We'd fought that night, hard. There were tears and frustrations. There were fears that we couldn't get past this, and me reassuring her we could. There were questions of intentions and questions of why.

Most of all, there was the realization we hadn't yet faced, even though we probably should have: we wanted different things in life.

And maybe, just maybe, our love wouldn't be enough to

bridge that gap.

Now, lying in bed, alone on Christmas other than Floyd, I think about last year. More than that, though, I think about today, and the regrets weighing heavily on me.

Why do I always back down when I want to step up? Why can I never man up, tell Lila what I need to tell her? Why do I always let her slip away when I want to grab on with everything I am?

Why don't I let myself hold on to happiness?

This morning, when Lila jumped up, I wanted to reach for her. I wanted to shove away the thoughts of her new boyfriend, of our goodbye, of all the things keeping us apart. I wanted to wrap her in my arms like I had done so many times and kiss away all the tension between us. I wanted to tell her I loved her, that I always had. I needed to confess to her I don't like who I am without her.

I was dying to tell her I'm still broken, still not worthy of her... but I'm selfish enough to want her back. I wanted to ask her to be patient with me, to help me get over my fears, and to help me be the brave man who deserves her.

But I didn't. Old habits truly do die hard.

Instead, I'd walked away from the only woman who ever understood me, who made me want to be better. I walked away from the only woman who devastated me when we broke up. I walked away from my past but also my future—if I was just brave enough to grab it.

So now, here I am, alone, Lila off with someone else instead of me.

Maybe I deserve misery after all.

CHAPTER THIRTY

LILA

"Hey, you," Oliver says, pulling me in for a kiss at the door of my apartment.

"Oliver, I didn't think you'd be back so soon," I say, truly shocked. I'm standing in sweatpants and my college T-shirt, my hair a disaster. Oliver wasn't supposed to be back until New Year's Eve.

"I just, damn I missed you." He heads into my apartment, jauntily strolling toward the sofa.

I stand at the door, still trying to overcome the shock of the sight of him. It's the day after Christmas, and I'm not ready for this.

I spent yesterday thinking about everything—thinking about what I need to do, about where I need to go from here.

And I know what I need to do. I just didn't think I'd be doing it so soon.

"Come, sit, tell me about your Christmas. How was it? Did you miss me?"

I smile, taking in Oliver's enthusiasm.

Over the past couple of months, we've gotten to know each other more than just from work. We've gotten to see what we could be together, and I've liked it. I really have.

But talking to Maren yesterday and in our subsequent conversations at Mom's house, I've come to realize one thing.

I'm happy. But Maren's right—it's surface-level happy. Because my true happiness has already been reserved for someone else. Whether or not we're going to be okay or make it, I can't string Oliver along. I can't keep pretending I'm over Luke, that I'm ready to be with Oliver completely.

"My holiday was good. But, listen, I need to tell you something."

He hushes me, putting a finger to my lips. "Me first," he says, and my stomach sinks.

"Listen, I know it's only been a couple of months, but being away from you over the holiday, it made me realize something I've known from the first time I saw you. I know you want to take this slow, and I know things are... complicated for you. But Lila, when I'm with you, nothing else matters but you. We're so good together. We're like this dream team of go-getters. We're good together. We're unstoppable. Lila, I love you."

I feel my mouth actually fall open. This was not how I envisioned this conversation to go.

"Oliver, I—"

He cuts me off. "You don't have to say it back. I just, damn, I needed you to know. I needed to tell you how I feel, and I needed it to be in person. It's why I cut my trip short. I realized I couldn't let the new year come along without you knowing how I feel."

I sigh. This is going to be harder than I thought. I feel the tears well because, in all honesty, I do care about Oliver.

It's just not enough. Why is it never enough?

"Oliver, the thing is, I've been doing a lot of thinking too. And you're right. Things are complicated for me. I want you to know that these past couple of months have been so great. You're an amazing man, and I felt myself falling for you. But, the thing is, I can't do this anymore. As much as I want to say I love you back, as much as I want this to work, it can't. My heart is still scarred, and the thing is, I think it always will be. I think I've already found my forever, even if it doesn't work out. I think I've found the one and only for me, and I just don't think that's going to change anytime soon. I'm sorry."

Oliver stares at me, the silence between us deafening. Finally, after a long, slow breath, he speaks up. "Lila, I know you're not over the past. But I can wait. I love you."

"That's the thing, Oliver. It's not fair. You shouldn't want to wait because I'm clearly not ready to move on."

He stares at me for another long moment. "Was I just a rebound?"

I bite my lip. I want to say hell no, which is what I've been telling myself all along. But I also know he deserves the truth. Tears start to fall. "I don't know, Oliver. I don't know. I just know I can't do this anymore. I'm sorry. I'm sorry I hurt you."

"It's fine," he says, but it's clearly not. He stands up, wiping his hands as if he's wiping them clean of me. "Merry Christmas," he says.

I want to say it's not Christmas, but I don't. I'm an asshole, it's true, but not that big of one.

He stomps across my tiny apartment, stepping over Henry who has slept through this whole torturous encounter, and slams my door so hard a picture falls to the ground.

Tears fall uncontrollably, and my vision is blurry. I know I did the right thing. But why does love make the right thing feel so bad sometimes? When is love going to get good again?

I sit for a long time in my misery, tears falling freely, feeling like shit.

Finally, it comes to me what I need to do.

I grab my bag and Henry's leash, and I go to do what I do best when I'm struggling with life.

* * *

"Three peanut-butter doughnuts, coming right up," Dot says, giving me a squeeze as she sets down the order for me and grabs a seat across from me. "I'm glad you're back."

I smile through the sadness and smudged mascara. "I was just in last week."

"I mean I'm glad the peanut-butter doughnut girl is back. I'm glad the real Lila is back."

I've already filled in Dot on everything—the breakup, the Luke Christmas situation, everything.

"I just feel so lost, Dot, you know?" I ask, taking a bite of a doughnut as Dot helps herself to the one usually claimed by Luke.

"I know. But you're on the way to finding yourself, I do think. It's a new year coming up. It's a chance to start over, you know? Get what you want this year, Lila."

"I think that it might be too late."

"You kids, never listening. It's not too late. It's never too late."

We sit and talk for a while about Oliver, Luke, Henry, and Dot's grandkids. We talk like old friends, which we are.

When I'm getting ready to leave, I turn to Dot and smile. "Thank you. Thank you for being such a good friend."

"Honey, you haven't seen anything yet," she says, winking at me. I'm not sure what that wink could possibly mean, and I'm not sure if I want to find out.

CHAPTER THIRTY-ONE

LILA

I'm tucked in on the sofa, my favorite sweatpants on and my feet tucked away into slippers. Henry's cuddled up to me on the sofa as I watch sappy holiday movies on television, all alone in my apartment.

It's been a couple of days since the Oliver breakup disaster, and it's been a couple of days since I've left my apartment. This is not a coincidence.

Despite my mother's annoying phone calls and Maren's insistence I need to get out and enjoy my holiday from work, I can't. Lila Morrow always has a plan, a direction, and an idea of where she's marching toward in the grand scheme of things.

Without that plan, I honestly don't even know how to function out in the real world.

Still, despite the chaos of my life right now, I don't feel as terrible as I thought I would. I feel a little bit... free, actually.

Sitting here, wasting away the evening with Henry, I've come to realize that life truly is about rolling with the punches, going with it, and feeling your way through. You can't always make rational choices or use your head to guide you.

Sometimes you have to trust your gut, your heart, and what feels right at the moment.

So, as the new year approaches, I vow to myself this is what I'm going to do. I'm going to stop looking to the future for happiness and start finding it in the here and now, whatever that looks like. I'm going to stop comparing my life to the meticulously planned timeline I set out for myself. I'm going to learn to just go with it, and smile at the surprises along the way.

But first, I'm going to spend another evening here on the sofa, doing nothing productive and enjoying every single second of it.

My phone rings, and I debate ignoring it. It's probably Mom wanting me to come over for dinner or complain about Maren. I pick it up, curiosity and annoying buzzing getting to me.

To my surprise, it's not Mom or Maren.

It's Dot.

"Hello?" I ask, wondering what's going on.

"Lila? Oh, thank God. I need you over here right away, please. There's been an accident and there's a dog who has been hit. We need you to get over as soon as you can. I think he's going to be fine, so don't worry, but he definitely needs to be checked out."

"I'm on my way, Dot. Be there in ten."

I flick the television off, run to my room to toss on a bra, change my slippers out for boots, and put on my winter coat.

Duty calls, and it looks like that flexibility is something I need to get used to right now.

CHAPTER THIRTY-TWO

LILA

"Dot, where's the dog?" I ask, running through the front door. She's standing behind the counter, smiling calmly, which strikes me as odd. Shouldn't she be in a panic? Shouldn't there be other people here, trying to help?

She comes from behind the counter as I breathe heavily.

"Honey, I'm sorry," she says, "but you two needed a shove. I can't stand it anymore."

"What?" I ask, confused, but Dot just gestures toward a table. I take a moment and realize Dot's is empty. Where is everyone? She should be open right now. This is always a place for teenagers and young couples to come sip coffee and ring in the holidays in a peaceful setting.

My eyes settle on something, though, in a familiar corner. The table, our table, is occupied.

By a familiar curly-haired man who looks just as awestruck as me.

Dot pulls me by the arm over to the table. "Dot, I can't…

are you serious?" I ask, a little pissed by her lies.

"Now listen, I know I lied to both of you. I'm sorry. But you two need to stop thinking it's too late and stop avoiding it. Your love isn't easy. I get that. My love with Louie wasn't either. We were different in so many ways, and we fought. We had different visions and we argued like crazy. We almost called it quits a few times, and we even spent some time apart. But you know what? Easy isn't always better. Sometimes the thing we fight the hardest is the best. I know you two have a lot of things to work out, but I believe in you. I knew from the first moment you walked through that door together you were real. You were good for each other. You were it. I don't want you two to let your pride or some stupid notion that you can't work through your issues get in the way. So suck it up and talk it out. I'm leaving now. Lock up when you're done."

I look at Luke, who is staring at Dot.

"Oh, and happy holidays," she says, smiling.

I look down at the plate of three peanut-butter glazed doughnuts between us, an awkward tension palpable as well. I smooth my hair self-consciously as I approach the table.

I can't believe she did this.

I can't believe he's here.

"So how did she get you here?" I ask quietly, almost afraid to raise my voice too much.

"Told me the roof was leaking and with the crowds of people, she needed a roofing expert."

I shake my head and smile. "She told me there was a dog

hit by a car."

"I didn't think Dot was so plotting," Luke says.

I shake my head. "So," I say just as he says the same thing.

We both sigh. Finally, I reach for a doughnut and take a bite. He does the same. "These things are so damn good," I say.

"What the hell is in her secret recipe?"

"At this point, with all her lies tonight, I don't want to know."

We both eat in silence for a long time, lost in our heads and confusion. I stare at him, feeling the butterflies stirring without even a word between us.

We finish our doughnuts, the third one still sitting on the plate. Neither of us makes a move, both staring at the table, not making eye contact. I wonder if Dot's plan will fail, if we'll get up and leave this place just as we came in… separately, alone, apart.

I wonder if too much has happened. I wonder if we're even the same people sitting here as we were before. I wonder if we could ever get back to the peanut-butter glazed doughnut eating, giggly couple we once were.

I wonder if I even want that.

Luke splits the last doughnut in half and hands it to me. We don't touch, and we don't joke. We simply finish our individual halves as if in ode to tradition.

"I should get going." The words come out of my mouth perfunctorily. I want to look at him and tell him I miss him, that I never stopped. I want to tell him I haven't been able to stop thinking about him or us since I walked out of that apartment for the final time.

I want to tell him that Dot's right, that we were so good together. I want to tell him I was a damn fool for insisting on a certain path for us. I want to tell him I don't care anymore if he's a little reckless with money or if he sometimes struggles to keep his feet on the ground. I want to tell him that he's not his dad and that he could never hurt me like that.

But I can't because the words are stuck in my throat. So much has happened, yet nothing has happened between us these past six months.

I stand, walking away from the table. Luke follows wordlessly. We walk out of Dot's, Luke locking up behind us. I feel tears forming, so I walk quickly, trying not to look back, the streetlight shining down like a beacon from the past.

I pause underneath it.

"Lila," he says behind me. It's said with a reverence, the single word floating between us in the freezing December night.

I turn to face him, the curly-haired man who, despite the past six months, I know better than I know anyone in this world. I see the familiar warm eyes that beckon me forward. Despite the distance between us, it feels like his eyes are wrapping me up. He steps toward me, bridging the gap. A silence freezes between us, the snowflakes gently falling onto us underneath the glow of the light. What should be a romantic scene is instead eerie, punctuated by an emotional distance and a fear of what will come next.

But then, Luke looks up at me, his eyes watery. He speaks, and it sends a jolt through me. "Look, Lila. Dot's right. I know things aren't perfect, and I know I hurt you."

"We hurt each other," I correct him, practically whispering.

"We did. And I know it's been a long time, and we've both moved on. But dammit, I miss you like crazy. I miss us and who we were together. I miss our breakfast walks and our Netflix binge-watching sessions. I miss your cold feet jolting me awake in the morning. I miss that weird-smelling shampoo in the shower and the way you always winked at me when I passed the salt. I miss everything about you." His voice, a reverent whisper, wraps itself around me in the deepest sense.

Tears fall now, the freedom of the admission to myself and to him releasing. "I miss you, too. I never stopped missing you. But what happened to us? How did this happen to us?"

"I don't know. I know there's a lot that's changed. I know we can't just go back to the way it used to be. Hell, I don't even know if I want to go back, because I know there was a lot wrong. But I miss you, Lila. I love you. I don't want to keep on like this if it means I have to keep on without you. I don't know what we need to do to fix this, and I don't even know if it's completely possible. There's a part of me, though, that thinks maybe it's not all gone. There's a part of me that thinks you might feel it too. I think that despite everything, we can find who we were together again. If we wanted, we could still be us, but better. We could be the us we always should've been."

I don't respond or try to rationalize what he's said. I don't search for answers or ask the hard questions. I don't work out the logistics in my head or think of all the ways this could go wrong. I don't ask for fancy promises or pledges from him. I don't ask for arbitrary discussions about forever. Instead, I listen to my heart and what it's been saying for the past six months.

With the streetlight illuminating the darkness above us, I lean in, my hand planted on the pole to steady myself. I lean in and let my lips find the familiar shape of his mouth, the beard I once asked him to shave feeling so good against my cold chin. Our kiss starts out hesitant, the kiss of two strangers unsure of their footing in the relationship. Soon, though, despite the frost in the air and in our hearts, we are home in the kiss. We find the familiar feeling we've been missing, and I'm entranced by the jolt between us. There's no denying it. The spark is still there, maybe even stronger. As his hand moves to my face and he grasps me just the way I like it, I melt into him, letting go of all the fears and frustrations I once felt. The wall between us cracks and then crumbles as his tongue dances on mine in a pattern familiar, a pattern craved.

"I love you, Lila," he whispers, his breath puffing clouds that drift between us. "I've lived my life thinking marriage was the enemy. But I've come to learn that a life without you is the enemy. I'll marry you tomorrow or next week or next year if that's what you want. Because a life without you isn't a safe life. It's just empty."

I catch my breath and calm my murmuring heart, giving a voice to the words etched into my being. "I love you, too. I've never stopped. And marriage isn't what it's all about. I thought it was. But this love we have doesn't need a ring or a promise of forever. It just needs you and me together. That's it. Marriage isn't for everyone, but what we have isn't something everyone finds either. I love you forever, ring or no ring."

"So we're made for each other, then? Soul mates after all?" he asks, and a huge grin spreads on my face.

"Soul mates," I say, grinning, and he wraps me in his arms.

Standing, staring at the town we call home together, I exhale for the first time in months.

After all this time, after all the doubts, I am confident now. It took us falling apart, trying to move on, and almost losing it all for us to figure it out. I'm thankful, though, that we did. I'm thankful we're here, right back here, where we should be. After all these heartaches and questions, there's just one thing I know as Luke's hand firmly grasps mine as if he'll never let go.

We're still us. We're definitely still us, and that's more than good enough for me.

EPILOGUE

ONE YEAR LATER

"Will someone please pass me another shot of whiskey?" Mr. Morrow asks as Will straightens my tie. Dean obliges, passing him the entire bottle.

"Did Lucy call again?" I ask, smoothing out my suit jacket.

"Yes. She only left five more messages this time about Grandma Claire's outfit and questions about the caterer. She also wanted to make sure your boutonnieres were correctly placed. Do I look like a wedding planner or something?" he asks before taking a huge gulp straight from the bottle. "I'll see you guys in a few. I have to get back to my spot. God help me if that woman mentions those damn boutonnieres one more time."

I grin, shaking my head, knowing Lila must be going about crazy right now.

In truth, Lucy Morrow is both elated that this day has come—and horrified that we wanted to keep it simple. Fifty guests, a small fire hall reception, and no limousine equates to debauchery in her book.

But at the end of it, Lila stood firm that she wanted things simple.

I think a part of her still wants to make sure it isn't over the top for me, which is crazy. I've told her over and over again I'm fine with whatever she wants.

After I put that ring on Lila's finger in the Park Lane waiting room back in June, she swore we could just elope and keep it simple. I wouldn't hear anything of the sort.

"Let's do it right, Lila. Let's make sure the whole family is involved."

So, here we are, getting ready to take that big step, the step I was terrified of for so long.

Looking in the mirror at myself now, though, I don't even remember who that man was. The man who was so afraid of commitment, of saying I do, of forever, is long gone. That man who two years ago messed up everything by swearing he'd never stand here, in this position, is long gone.

The man who was afraid to chase his dreams is long gone, too. I've worked on my last roof, this summer taking my career on a new path. I'm living my dreams in all ways, going on tour this spring with a well-known band. I'm singing full-time now.

And I'm with Lila full-time now, forever, for good. Everything I was too afraid to believe could happen came true.

I'm a lucky man in so many ways.

It's so symbolic that we're getting married today, on Christmas, the day that was the beginning of the end of us… and now the beginning of forever.

I guess, in a way, our breakup changed me. It made me stronger. It made me realize, above all, that there were scarier things than wedding vows and promises.

Like losing Lila.

It's been a long road to here. There were so many details to work out after that night at the streetlight. There were hurts and fears to overcome.

Still, we did. We found our way back. We found that, even after we'd cracked apart and dissolved the relationship, it was never really gone. We weren't the same Luke and Lila as when we started—but that was a good thing. We were better. We were wiser.

We were more aware of what we had to lose and how much we didn't want that to happen.

"You ready, bro? It's about time," Evan says, slapping me on the shoulder.

I turn to him, smiling. "I'm ready. Let's do this."

We head out to the altar, and I find my place, looking out at all the people who matter most in our lives.

Grandma Claire is already seated up front, Trixie on her lap—of course. She's wearing a red strapless dress with a hot pink hat. I'm feeling like this wasn't the outfit she was supposed to wear. She blows me a kiss from her bright red lips as the organ music begins to play.

"I love you, Luke!" she screams, to the preacher's chagrin.

"Love you too, Grandma Claire. You're beautiful," I yell back, ignoring formalities. Grandma Claire blushes and winks.

As the music begins, Charley leads my mom down the aisle to her seat. Lila's mom is on the other arm. The two look beautiful. Mom blows me a kiss as well, and I smile. Once they're in the pew, Charley gives me a thumbs-up. I notice Lucy scowling at the sight of Trixie, but she apparently decides she has to just go with it.

The bridesmaids are next, Scarlet, Zoey, and Maren as the matron of honor. They look gorgeous in their red dresses, poinsettias in their arms. Everyone is all smiles, perhaps because they thought this day would never come.

Henry is next—the ring bearer of course—pulling a wagon with baby Sophia, Will and Maren's daughter. Will's mom walks beside the wagon as a precaution. I grin as everyone fusses over the sight.

And then it's time.

The doors open, and she's there, right there, walking toward me.

For so many years, I'd feared this moment, made it out to be this terrifying lie. Standing here, emotion sweeps over me and I realize I was a fool.

I was a fool to think the sight of Lila walking toward me, waiting to promise forever to me, would be anything but beautiful.

She ambles toward me, and I hear our friends and family members rise, but I don't worry about them. I can't take my eyes off the vision coming down the aisle. I want to sear the sight into my memory.

The woman who stole my heart over a dying cat, who agreed to go on a date with me at the gym, who missed part of our first date because of a pager, is going to be my wife, be my forever. The woman who makes me want to be a better man, who supports my crazy dreams and pushes me to find happiness is going to be by my side for the rest of my life.

We are going to be Luke and Lila for good.

There's no fear, no desire to run away. There's no worry that I'm going to follow in my father's footsteps. As Mr. Morrow puts Lila's hand in mine and kisses her cheek, as I feel the touch of that familiar skin on mine, there's nothing but sheer joy that my best friend, the woman who completes me, my soul mate is here with me ready to say "I do."

I kiss Lila on the cheek and whisper an "I love you" as we head up the steps to stand in front of the preacher, in front of our family, and in front of God to commit ourselves to each other. As we do, I turn around for a second to the other familiar face in the crowd.

Dot.

She's wearing a beautiful green dress. I give her a smile, and she winks at me.

I turn back to the ceremony, to the words, and to the forevers I promise.

We say our vows, which we've written ourselves. When it's my turn, I turn to the woman who changed everything for me, and I spill my heart out for her.

"When you came into my life, Lila Morrow, I didn't

know how broken I was. I was this fool wandering through life with no purpose or sense of direction. And then there you were. You saved so much more than Floyd that day. You saved me. You made me realize that love was beautiful and worth it. I knew from that first day there was something about us. Standing here today, in front of our friends and family, I promise to always remember that there is truly something special about us together. I promise even on our worst days, on days when we feel like throwing in the towel, I'll remember what I knew from that first day—we're good together, so good together. I promise to love you and support your dreams. I promise to stand beside you when the road gets rocky, and I promise to pick up the crumbs of our relationship when we fall apart. I promise to always remember we're better together than apart, and I promise to give my best self to you, every day, for the rest of our lives. Above all, I promise to remember that you are and always will know the song in my soul, and I promise to know yours."

With that, the preacher ushers me to the back of the altar, where I've stowed my guitar.

As Lila stands in her spot, tears streaming, I play the song, our song, "Under the Streetlight."

It's more than just a song. It's a promise. No matter how many stages I play on or how many crowds know my name, there will be no better moment for me than this one. There will be no other performance that means this much.

When we get lost, when we feel like it's not worth it, we'll remember that symbol of us, the light in the darkness, the place where so many times, we realized our dreams are with each other.

The preacher finishes the ceremony and I kiss my bride, a passionate kiss we've waited too long for. We run out the back of the church, Mr. and Mrs. Bowman, and Grandma Claire lets out her signature yee-haw.

"We're married. I can't believe it," Lila proclaims, leaning on my arm.

"I can," I say, smiling. Because I can. It took me a while to get here. It took us a while to get here. It took me a while to realize the truth.

With Lila, I'm able to get over the past and my fears. With Lila, her happiness is my happiness.

With Lila, everything is possible, and I want to hang on to that forever.

* * *

"Ho ho ho, Merry Christmas!" a voice bellows as Lila and I clink glasses at the head table, finishing our dinner.

"I didn't know you invited Santa Claus!" Grandma Claire shouts, a huge smile on her face at the table in front of us.

"Santa Claus" rushes into the reception, handing a small gift to Lila and me.

I see familiar eyes behind the costume and laugh.

So this was where Charley went when dinner was being served.

The deejay plays some holiday music, but stops it as Charley—er, Santa—takes the mic.

"I just want to say congratulations to the beautiful couple we're celebrating tonight. I haven't been in this family long, but I can honestly say it's a family filled with love. Welcome to our family, Lila."

I smile, handing the gift to Lila to open. She peels back the paper, and reveals a key. She looks at me, confused. "What is it?"

"I don't know," I say, eyeing Charley and then Mom.

"Your mother and I thought it was about time you two get a new place, since your place isn't quite what you had before," Charley says.

It's true. We've been living in Lila's apartment, which is a little bit small—and let's just say the neighbors above us like to have a screaming good time. It's a far cry from the first place we had.

"I don't understand," I say, staring at him.

"It's not much, but you see, I have this rental property across town. It's yours." His words are simple, but they shake me to the core.

I pause, wondering if I've heard him right. "What?"

"It's yours, son. Make lots of great memories there."

I'm choked up now, and Lila gasps.

"Is this for real?" she asks.

"I think so," I say, as we stand from the table. Mom and Charley rush over, and we are wrapped up in a group hug as the rest of the guests clap.

"I can't believe this, thank you," Lila says.

"Thank you," I say, also touched by their kindness.

"You two are just beautiful together. You deserve a place

to call home for good," Charley says, grinning behind the beard.

I look at the kind eyes of the man who came into my mom's life later in life, who came into *our* lives later in life, but has made such an impression all the same.

I see in Charley the kind of man I wish my father had been, the kind of man I hope to someday be for our kids.

"I love you," I say to Charley.

"I love you too," Charley says. "Glad to be part of the family."

"All right, all right, enough sappiness for one day," Scarlet says, rushing up to hug us now too. She smiles. "Love you, big brother and Lila. So glad you two are finally hitched. Now can we get this party started?"

Some glasses tap, and Grandma Claire lets out a rebel yell. I point to the deejay who changes to some fast-paced music, and everyone hits the dance floor.

Grandma Claire is twerking, and even Lucy is letting loose—I think her husband spiked her drink to get her to calm down.

Scarlet and John dance beside Lila and me. Evan and Zoey are getting a little close, and even Henry has wandered out onto the floor.

All around us, the ones we love, the people who matter most, surround us, celebrate with us, and cheer us on.

"This is the best Christmas we've ever had," Lila whispers into my ear.

"Honey, you haven't seen anything yet," I say, winking, and lean down to kiss her hungrily.

"Will you two get a room?" Maren asks, sneaking up beside us.

I finally pull away, and Maren shakes her head. "Anyway, aren't you glad I dragged you to Zumba?" Maren asks Lila.

Lila scrunches her nose.

"From what I heard, you two were on the banished wall after I believe someone used the phrase 'Zumba bitches.' In reality, I'm married to an outlaw," I say, kissing Lila on the cheek.

Lila smiles, shaking her head. "Well, you're the one who chose to be soul mates with a rebel, you know."

"And I wouldn't have it any other way. Now come on, let's hit up the cookie table."

I wink at her, and we head over to the cookie table—which doesn't have a single cookie on it.

"Three please," I say, and Dot just smiles a huge smile from behind the mock Dot's Doughnuts counter.

"You two are made for each other," she says, handing us our plate of three peanut-butter glazed doughnuts.

"Yeah, I think we might be," Lila says, leaning in to take a bite of one of the doughnuts in my hand.

When we each finish our first, we split the third right down the middle, heading back to the dance floor for a little bit more partying and a whole lot more forever.

"Still us," Lila says, leaning into me as we make our way back to our wedding, to our party, and to the forever sitting before us.

"Still us," I reply, nodding and thinking about how glad for that I am.

ACKNOWLEDGEMENTS

First and foremost, thank you to Hot Tree Publishing for giving my writing a place to call home. Becky Johnson, you work tirelessly to give your authors a supportive family to help them chase their dreams. Your devotion to the romance genre and your vision for the future is inspiring. Thank you to everyone else who helps make me make my stories their best version, including Liv, Justine, Peggy, all the beta readers, and all the amazing authors. I am truly blessed to call myself a Hot Tree Publishing author.

Thank you to my amazing parents for always supporting my dreams and teaching me that words are power. Thank you for all your love and encouragement.

Thank you Grandma Bonnie for always being a believer in my writing and supporting me.

Thank you to my husband for being my rock when days are tough and for making me laugh. You always encourage me to keep dreaming and to just keep going, even when I feel like giving up. You have shown me that love is beautiful and real. You are my best friend, and I am so lucky to have found you at such a young age.

Thank you to the teachers who shaped me into the writer I am today. A special thanks goes to Tom Kunkle, Diane Vella, Sue Gunsallus, and all of the professors at Mount Aloysius College.

I want to thank all my coworkers and friends who go above and beyond to support my dreams. Thank you to Christie James, Alicia Schmouder, Lynette Luke, Jennifer Carney, Ronice Sceski, Maureen Letcher, Kelly Rubritz, Kristin Books, Jamie Lynch, Kristin Mathias, Heather Jasinski, and Deborah Biter. Thank you to Kay Shuma for believing in my stories before I even believed in them myself. Your kind words always encourage me to keep writing. Thank you to my amazing in-laws, Tom and Diane, for supporting my dreams.

Thank you Lisa Sprankle and Jennifer Lilly from Bradley's Book Outlet for supporting my author journey and helping me share my books with the local community.

A special thanks to all the book bloggers and reviewers who help me share my words, especially Tome Tender, Nerd Problems, Once Upon a Page, Books & Bindings, Elizabeth Cole for Nerd Problems, and everyone else dedicated to spreading the words about books.

Thank you to all the readers and fans for taking a chance on a small-town girl and believing in her words. Thank you for sharing your kind remarks about my characters and stories. Thank you for helping me live my wildest dream.

Finally, thank you to my best friend, Henry, for reminding

me that unconditional love is real. I hope we have many more years of lounging on the couch together, dancing in the living room, and eating way too many cupcakes.

ABOUT THE AUTHOR

An English teacher, an author, and a fan of anything pink and/or glittery, Lindsay's the English teacher cliché; she love cats, reading, Shakespeare, and Poe.

She currently lives in her hometown with her husband, Chad (her junior high sweetheart); their cats, Arya, Amelia, Alice, Marjorie, and Bob; and their Mastiff, Henry.

Lindsay's goal with her writing is to show the power of love and the beauty of life while also instilling a true sense of realism in her work. Some reviewers have noted that her books are not the "typical romance." With her novels coming from a place of honesty, Lindsay examines the difficult questions, looks at the tough emotions, and paints the pictures that are sometimes difficult to look at. She wants her fiction to resonate with readers as realistic, poetic, and powerful. Lindsay wants women readers to be able to say, "I see myself in that novel." She wants to speak to the modern woman's experience while also bringing a twist of something new and exciting. Her aim is for readers to say, "That could happen," or "I feel like the characters are real." That's how she knows she's done her job.

Lindsay's hope is that by becoming a published author, she can inspire some of her students and other aspiring writers to pursue their own passions. She wants them to see that any dream can be attained and publishing a novel isn't out of the realm of possibility.

WEBSITE: WWW.LINDSAYDETWILER.COM

FACEBOOK: WWW.FACEBOOK.COM/LINDSAYANNDETWILER

TWITTER: WWW.TWITTER.COM/LINDSAYDETWILER

GOODREADS: WWW.GOODREADS.COM/AUTHOR/SHOW/13508159.
LINDSAY_DETWILER

AMAZON: WWW.AMAZON.COM/LINDSAY-DETWILER/E/
B00TNAVBSS

NEWSLETTER SIGN UP: WWW.TINYLETTER.COM/LINDSAYDETWILER

OTHER: WWW.YOUTUBE.COM/CHANNEL/UCVZ8HP-
EESFMPRJUG0A4ZZA

ABOUT THE PUBLISHER

Hot Tree Publishing opened its doors in 2015 with an aspiration to bring quality fiction to the world of readers. With the initial focus on romance and a wide spread of romance subgenres, we envision opening up to alternative genres in the near future.

Firmly seated in the industry as a leading editing provider to independent authors and small publishing houses, Hot Tree Publishing is the sister company to Hot Tree Editing, founded in 2012. Having established in-house editing and promotions, plus having a well-respected market presence, Hot Tree Publishing endeavors to be a leader in bringing quality stories to the world of readers.

Interested in discovering more amazing reads brought to you by Hot Tree Publishing or perhaps you're interested in submitting a manuscript? Head over to the website for information:

WWW.HOTTREEPUBLISHING.COM